FLIGHT

BY

Jean Grant

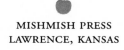

MISHMISH PRESS
LAWRENCE, KANSAS

FLIGHT

For information contact Mishmish Press
1308 Jana Drive, Lawrence, KS 66049
or email expatjean2@gmail.com

www.jeangrantwriter.com

FIRST EDITION
Cover by Tania Hurt-Newton
Book designed by Audrey Taylor
Author photo by Mieke Huijts

Library of Congress Control Number 2016918948

ISBN 978-0-982507445

For Bob Fraga who lights my way.

Each star hath a companion star
By its light to see

Mahmud Abu Al Wafa

Flight

A novel of Beirut and the French Countryside

by Jean Grant

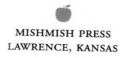

MISHMISH PRESS
LAWRENCE, KANSAS

Chapter 1

Exactly a year ago, April 13, 1975—unlucky thirteen— a scuffle outside a church and the killing of four Christian militiamen led to a dirty payback with twenty-eight Palestinians dragged off a bus and shot. Since then, the deadly tit-for-tat had not stopped. In the past week, twenty-four ceasefires collapsed. A boom, crash or thud propelled everyone away from the windows. Today, after five days of dawn-to-dusk curfew, the rival militias declared another ceasefire.

Finlay Fortin, released from what felt like house arrest, climbed into his orange VW bus. His daughter Anouk had nicknamed it Cinderella's Coach when she was a little girl. Now, at fifteen, she decorated it with decals of daisies and peace symbols and hung blue donkey beads from the rearview mirror to ward off bad luck. Finlay yearned to leave the heat, noise and bustle of the city and head up to the mountains, where the air was crisp and clean, scented with golden mimosa. But he was answering a more immediate need. They were low on food, so he drove to the grocery store, which was jammed with shoppers. For once, there were tin cans on the shelves, fresh produce, and lamb and beef on the meat counter. All that, but not what he most desired—fragrant French bread.

On their way home, his wife Maureen—she liked to be called

Mo—rummaged through the gear in her photo bag: filters, light meter, flash, lenses and lens cleaners, along with the red bandana she carried in case of tear gas. "Hey, I'm almost out of film. Can we swing by the photo shop? It'll only take a sec." She turned around to the back seat, where Anouk was swinging her feet over the sacks of groceries on the floor. Stalks of celery stuck out from one of the brown paper bags. "Okay with you, Sunbeam?"

"Yeah."

Finlay turned onto Bliss Street. Amid the blares and beeps of the backed-up traffic, he looked for a parking space. Cars were parked bumper-to-bumper alongside the curb, but eventually Mo saw a spot. As he edged the VW bus back into the space, the cars behind them honked, and Anouk pressed her hands over her ears.

"Wait here, I'll be back in a flash." Mo jumped out of the front seat.

"I'm coming too." Anouk slid open the door of the bus.

"Don't," Finlay shouted after her. But she was already gone. He watched the two of them hurry past the stone houses with their arched windows and pillared balconies. A tasseled donkey harnessed to a barrow hee-hawed and pawed the pavement. He recognized its driver. Before being assigned faculty housing, Finlay used to buy their cooking and heating gas from him and lugged the canister up the dusty stairs to their third-floor apartment. The campus was safer, and he was grateful to have moved there, especially with a daredevil teenager.

He watched as Anouk followed her mother into Zamil's Photo Store. Anouk seemed unfazed by the troubles. Her heart's one desire was that the boy next door would invite her to his graduation dance. If Danny did, Finlay had decided to let them borrow Cinderella's Coach. He had bought it secondhand when Anouk was seven, and he'd let her name it. It seemed only yesterday.

Drenched in perspiration, Finlay rolled down the window but

quickly closed it because of the fumes of car exhaust. They came out of the store, Anouk in her pixie cut and bellbottoms and Mo with her camera bag slung over her chest. Shouts erupted from the lane, followed by bursts of machine-gun fire. Finlay leaped out of the bus. "Mo! Anouk!" he yelled, waving his arms.

"Stop!" he bellowed with a familiar sinking feeling as he saw his wife rush toward the lane with Anouk following her. Was Mo pretending she didn't hear? Or had she gone totally nuts this time? Chest pounding, he raced after them. The firing grew louder, and they darted behind a wall of cinder blocks with sandbags propped in front. Just as he arrived, Mo exposed her head and hands as she steadied her camera on the top of the wall.

Finlay grabbed Anouk and flattened her body with his. Lying that way, he noticed how much bigger he still was. Shots rang out. A scrawny youth in jeans and a red-and-white-checked keffiyeh fell screaming onto the pavement, his arms outstretched. Blood streamed down his right leg. Three men in dark pants ran off, clutching submachine guns.

With anger making his limbs stiff, Finlay hustled Anouk and Mo back to the VW bus. Once they were safe inside, he screamed at Mo, "Don't you have a brain in your head? They could have shot you both." He breathed hard and fast.

"Dad, don't shout. Please. We're okay."

Mo didn't reply. She pressed against her side of the VW bus as far from him as possible. He couldn't bear to talk to her or even look at her. The silence was like the pall that had fallen over their marriage. He couldn't take much more. The feeling was mutual, as he well knew. As soon as they got home, Mo locked herself in the darkroom.

At supper, all of them sullen, they chewed on stale bread. Finlay wasn't going to be the first to speak. For once, he wasn't going to make things right. Anouk asked to be excused and left her bowl of lentil soup half eaten.

"There's ice cream," he said.

"Who cares? I can't stand it when you guys give each other the silent treatment." She stomped off to her room.

He turned to Mo. "You don't get it, do you, the danger you put our daughter in?"

That hit the target. "I'm sorry. I wasn't thinking. You're right," she said as though this was the first time. "But the shots I got are striking. I was worried maybe they'd be overexposed or blurred, but they're crystal clear." She smiled with pleasure. "I was lucky to be on the spot. I'd hate to have someone beat me to the scoop."

He thought of all the ways she could get herself killed: stepping on a landmine, getting caught in a crossfire, run over by a tank, or hit by a mortar or rocket. She knew the risks she took were hard on him, but when he begged her not to take so many chances, she smiled and said someone had to.

But did it have to be her? Couldn't someone else give a voice to the afflicted? He didn't have the energy to bring it up again, although their brush with death left him hollow and afraid. It was the first time that Anouk had deliberately put herself in danger.

Mo went next door to visit her best friend, Molly Delacruz. The Delacruzes had been their host family when they arrived in Beirut, and they all hit it off right away. Although Danny was three years older than Anouk, he liked her, or at least put up with her. As for himself, he and Juan became drinking buddies, the first such friendship he'd had. How he missed him! Thinking of his friend made Finlay feel hollow and afraid. Always the two families spent the holidays together. This was their first Easter without Juan.

Finlay cleared the table, and then he opened up Hemingway's *For Whom the Bell Tolls* and read until he became drowsy. By the time Mo came back from the Delacruzes, he was already in bed. She undressed in the dark, got in beside him, and nudged his heel with her toe. "Are you asleep?" she whispered.

He grunted. She wasn't forgiven just because he had lost himself in fiction for a few hours.

"About this afternoon. I didn't realize Anouk was following me. I'm sorry. Turn on your side, okay?"

She massaged his back, making little circles up and down either side of his spine. After a while, he pulled away and sat up.

"How's Molly?" he asked.

"Blue."

"Stands to reason. It's only been a month since Juan— Poor guy. I keep thinking about him."

"So, don't think about it."

He could feel the small shrug she gave.

"Aren't you ever scared?" The question slipped out of his mouth.

"Usually it's over so fast. Bingo! And whew, I'm still there. When I hear the bullets whistling, I get a little shiver. Then I'm setting the f-stops and stuff, concentrating on framing the shot, and I don't sense any danger."

An edge crept back into his voice. "I can't fathom that."

"I didn't make Anouk follow me." Mo abruptly got out of bed and left the room. She might as well have slammed the door.

She was reckless. His mum had been the same way, and he'd hated that too. Was it his fate to have his wife turn into his mother? Did he deserve that?

Some time later when she came back to bed, he was still awake. She touched his arm. "You're right. I shouldn't let myself get carried away. I'm sorry."

"What if it happens again? Anouk might not be so lucky."

Mo drew a crisscross on the bodice of her nightgown. "I won't be so stupid a second time. Cross my heart and hope to die." She laughed, a small bitter laugh.

"It's not funny." He turned on his side away from her.

In the middle of the night he got up. He had developed insomnia, and any hint of light woke him. Mo had forgotten to turn off the amber safelight in the darkroom. The acrid fumes of the chemicals made the room unpleasant. Standing in her private space, he unclipped the prints hanging from metal clips and flipped through them. He paused at the shot of a boy in a black T-shirt with a white cross; the lad was shouldering an M16 with a decal of the Virgin Mary on it. Finlay pressed his lips tightly in anger. To get the shot, Mo must have crossed the Green Line, the dangerous barricade dividing the city. Now that she was determined to make a name for herself, she was becoming foolhardy.

He switched off the light and left the darkroom. He regretted having set it up for her. Yet he had felt so good about it at first—the workbench with enlarger and easel, and on the shelves below, tongs, timer, developing trays, and gallon-sized bottles of bath and fixer. At the time he had considered the darkroom as a form of protection. It meant she didn't have to venture off to some photo lab during curfew. Still, he had been a fool to encourage her career. Both his life and Anouk's would be pleasanter if Mo devoted herself to them rather than to her career. Was that selfish of him? He supposed it was.

In the morning, there was hot water. He showered and toweled himself dry. As he opened the medicine cabinet to get his shaving kit, he knocked down the plastic disk containing Mo's birth control pills. The sight of it riled him. Of course, she had more right to what happened to her body than he, but did his yearning for another child count for nothing? He resented how obdurate she was, but he lacked the energy for another argument.

He held the badger brush under the water and then swirled it around the shaving bowl to work up the lather. With his late father's razor, he shaved in swaths from cheekbones to jaw. The bone handle felt smooth in his grasp. Papa must have brought it to Canada when he emigrated from France. Finlay stretched out his chin, shaved his neck, and made a second pass over his cheeks, working up against the stubble. He glanced in the mirror; he was beginning to look like his father. He had the same dark curls and pointed nose. The scent of the aftershave reminded him of Papa's reminiscing about the lavender bushes in front of his ancestral home in France, where he'd been born. The last time Finlay had seen him alive, Papa asked him to visit Espérac; Finlay only promised that he'd remember his wish.

Finlay tucked his shirt into his khaki pants and knotted his tie, blue with a tiny chevron print. He made the bed, pulling the paisley spread up tight, and drew aside the filmy curtains. Below, a fishmonger in dark baggy trousers was hawking silvery sardines in a basket he held in his hand. In guttural Arabic, he called, "Fish! Fish! Very cheap!"

Mo was doing her morning yoga, and Anouk had already left for her morning run. Finlay made toast, brewed himself coffee, and put the kettle on for Mo's herbal tea. They were out of milk, but he'd buy some later. After setting the table on the balcony, he leaned against the turquoise railing and stared toward the east. It still rankled him that she had ventured to the other side to get the photo of the Christian gunboy.

A sudden movement caught his eye. On a fishing boat near the rocky shore, one of the men flung something overboard, and water sprayed up. Pfft, Pfft, Pfft. The youngsters who were waiting for their school bus ran to the sea railing. They cheered as fish floated to the surface inside a blue net. A tremor went downward from Finlay's left eyelid, and he sucked in his cheek to quell its quivering. Dynamiting for fish was illegal, but who was following the rules these days? The city was a war zone.

The fishermen were hauling in the net when Mo came onto the balcony. In her sundress, she looked like a child bride. At the small

table, she poured herself a cup of tea and sipped it as she glanced
at the paper.

"Anouk should be back by now," he said.

"Don't worry." Mo turned the page of the paper. "She'd outrun
anyone who tried to stop her."

What was the speed of a bullet? Did anyone outrun that? He
forced down a spoonful of the bran cereal.

Mo tapped her finger on the picture of a boy in a blue soccer
outfit; his arms were pitted from shrapnel fragments. "I wish I'd
taken that."

"It's sickening."

"Nice focus, though. Lighting's good, too."

Her nonchalance made him grit his teeth. "That photo of the
kid with the big cross on his T-shirt?"

"What about it?"

"You know what."

"Okay, so I took a chance."

"You're asking for trouble over there."

"I have to go find the news." She peeled a banana, gave half to
him, and ate the other half. She passed him the paper as well, got
up from the table, and crouched by the flower boxes. He glanced
at a story about a bicentennial flag stolen from some observatory
in New Hampshire and put the paper down. He'd been trying
to avoid the news lately. It made things seem even more out of
control.

Bent over the red geraniums, Mo was pulling off the faded
blossoms and yellow leaves. As she dropped them over the railing,
he stared at the back of her legs, still slim, her ankles narrow.
Unlike Molly and most of the faculty wives who had gone thick
in the waist, she was as slender as Anouk. He looked up in relief
as his daughter bounced onto the balcony in her short shorts and
Snoopy T-shirt.

Mo stopped deadheading the geraniums. "Breakfast is at seven," she said in her firm voice. "Your father was starting to worry."

"Sorry, Mom. Sorry, Dad."

"Remember for next time," she said.

"Okay." Anouk slipped into her place at the table and sliced a banana onto her cereal. "I need to get to school early. In homeroom I get to choose the 'Quote for the Day.'"

"Say again?" Mo turned, secateurs in her hand.

"I'm still trying to decide which one. What do you think of this one? A guy on death row gets asked for his last wish. 'A bulletproof vest,' he says. Clever, huh?"

"That's not funny," Finlay said.

"Dad, give me a break. Here's one I got from Danny. It's Malcolm X. 'Cool it, brothers.' He said it just before they shot him."

Finlay jiggled her elbow. "Lass, can't you find something more cheerful?"

"Dad, it's not just me. We're all doing last words. Think I'll go for the Malcolm X." She wolfed down the rest of her Cheerios and hurried off, arms loaded with books, her cap of black hair shining in the sun.

Mo put down the clippers and came and sat down beside him. "Is the gallows humor bugging you?" she said, not unsympathetic.

"Remember when your mother passed away? And my papa? Anouk sobbed her heart out. Now she skates over deaths as if they're scratches on ice."

"Yeah, but that shell protects her," Mo said.

"We need to get her out."

"Look, we've already gone over this. Anouk doesn't want to leave." Mo stood up. "Me neither. Those shots I took yesterday, they'll be in New York by tomorrow. Maybe I'll strike it lucky this time."

"You're spending a fortune on that fancy delivery service."

Her pink cheeks flushed. "Speed counts. That peace march the snipers fired on? If I'd got something in faster, AP might have taken it. " She stacked the bowls. "Look! I can't stop now. Once Congress sees how bad it is, they'll—"

"You're tenacious, but—"

"You used to admire that in me."

Her chair rasped against the terrazzo tiles as she carried the bowls into the kitchen. He went to the iron railing of the balcony and stared out to sea. During their home leave in the States, she had made the rounds of editors to show her portfolio. Finlay didn't like any of the pictures. These included a teenager, blood gushing from his chest; a toddler on a mattress with a print of red roses, his face covered by a sheet; a girl in pigtails wearing a yellow-striped uniform lying dead on a classroom floor under a map of the world on the wall. That kind of picture. Mo asked to be taken on as a retainer, but her editors told her to freelance for a bit longer.

"People shouldn't give in to despair" was her mantra. She cultivated the Associated Press's bureau chief in Beirut. Red-cheeked and plump, Bill Newton took her on as a stringer. AP published her picture of rain-drenched gunboys cradling their machine guns under black umbrellas as they huddled behind sandbags. AP bought her shot of two gorgeous women in a red convertible staring up at an apartment building with shattered windows and walls pockmarked by bullets. AP ran what she called her "Pieta piece"—a mother with a toddler in her lap, his cheeks pitted by shrapnel. She was paid per photo. It wasn't much, but she felt encouraged. A month later, catastrophe struck—Bill Newton disappeared.

Thinking about Bill made Finlay's tic start up. He sucked in his cheek and strode into the kitchen. "Mo, we need to talk."

"What now?"

"What happened to Bill could happen to you."

The telephone rang. "Hello," Mo said, as though glad to escape.

Finlay gazed past the sink filled with dirty dishes through the window toward the Mediterranean, flat and gray. At first, he was the one who had wanted to come to Beirut, to live in a place where no one talked about Vietnam or used words like gooks, grunts, and body bags. For two years or so they enjoyed relative peace with only the occasional sonic booms set off by Israeli pilots to remind Beirutis who was boss. Mo kept up her photography, taking pictures of Anouk and the city. One April she accompanied his Arab-American literature class to Gibran's birthplace, near the site of the biblical Cedars of Lebanon. The bus snaked its way up the road. When they arrived, she had the students join hands as they circled one of the five remaining massive millennial trees. She sent the photo on spec to the *Chicago Tribune*, and they bought it.

Later, when Egypt's president Gamal Abdul Nasser died, a thousand men paraded down the Corniche and chanted to the beat of drums, "Gamal Abdul, Habib Allah—Nasser, Beloved of God." When AP bought the photo, Bill Newton took her under his wing. She began to hang out with the journalists at the Commodore Hotel. "My gang," she called them. She seemed to enjoy their company more than his, he thought.

She hung up the phone and came toward him. "Hey. There's news," she murmured, her hazel eyes shining.

"Have they found Bill?"

"I'm sorry. Not yet." She scrunched her pale forehead. "Look, here's the thing. Now don't get all upset, but that was AP calling from New York. They like my stuff. I've got my foot in the door," she said triumphantly. "Any day now, they'll take me on as a regular."

"God, you're ambitious."

"I know what I'm doing."

"So you say. How about Bill?"

"He'll turn up. It's only a matter of time. Finlay, don't look at me that way. I'm not a monster. That photo you objected to, the one of the gunboy with the cross on his T-shirt? AP liked it."

"You'll get yourself killed. There are plenty of gunboys here. You don't have to go rushing off to the other side."

"No one as cute as that Che Guevara lookalike." Mo smiled. "Sideburns, too, but not as thick as yours." She ran a finger down one of them.

His throat felt so tight he could barely squeeze out the words. He took her hand. "Be careful. Please."

"You'll see. Everything will work out." She stood on tiptoe and twined her slender arms around his shoulders. "Don't worry."

"Take care," he said.

"You too. Take care."

That's what everyone said— instead of "Bye," or "So long," or "See you later"—but only Mo said it with a cutting edge. He supposed he should appreciate the irony. Wasn't that what he taught every day?

As he climbed the stairs to Upper Campus, the April sun felt hot on his back, the iron railing warm under his hand. Anemones, iris, and larkspur bloomed on the hillside by the chemistry building. Coeds in miniskirts and heels hurried past, late for their eight a.m. classes. A few students were studying under the massive banyan. When Anouk was younger, she and Danny would shimmy up the tree, grab its roots that hung down like stalactites, and swing out screaming in wild abandon.

In the English Department, Finlay got a cup of coffee and carried it to the office that was now all his. With the onset of the troubles, his office mate left in the first evacuation, and Finlay moved his desk to where Tom's used to be —kitty-corner to the door. Finlay looked out the window. Everything was normal on Bliss Street. Metal shutters screeched as shop owners pushed them up. The beggar in the brown suit was in his regular spot, cigar box for alms slung over his chest, white cane in hand.

Finlay drained his coffee and set to work. He finished grading a set of freshman essays—he'd already spent five or six hours on them. Several students had not yet turned in their papers, but his department head didn't approve of giving extensions. Short and straitlaced, he railed against what he called "lowering standards at the premier institution of learning in the region."

After Finlay had finished all twenty essays, he unlocked the bottom drawer, where he kept his soft-covered register and entered his students' marks. As he put back the grade book, he happened to glance at the picture on his desk. It was one he had taken two years ago. Mo, her arm around Anouk, was looking straight into the camera, her ginger hair in a thick rope, freckles scattered on her pale cheeks and her hazel eyes wide-set and aware; Anouk was grinning, teeth armed with metal braces. A line from Francis Bacon sprang to his mind: "He that hath wife and children hath given hostages to fortune." Remembering the incident yesterday, he grabbed the photo on sudden impulse and shoved it in the drawer.

At his eleven o'clock in Nicely Hall, he set his satchel on the table at the front. A girl apologized for missing the previous class—a gunfight in her neighborhood—and Finlay allowed her an excused absence. He took roll, and as he called their names, the students raised their hands.

"Bilaad, Jawad; Bitar, Albert; Dajani, Michel; Farag, Randa. Zakharia, Emile."

Finlay spotted the pistol under Emile's chair. That was his rule during the troubles: guns had to be out in the open, not concealed.

He picked up a piece of yellow chalk and started class by writing a line of poetry on the board. Today, instead of the verse by the poet Adonis he had intended, he wrote a line from e.e. cummings:

"Listen, there's a hell of a good universe next door. Let's go."

Nabeel, sitting in the back row, raised his hand. "Professor, isn't that subversive?"

Finlay smiled. "Much poetry is," he said. He delivered his lecture, but it didn't go well. His students were fidgety, and with the unrest in the city, it wasn't surprising. When the bell rang, they filed out, the boys joking and trying to impress the girls. He erased the chalkboard and brushed the chalk dust from his shirt cuffs. As he tucked his books in his satchel, he noticed Emile's gun still beneath his chair. Thickness clogged Finlay's throat as he picked it up. The revolver had the heft of a dead rat and felt cold to his touch. He was tempted to leave it for the janitor to handle, but Emile might need it.

Finlay found him in the Milk Bar under the grape arbor, flirting with Randa. Finlay unbuckled his satchel and held it open. "You forgot this. Here."

Emile slipped the gun into his holster. "My father got it for me."

Randa's ringed hands fluttered. "Emile needs it. Really. Two weeks ago at the Green Line, the other side grabbed him and stuffed him in the trunk of a car."

"No big deal." Emile kept up a manly presence. "They didn't keep me long."

Randa turned to Finlay. "He was lucky. Sometimes people don't want to bother with taking hostages. They just want to shoot somebody. Anybody will do."

Finlay couldn't help but admire her unflinching acceptance of the situation they were in.^

On leaving campus, Finlay headed down Bliss Street. He thought he heard someone call his name, and he spun round. Seeing nobody, he started walking again. Again he heard someone call, "Professor Fortin."

It was Zaki. Tall and rangy, he emerged from underneath a

dirty white Chevrolet. Before the troubles, he had taken freshman English with Finlay. Zaki was passionate about Milton. Zaki had contrasted his life, "beholding the bright countenance of truth in the quiet and still air of delightful studies," with that of his grandfather, a man so poor he was reduced to digging a well in the rocky ground by hand, yet all the while, praising Allah for his blessings.

When the troubles began last year, Zaki's father was yanked off a bus at a roadblock and killed for believing in the wrong religion. To support his family, Zaki dropped out of school and joined a militia, but he had worked as a gunboy only a week before he got his trigger finger shot off. Now he made ends meet with a part-time job as Mo's fixer, driving her around and translating for her.

"What're you doing?" Finlay asked.

Zaki brushed off his pants. "Favor for a friend. Checking for a car bomb. Nothing there."

They ambled along Bliss Street, cars lining the curb, Mount Sannine in the distance, still snow-capped this first week of April. The light at the corner was red, and while they waited, they both heard music coming from a balcony. "Fairuz?" Finlay guessed.

"Yes. Singing she loves Beirut with all her heart. Don't we all?" Zaki said with a tinge of irony. "Frankly, I'd rather go to America."

"To make your fortune?"

"Of course. And you, Professor? You will stay here?"

"For the time being. We're fine." They weren't, but he didn't want to talk about it. Driving for Mo, Zaki was privy to her complaining and some of it was likely about him.

Zaki raised his eyebrows. "Are you sure?"

"Sometimes little things get me down. The——"

"You're right to worry. Lots of bombs these days. And you suffer alongside us. So kind of you. To teach. To abide with us." He put his hand to his heart, and Finlay felt touched.

On Bliss Street, American cars were parked bumper-to-bumper outside the shops, apartment buildings, and three- and four-story houses.

"Shoeshine?" A boy looked up at Finlay from the square of cardboard where he sat on the pavement. He waved his shine rag, his hand grimy with shoe polish.

"Not today. Tomorrow maybe," Finlay said. He and Zaki strolled on past the fast-food restaurants that lined the street. In front of Khayat's Bookstore, Zaki paused to peruse the window display of the latest books. "Mind if I go inside? I need to pick up a book."

"No problem. I'll wait," Finlay said.

Women in summer dresses crowded the street. He liked looking at them. One had a gardenia in her long black hair. The heat of midday had passed, and it was pleasant on the shady side of the street. Two elderly men sat hunched over a backgammon board. Opposite, a wall ran the length of the block and enclosed the University. A few feet away, in front of Uncle Sam's Fast Food, Finlay noticed a red Karmann Ghia parked on his side of the street. The sports car had low, sleek lines, and he idly wished he could afford it. Two little girls in school uniforms were playing hopscotch in the alley. One tossed a stone toward the chalked spaces, hopped from square to square, and bent to retrieve the stone. It made Finlay nostalgic. That first year in Beirut, Anouk had loved to play hopscotch with her friend Jilly, both of them singing, "Skip to my Lou, my darling."

He was distracted from his reminiscence as a fellow crossed in front of him, sidled over to the side of the car, and tossed in a package. The guy had a Groucho Marx mustache, slicked-back hair, and a black-and-white keffiyeh twisted around his neck.

When Zaki came out of the bookstore, Finlay was about to point out the man, but the boy had other worries. "Everything's getting worse," he grumbled. "Strikes, curfews, water shortages, snipers, and now I can't even buy a book. The port is still closed. Who knows how things will end?"

As they walked side by side down the street, he told Finlay a fable. "If you plop a frog in a pot of boiling water, it has the sense to leap out. But if you set it in cold water, it'll paddle around, and as the water heats to a boil, the poor thing will be cooked alive."

Finlay rolled his eyes. He had heard this story so often.

Right at that moment, an explosion boomed. People started running.

Finlay gasped. "That car. The red sports car. It's rigged—"

"Wait," Zaki said, putting his hand on Finlay's arm to restrain him. "Sometimes one follows another."

A few minutes later, they sprinted toward the car. In the alley, glass shards littered the chalked rectangle of the hopscotch game. The girls were gone. The military police, the Red Berets, hemmed in the man with the mustache. Blood ran down his right arm.

"What happened?" Finlay asked.

"He screwed up. Just gave us a scare. Didn't know what he was doing, thank God," the Red Beret said.

"Have you seen two little girls?" Finlay asked in a panicky voice.

The Red Beret pointed to the shoeshine boy. "Ask him. He was the one who alerted us."

Finlay looked about wildly. At last, he spotted the girls. They held strawberry ice cream cones as they stared at the shattered back window of the Karmann Ghia. The taller one wore a gold heart-shaped locket and tiny gold studs in her ears. The other girl bent to lick some ice cream that had dripped onto her wrist. Their nonchalance rankled him. It was by sheer luck that they weren't dead. If Mo had been here, she'd have whipped out her camera to photograph the scene. As a war photographer, that was what she was paid to do. She knew the risks. Anouk did not. And she had become blasé about the danger.

They had to get her out.

Chapter 2

When she got home from school—it was a half-day because of Good Friday—her mom was shut up in the darkroom. Anouk slid through the beaded curtains to her room and sprawled in the green beanbag to do her homework. The hardest assignment was the study sheet on Antigone. She'd been doodling in class—all the swirls of a prom dress— and couldn't recall the theme of the play. She wasn't even sure exactly what a theme was. She wasn't smart like Danny, but at least she had friends, especially Jilly, who was popular. He just had her.

He was too busy with his peace stuff and taking care of pigeons for a biology professor who had evacuated to the other side of the city. Once, after a lot of begging, he let her help. He fed the birds, opened the small door in the hutch and let them go free: fantails, Jacobins, rock doves, tumblers, capuchins, and frillbacks. He'd taught her all their names. He was smart, tall too. He could have been a forward for the basketball team, but he wouldn't even try out. His excuse was that he objected to the team being called the Warhawks. He didn't have a lick of school spirit.

She did. She was proud of having made cheerleader. She had a flat back, perfect posture, and weighed only a hundred and two pounds. Every squad needed an angel, a girl light enough to send flying through the air. All she had to do was to keep her muscles tight until someone caught her—it happened every time. She was mostly over her crush on him, but she couldn't help but wish Danny would be the one to try to catch her.

The doorbell rang. He had come to work on their bandage project. Last weekend, they had gone door to door to all twenty-one apartments to collect old sheets, which they sterilized in her mom's spaghetti pot. One for a double-bed made fifty-five bandages, each three inches wide, while a single made about thirty-five. They went to the kitchen, and Anouk found him a pair of scissors in the junk drawer. Sitting at the kitchen table, he picked up a sheet, slit the hemline and ripped. She turned the radio dial from its usual spot on the BBC to her favorite deejay and took a strip of fabric to roll. The edges were frayed, but that didn't matter. She turned the cloth over and over, keeping the roll taut.

"Bet we'll have five hundred when we're done." Danny squeezed a roll in between the others in the carton to go to the Red Cross.

"Zaki, the guy who works for my mom, says we need thousands."

"We'll get them. It's bad enough that people get shot; they shouldn't have to bleed to death, too."

She told him about the guy who got shot in the lane behind Zamil's Photo Store.

"Hard," Danny said.

"I think the guy just got it in the leg, but my dad rushed us out before I could tell."

"I'm sure his friends came back for him."

Anouk got up to change the station on the radio. "Hey, you want to see something cool? I'll show you my mom's shots of that camp where Zaki lives."

"Yeah, but we shouldn't go through her stuff."

"She wants the whole world to see them, so why not us?"

"Still, it won't hurt to ask," he said.

Mom, who was in the darkroom, actually looked flattered and gave her a manila envelope where she kept recent prints. Back in the kitchen, Anouk untied the red string around the clasp and spread the black-and-white photos on the table. Danny flipped through them: men hunched on stools playing backgammon using an upside-down orange crate for a table; Zaki's shack, stones weighing down the tin roof; and inside, sleeping mats stacked against the wall where a map of Palestine was tacked up. She passed Danny a picture of a skinny woman in an ankle-length white dress with red embroidery. "That's Zaki's mom. Nice dress, huh? She changed just for that shot."

"I like it that she's proud."

"Zaki's that way, too. He used to be in one of my dad's classes before the troubles. Dad says he's smart as a whip."

Danny picked up the photo of a man on a stretcher. "Poor guy."

"But he'll go to heaven."

"That's naive. Heaven is what we're supposed to make here on earth."

"Still, there's gotta be something afterward. Like after we lose our baby teeth, the real ones come in."

"Next thing you'll believe in zombies." He gave her a big creepy smile and made his green eyes grow huge; he clenched his fingers into claws, and, making retching noises, staggered toward her. She laughed hysterically.

Afterward, he invited her over to see his peace installation. She'd been to his room often, and she liked everything about it: the red poppy print curtains, the white shag rug, the photo of him hiking along some pilgrimage trail in Spain. He showed her the acceptance letter from Swarthmore College, where he was going to take classes in Peace Studies in the fall. Lined up on his desk were tin cans, full of nails, screws and bolts, along with spools of string and wire. Stacked on the floor were shoeboxes filled with hunks of shrapnel and bullet casings. Then she took out a couple of the brass casings, put them to her ears and said he could make her earrings from them. She liked flirting with him, but he barely noticed.

He showed her the knee-high sculpture he called, "The Tree of Death." A length of lead pipe made the trunk of the tree, and painted hunks of shrapnel hung from the wire branches. She touched a jagged edge of the shrapnel. It felt cold. "Where did you find this stuff?"

"On the beach. And from Jimmy."

"That little kid?" She fingered a red casing.

"Yeah. He gets it on the playground."

"What did you trade him for?"

Danny squirmed. "Three firecrackers."

"That's not enough."

"Jimmy thought it was."

She wasn't going to argue. She tightened a wire loop around a cartridge shell. "Why don't you use one of my mom's shots for the top?"

"No way."

"Or one of Jimmy's GI Joes? Sort of like the Angel of War."

"Too tame. Maybe I'll find something gruesome on the beach."

"Want company?"

"Better check with your mom."

Danny was like that, always wanting her to stay on good terms with her parents, which seemed odd because he was such a rebel. Maybe it was because Mr. Delacruz was dead that Danny appreciated her parents taking him under their wing, especially her dad.

"Okay, okay," she said. When she got home, she knocked on the bathroom door. "In a sec," Mom said, but it was several minutes before she came out. She gave her permission, reminded them to watch for snipers and come home if they heard firing, gave Anouk a quick hug, and went back into the darkroom. It was a brush-off and made Anouk feel blue. Jilly's mom would have said no. She was such a safety fanatic that she was making the family leave, but at least she cared. She might have even asked to go with them to the beach. But Mom was always too busy. Why couldn't she ever see how it felt? There was nothing to do but suck it up. Anouk took a deep breath and left.

The beach was deserted. They stood on the pebbly sand, looking out to sea. It was blazing hot, and Danny took off his striped jersey. He found a stick and drew a peace sign in the sand. They combed the shoreline, littered with scallop shells, old tin cans, and a rusty bike chain. She found a yellow ducky and a collapsed beach ball. Nothing right for the tiptop of the Tree of Death.

"Keep your eyes out for a starfish. That'll work. We can paint it black and call it the dark star." He wound the bike chain and dumped it into the garbage bag he'd brought from home.

They stumbled across beer bottles, stray bits of Styrofoam, and rusted batteries. She found a piece of green sea glass and held it up to the sun. "I get to keep anything pretty, okay?" She stuck it and the ducky in her backpack.

He poked a sea urchin's black quills with his stick.

"Lucky you didn't step on it. Maybe that's your nasty thingy for the top."

"Too small," he said.

"You're awfully finicky. See that over there?" She kicked off her sandals, waded into the water and fished it out of the seaweed. It was a Barbie, nude except for one high-heeled shoe. She came back to shore and showed it to him. "Hey, let's find her a Ken doll and put a 'Make Love Not War' sign beside them. Good idea, huh?"

"Too tame. Too cute." He hurled the Barbie into the sea, and it bobbed in the white-crested waves.

"Hey!" She jabbed him in the ribs as a great idea came to her. "I know where you can get a foot!"

"You're kidding?" He stared at her, his eyes a stormy green.

"For real. I heard about it at school. Still in its sneaker."

"Gross." He scrunched up his face.

"Yeah, but gross is what you need. Right? It's down by the harbor near the Blue Destiny Hotel. We could go there and be back before supper."

"Your dad would have a fit."

Her father had set limits as to where she was permitted to go. Last month, he had sat her and Danny down with a map of the city, drawing her boundaries in red ink: Anywhere on campus was allowed; she could go along Bliss Street and up Jeanne d'Arc to Hamra; and she could walk down to the lighthouse. But going a single block east of campus, even to the American Embassy, was forbidden.

"I don't see why Dad's so strict with me. My mom goes wherever she wants."

"It's for her job," Danny said.

"We could take Cinderella's Coach."

"Better ask your dad first."

"He's at the office." She kicked the sand.

"Let's check with your mom."

She didn't want to face that closed darkroom door again. "No can do."

"About that foot." Danny's eyes bored into Anouk's. "Whose foot was it? Where did it come from? Sure you're not kidding?"

"It's there. All the kids said so."

"But what's their basis for saying that?"

"Who knows? Honestly, you're so picky."

"Just because everyone thinks something doesn't make it true. Maybe it's not a foot, but something else the size of a foot, say a dead squirrel."

"How're we going to know if we don't check it out? You tell me that."

He didn't look the least bit enthusiastic. They walked along the shoreline back to the stairs that led up to the Corniche, where they passed one of his peace wreaths, a ring of olive branches decorated with origami paper cranes. He said it was one of his best, but a woman carrying a bag of oranges passed it without giving it a second glance.

"See, it's too tame," Anouk said. "A real foot, all bloody, would shock her. You gotta jolt people. That way they'll do something to stop the troubles."

He shrugged. "Maybe you're right." He made her go home to ask her mom for permission to take Cinderella's Coach while he waited in the parking lot.

When she got to their flat, the bathroom door was closed, so Anouk grabbed the car key, a plastic figurine in a blue princess dress, from its hook by the front door, ran down the six flights of stairs, and gave it to Danny.

"This is girly," he said.

"It's a joke. It's to match the VW bus. Cinderella's Coach, get it?"

"I don't have a license."

Now she was caught up in the idea. It was an adventure. "It'll be practice for your driving test. We'll drive over, grab the foot, and hurry back. Nerves of steel, right?"

"OK, OK," he grumbled. In the driver's seat he went through the ritual: check mirror, release handbrake, put the key in the ignition, move into gear, check the blind spot. He drove through campus and turned onto the Corniche, where little kids were pedaling their tricycles up and down the broad sidewalk. Soon he was cruising toward the harbor, where container boats were lined up waiting to be unloaded. He shifted gears to fourth and fifth, going faster as they passed the American Embassy.

There was a boom, and Anouk jumped.

"Only a sonic boom," he said. "Israelis saying, 'Hi.'"

"Don't you hate it when they do that? Still, it's not fair to hate anyone, especially not them. The Holocaust, remember?"

"They're awfully mean to the Palestinians." He stopped for a red light.

"Lay off the politics." She enjoyed talking to Danny like that as if he weren't older and smarter.

A half-mile down the road, she spotted a parking space. "Okay, over there," she said.

"You'd better be right about that foot." He grabbed the black bag in which to stash it, and they clambered out of Cinderella's Coach.

On the beach, a few feet from a rowboat leaning on its side, a black cat gnawed on a mullet, tugging the flesh from the bones. It was revolting. The foot might be too. She didn't feel so sure about it now, but she didn't dare tell Danny that after having dragged him here.

"Hey," he shouted to her. "We haven't got all day."

"Wait up. I'm coming."

They hunted a half-hour for the foot. She thought she saw it next to some blue fishing nets, but it was just a water bottle. "There's got to be a foot somewhere around," she said. "A severed foot. In a sneaker. Everybody said so."

"Well, everybody got it wrong. Dead wrong." He scowled. "Vamonos."

Dark clouds scudded across the horizon and waves smashed against the boulders as they plodded through the ribbed sand until they arrived at the steps leading to the sea road. They stopped to rub the grains of sand off their feet.

"Shit. I got gunk on me," Danny said. She dug a tissue out of her pocket and handed it to him. He rubbed, but the tar stuck, a black smear on the side of his ankle. "I knew we shouldn't have come. You believe everything you hear. Like some little kid."

That stung, and she didn't feel she deserved it. "Well, don't blame me. Everybody said there was a foot."

He rubbed harder at the tar. "Everybody was f—ing wrong."

"Someone must have got to it before us," she grumbled. "Anyway, what's the big deal? A lot of kids think you're weird to be such a peacenik."

"Why do you care what they think?" He heaved the trash bag over his shoulder.

"You always think everybody's wrong, and you're right. Maybe it's the other way around."

He stopped short and turned to her. "But there are better ways to live. You have to do what you think is right, not what other people think. My mom once told me about this old lady, Peace Pilgrim. She's walked thousands of miles with only a comb, a toothbrush, and a pencil. She keeps going until someone gives her food or a place to sleep. She tells people about peace. And know what? She's still at it."

"Yakkety yak. That's some weird old lady."

"At least she's trying. But you just want to be popular."

She wasn't taking that from him, the hermit. "So, is that a crime?"

"I admire that old lady. You shouldn't make fun of her." He plodded ahead.

"Wait up."

He kicked a stone. "There's something else. I shouldn't say this because your dad is great. But in this one shitty way, you're exactly like him. He never says what he thinks. It's always, 'Hemingway says this,' or 'so and so says that.'"

"I'm not like that!"

"You are, too. With you, it's always 'everybody says,' or 'everybody thinks.' Who cares what everybody thinks? What do you say? What do you think? That's what counts."

"Oh, just shut up. You're wrong about my dad. He doesn't do it to show off. He can't help it. All those dead writers, they're like part of him."

They were almost back at Cinderella's Coach, and in the distance she noticed two men slouching against its side. They wore white shirts, gray pants, and black lace-up boots.

"Hey, get a load of them." She nudged Danny in the ribs. "Except for the boots, they could be teachers."

"No way. That guy's got his shirt unbuttoned halfway down to his belly button. Gross."

As they got closer, she saw the thick gold chain on his bare chest, and the gold rings on his fingers. The other guy was bald, and his belly ballooned out over his pants. She grabbed Danny's arm. "Goldfingers and Fathead," she giggled.

Fathead advanced a step toward them. "Please," he said, his voice quiet. He kept one arm behind his back like Dad at Christmas when he'd lean down and say, "Guess what I've got?" And laughing, he'd shout, "Marzipan," and pull out the box of sugary almond candy.

"Yes?" Anouk smiled her cheerleader smile.

"Please. One moment, please." Fathead drew his hand from behind his back and slowly, casually waved a pistol—not at them, but downward at their shadows on the sidewalk.

Her hands flew to her mouth. She couldn't take her eyes from the funny little gun, black and oily, no bigger than a cap gun.

"You." Fathead swiveled the pistol, so it pointed at Danny's ankles. "Give my friend the key, please."

Anouk let go of Danny's arm, and he dropped the bag with the stuff for his peace installation. Reaching into the pocket of his Bermuda shorts, he fished out the key. Goldfingers grabbed it, got into Cinderella's Coach and pulled shut the yellow-and-green checked curtains at the windows.

"You, little one," Fathead said to her in a greasy voice. "Little one, you may go." He edged around so that he was behind Danny. Fathead waved the gun as if it was a flashlight, and he was lighting her way across a dark street. When she didn't budge, he yelled at her to leave; his voice was harsh. She shook her head. He nudged Danny forward, the muzzle in the small of his back.

"Yallah!" Fathead snapped, his finger on the trigger. "For the last time, leave."

Danny just stood there, pale as could be, a sick expression on his face.

She stumbled across the street, terrified for Danny. When she made it to the other side, she looked back. Fathead's pudgy fingers were in Danny's black curls. He shoved him head first onto the mustard vinyl in the back of Cinderella's Coach, and the van drove off in a plume of white exhaust.

Chapter 3

She rushed to the front desk of the Blue Destiny Hotel. Panting, she hit the service bell. The desk clerk continued sorting the mail, his back to her, so she dinged it again, repeatedly.

"Sorry, I didn't see you come in," the clerk said, turning toward her.

"Hey! Please help! We need to call the police."

The telephone rang, and the clerk lifted the receiver.

She pressed the bell again. "My friend's been kidnapped. Call the —"

"I doubt the police would help."

"Just call them. Please."

"Shouting won't help," he said.

"Damn it all!" she cried. She had never sworn before, and she half-expected her father to appear and reprimand her, but the bellboy kept on pushing a luggage trolley, and the clerk glared at her as he kept talking on the telephone.

She raced out. On the Corniche, everything seemed the same: the taxis honking, the stench of diesel and exhaust fumes. The one thing different was that Cinderella's Coach had disappeared into thin air. She ran on despite the stitch in her left side. At the university's Sea Gate, she took the shortcut across the soccer fields.

At the Faculty Flats, the electricity was off, so she trudged up the stairs. On the sixth floor, hers and Danny's, she paused outside his front door on which he had stuck a nuclear disarmament decal. Feeling sick to her stomach, she sneaked past it to #602.

Once inside, she hurried to the toilet bowl and retched. She splashed water on her face and washed her hands, but she couldn't get the tar off. The smell made her more nauseous. She went to find her mother. The darkroom door was closed, but she pounded on it. "Mom, something happened," she whimpered.

"What now?" Her mom sounded impatient.

"Danny. Some guys grabbed him," Anouk sobbed.

"Calm down. You're shaking like a leaf."

"And it's all my fault. I took Cinderella's Coach."

"What?"

The front door opened, and Anouk darted to it. "Daddy, something's happened. Something awful." She blurted out the awful story and bawled like a baby.

"Look, we can break down later." Mom ticked off her plan of action. "First, we tell Molly. Next, we call the university, and they'll call the police. Then we—"

"The police won't help. That's what the man at the hotel said."

"Well, Danny's an American. That makes a huge difference." Mom opened the directory of expatriate faculty and ran her finger down the column of administrators until she found the dean's number. Dad called him, and they went next door.

The instant Mrs. Delacruz opened the door, she asked about Danny. "It's past curfew. I'm worried. Usually he's so good about calling when he might be late."

"That's why we're here," Mom said. "Look, we've got terrible, terrible news. We better go inside." As they entered, Anouk smelled the chocolate chip cookies. In the living room, Mom gave her a little push as if to tell her to hurry up while Dad got the red alpaca wrap from the back of the sofa and placed it around Mrs. Delacruz's shoulders. Anouk twisted the red-and-blue friendship bracelet Danny had given her last year. "Something bad happened. And it's all my fault." She turned to her mother. "Mom," she begged. "You tell her."

"Mo, what's happened?"

"Here's the thing. Danny's missing. There's no easy way to say it. He was kidnapped, it seems, but we'll find him, and we won't leave you." Her mom spoke in a rush. It was like when she ripped the adhesive tape off a sore.

"What? What's that? Kidnapped, you say?"

Anouk bowed her head. "Um. Well, um, Danny and I, we were coming back from the beach, we'd been collecting stuff for his peace thingies. And then, well," she blubbered. "These creeps grabbed him."

"No, sweet Jesus, no. It's not true. It's not. I'd know if it was. It can't be."

Anouk sat alone on the sofa and wished she could run somewhere far away. A scallop shell with a red cross on it lay on the table. Danny had told her about it—something about a pilgrimage, but she couldn't remember what.

After what seemed like hours, the Dean arrived with a Lebanese man, an official from the American consulate and a pair of policemen. They sat at the kitchen table, where one of the police had set up a portable typewriter. The other policeman grilled them while his partner typed out their answers.

"What was your son's blood type? Where's the boy's father? The year and registration number of the VW bus? Its color?"

"An offer of a ransom might get him back faster," her mom said.

"U.S. government policy is firm. No concessions to terrorists. We expect the host government"—Mr. Brown glanced at the Lebanese official—"to exercise its responsibilities to protect those in its territory. We expect the boy to be released as quickly and safely as possible."

The policeman turned to Anouk. "Could you pick the kidnappers out of a lineup?"

"I'm not sure."

"Were they Arabs?"

"I can't say for sure."

"Were they light or dark-complexioned?"

"Normal. One of them wore a bunch of rings on his fingers, and the other guy was fat."

"How long was their hair? What color?"

"I don't know. I just don't. All I remember is their black lace-up boots."

Mrs. Delacruz covered her face with her hands. "How can this be happening? He's going to be eighteen next week. I didn't know what to buy him for his birthday. And now—" She rocked back and forth, whimpering.

"Look. We'll find Danny." Her mom put an arm around Mrs. Delacruz. "What Mr. Brown said about not paying a ransom, that's the company line. There are ways of handling these things— say, the consulate arranges for a visa, or for some hotshot's kid to go to school in the States. The Dean puts in a good word. That kind of thing. Sometimes other countries help out too. You'll see. It'll be okay."

When they got home, Anouk shut herself in her room and stayed there. Dad set a plate of spaghetti at her door, but she didn't touch it. At three in the morning, she was still awake. When she peeked out, she saw a light on in the darkroom. Mom was there sorting through her box of old contact sheets. In the morning, she made an 8 X 10 print of Danny, her father had seventy-five photocopies made, and that afternoon the three of them went around the neighborhood pulling off the "Lebanon Love It or

Leave It," and the "Leaving Town Sale" signs from the telephone poles. In their place, they pinned his photo followed by five lines of thick type.

MISSING PERSON.

Daniel Delacruz (nickname Danny)

Age: 17

Height: 2 meters. Weight: 56 kilos.

Black hair/green eyes

Reward Offered: 50,000 Lebanese liras

Chapter 4

A few nights later, Finlay was awakened by a whirring sound, and when he got up to check, he found Anouk in the bathroom with the hair dryer, aiming it at the wet splotch on a sheet. He guessed what had happened and put his arm around her. "Sunbeam, it's okay. Dump those old sheets in the tub, and we'll put on some fresh ones."

When he came back with them, she was standing in her room looking blue. As they tucked the sheet corners in on either side, he tried to comfort her by saying it wasn't her fault, and it could happen to anyone. In the morning, he pulled the wringer-washer from its place in the corner of the kitchen, opened the metal drum, and loaded her sheets along with the rest of the week's laundry. The old washer bounced on the floor, leaking sudsy water. When the clothes were done, he dumped the wet sheets and the clothes in the laundry basket and took it up to the roof, where a dozen lines were strung along tall metal posts. He pegged up the sheets and assorted underwear, shorts, skirts, and T-shirts.

Afterward, he walked to the railing to look out over the city. The quiet felt eerie. Across the street on the rooftop gym of Anouk's school, boys about Danny's age dribbled basketballs and practiced their layups, jump shots, and slam-dunks. High up, pigeons wheeled in the sky while far below, armored trucks sped down the seaside promenade. To the east, plumes of smoke rose. The television antennas sprouting from the roofs of apartment buildings crisscrossed the sky. In some of those buildings, snipers were keeping watch; Finlay pictured a child's eyes centered in the crosshairs of a gun. He tossed his head to shake off the image and turned in the direction of the Phoenicia Hotel. He had heard that militiamen had shot out the plate glass windows in the upper floors so they could fire rockets at the enemy forces holed up in the Holiday Inn. The Battle of the Hotels, they called it.

Anouk once said that you could see how light travels faster than sound. First, you saw the black smudge on the side of the building, and only afterward did you hear the boom of the rocket smashing it. She'd learned that in physics class. Her detached analysis bothered him. Finlay wanted to tell her that people were dying, that they deserved proper attention. He worried that she didn't care. At least, the bed-wetting proved otherwise.

In the afternoon, he and Mo went up to the roof to get the wash. As he took down a pair of gym socks, he thought of Anouk's mad quest for the foot. He turned to Mo. "We should leave."

"It's only been four days since Danny was taken. Don't let's waste our energy worrying. He'll turn up."

"Your Bill Newton died." Finlay unpegged Anouk's favorite T-shirt, one with a print of red poppies.

"That's different. Bill's a big shot. Danny's just a kid. Beats me why anyone would grab him. And why take Cinderella's Coach? It's old as the hills."

She was trying to rationalize the unfathomable. "If something happens to Danny, it'll damage Anouk." He took down her sheet with its print of gamboling kittens. It felt warm in his hands.

"Here, I'll help." Mo came toward him, and they stretched the sheet taut, doubled it lengthwise, folded it in half once, and then again.

"About Anouk." Finlay placed the folded sheet in the basket. "Except for school, she hasn't left home since those goons grabbed Danny. She's terrified of running into Goldfingers or Fathead, and she avoids Molly like the plague. She blames herself for what happened."

An explosion boomed.

"Another little visit from our neighbors to the south," Mo said, her voice ironic.

He searched the sky but saw no Israeli jet. "It's not a sonic boom. Maybe a car bomb?" He grabbed the basket, and she sprinted after him down the stairs.

School was dismissed early that day because of the fighting, and when she got home, Anouk complained about getting extra homework. "It's not fair," she said.

"Better get started on it," Mo said.

Anouk made a face, sprawled on the living room floor, and opened her biology textbook. She scribbled notes for a while and looked up at Finlay. "Know what? I wish I'd inherited Mom's looks."

"You did," he said, surprised. "You're slender and have your mother's eyes and mouth."

"She'd be prettier if she wore lipstick."

Mo put down the length of cotton that she was cutting into diamond shapes for patchwork. "Not my style, Sunbeam."

"So? Change your style."

"Don't talk to your mother in that tone of voice," Finlay chided.

Anouk apologized in a sullen voice and slouched off in the direction of her room.

Mo turned to him. "Anything in the mail?"

He had been holding back the news. He'd wanted to present it at the right time. "A job offer in Montreal."

"Cold up there." She cut another patch and added it to the pile.

It was the third offer he'd received; he was a lucky man, his colleagues said. Jobs teaching English were hard to find. Montreal was home in a way, but there was trouble there too: French Canadian separatists hiding bombs in mailboxes. Was there no peaceful spot anywhere on earth that wanted him?

"We're better off staying put." She wet a piece of thread, slipped it through the eye of a needle, and began to hem a red patch.

He recognized the fabric. It came from the maternity dress he had bought last November when she was in need of cheering up. He had assumed it was morning sickness that was depressing her, but it was the pregnancy itself. She aborted the baby at three months and told him only after the fact.

"I wish you'd kept the child," he blurted out.

"What?" She flinched. "Don't, please. I can't deal with babies. Let the children of the world be Anouk's brothers and sisters."

"We could have another."

"Please, not that again. I put in my time with Anouk. With just her, I can still do my work; with a baby, it'd be impossible."

He glowered at the red patch in her hand—little Freddy snipped into diamonds.

"Maybe you need a hobby too. Busy hands calm the mind."

"What are you going to do with that quilt?" he asked.

"It's a Shining Star pattern. I'm planning on giving it to a refugee family."

"Anouk might like it."

"She's got three already. Refugee kids don't have any."

"But she's ours." Our little girl, he wanted to say, but Mo would think him maudlin.

"What's she supposed to do with another spread? You tell me."

He pictured his wife six months pregnant and beautiful. If she had let nature take its course, at this very moment he could have touched her belly and felt their baby kick. He twitched and sucked in his cheek. He had lost that battle. There was no point rehashing his grief.

He went to the kitchen to prepare some pizza dough. Working with his hands to form the dough, he was able to regain his equanimity. After he had set the dough to rise, he took his cup of coffee out onto the balcony, where Mo was sipping herbal tea. She slapped his hand playfully. "You know caffeine is bad for you."

"Where's Anouk?"

"Down in the basement. All the kids are there, she says. I better check on them in case they got it into their heads to streak or something."

"Anouk's too shy for that. Thank God."

Mo grinned. "Oh, come on. Even Snoopy streaks. Think of it. If thousands of us streaked across the Green Line, that might wake people up. That's one picture I bet I could sell."

After she had left, Finlay worked on his lesson plans until it was time to punch down the pizza dough. It wasn't as satisfying as making bread. Nothing was. He spread on the tomato paste, added the toppings—olives, pepperoni, and cheese— and set the pizzas in the oven. Once they were sizzling, he carried them to the basement.

Mo seemed relieved to see him. Apparently, when she had arrived, the boys were screaming "touché," lunging at each other with gym mats while the girls snickered over the naked women in a dusty *National Geographic* they'd found. She calmed the boys down and gave the girls her pep talk about nudity and respecting human dignity.

He sliced the pizzas in the dim light, and it was quiet while they ate. They had just finished eating when the sirens sounded again. Instead of staying put, Mo got up to leave. "Please wait until the all clear," he said.

"Here? In the dungeon?" She rolled her eyes.

He hated it when she called it that.

"Too stuffy for me. And, as I've told you a thousand times, I need to do my work."

Shortly after she left, the electricity went dead. Finlay lit candles and had everyone sit in a circle, and one of Danny's friends played, "We Shall Overcome," on his guitar while Anouk and her friends sang along.

Finlay lay down on one of the mats and soon dozed off. In a dream, he found himself waist-deep in pink hollyhocks, caught in a snow globe. A bosomy woman stood at a nail-studded door of a half-timbered house. Her fair hair was gathered in a purple and gold net, and she held a snail in her open palm, its horns wavering. He reached out his hands to her, but she vanished, as did the house, built of stone, an ancient beauty with a high-pitched roof. Papa was standing there, arms outstretched in welcome.

Finlay awakened. It was a recurring dream and always gave him twinges of guilt, because he was sure his father would have liked his only grandchild to know the pleasures of French life: their passion for hunting snails and mushrooms, their elegant ways, and their love of the table.

Finlay thought back to the worst day of his life, the day Papa died. It was spring break at the college, and he had gone home to Montreal for a visit, leaving Mo and Anouk in Kansas. It had been snowing. While Papa cooked the noon meal, a beef bourguignon, his mum drank glass after glass of red Merlot. She complained about the weather, unusual for late March. "Another wee drop to warm me up," she said. Papa poured another glass. "Foul weather can't stop the wine from tasting good," he said. An hour or so later, he got a toothache.

"Maybe it's a loose filling or a cavity." Mum gave him an aspirin, but it didn't help. They each had a glass of whiskey. Papa clamped his hand to his cheek, and when he could bear no more, Finlay offered to take him to the dentist, but Mum insisted he needed the time to prepare for his classes and said that she would drive. For the rest of his life he would regret having allowed her to do so.

When his parents had still not returned by the time he finished his class prep, he put on his mittens and red toque, got the snow shovel, and cleared the path. As he was finishing, a policeman arrived, badge shiny against his dark snow-speckled parka. "Let's go in out of the cold," he said. In the vestibule, he broke the news. There had been a car accident and his father had died in the ambulance on the way to the hospital.

Heaviness had wedged like a boulder in Finlay's chest. He stared at the policeman's black galoshes as they dripped onto the black-and-white tile hexagons of the vestibule. The man's glasses must have fogged in the warmth, for he wiped them dry with a handkerchief.

"And Mum? My mother?"

"Mrs. Fortin told us we'd find you here. The hospital is keeping her for observation."

"Will she—"

"She'll be okay. A few lacerations."

Now, years later, in the basement shelter in the mild dawn of a spring day, Finlay lay quietly in the dark. After a while, he twisted the pink balls of wax from his ears and set the plugs in their plastic box. The power was back on, and by the light of the twenty-watt bulb dangling from the ceiling, he watched Anouk, her small body curled in a fetal position beside him. He closed his eyes. God protect her. He burrowed under his sleeping bag for his flashlight, propped himself on an elbow, and opened Hemingway's *A Natural History of the Dead*. Apart from the occasional gush of water down the pipes, the silence was profound.

When the sun pierced the strips of duct tape that crisscrossed the grimy windows, he could make out twenty or thirty people arranged in family clusters. Molly Delacruz was a few feet from him, a space on the floor beside her where Danny should be. Mo hadn't come down. He was the only one without his mate. Finlay hoped he hadn't screamed in his sleep. She claimed he sometimes did. Still in his blue-and-white striped pajamas, he picked his way around the bodies, bending his head so as not to hit the joists. At the far end of the basement, he pulled open the steel door and trudged up the dusty steps. In the gray light of dawn, he listened for the Kalashnikovs: not a single rat-a-tat-tat. The militiamen, gunboys as Mo called them, were snoozing off the night's work, and it was too early for snipers. Mo and Anouk were safe, but that hardly comforted him. For how long? was the question.

C h a p t e r 5

On the first of May, Finlay's father used to buy lily of the valley. A single sprig brought luck and bliss all year long—so Papa had told him. Curiously, the Lebanese carried on the custom even though the French mandate had ended long ago. When the Fortins first arrived, he wanted to send Anouk to a French school in East Beirut, on the other side of town, so she'd become more fluent in French. Mo nixed it, which turned out to be a good thing, for the troubles would have prevented Anouk from traveling there safely.

As he got out of bed, Mo stirred, eyes closed, ginger hair spread out on the pillowcase, a slender arm on his side of the bed. When she looked like that, defenseless, he loved her; he swore he did. He got dressed and set off for the florist on Jeanne d'Arc Street.

It was a balmy spring day. Outside the shop, dahlias and delphiniums, roses and gladiolas stood in big aluminum containers. He went in and bought a bouquet of lily of the valley, and the clerk wrapped the tiny bell-like blooms in green tissue. As Finlay left the shop, a pickup truck jammed with men, women, and children passed. In back, the cargo area was piled high with sofas, air conditioners, bookcases, cartons, and mattresses; the iron legs of a bed frame jutted into the sky. Were they Christians—what a Muslim colleague called "those troublesome Maronites"— escaping to East Beirut? Or Muslims who had fled that side of the city to find shelter in West Beirut? In times of trouble, it was safer to be with your kind. Even in his class, no one wanted to cozy up beside a classmate he might later be required to murder.

As the pickup truck passed, Molly swam into view on the other side of the street. She had suffered terrible blows, the death of Juan and now Danny kidnapped. Wretched in the presence of her pain, Finlay was tempted to slip into the alleyway to avoid her. But that was cowardly. He tightened his hold on the bouquet and crossed the street. Molly's red hair flew out in all directions, and her eyes were the same haunting jade color as Danny's. On impulse, he put the flowers in her arms and told her about the French belief that lily of the valley brought luck. He wanted to say he felt the profoundest sympathy, but she might take it to mean he assumed Danny was dead, so he said only that it must be rough for her.

Molly dipped her head to breathe in the fragrance of the bouquet. He was afraid she might cry, but she didn't, and as she headed back to campus, her step seemed to him lighter, and her bangles jingled. He returned to the florist to buy flowers for Mo. As he selected a bouquet of lily of the valley, the smell of the white lilies in a funeral wreath on display overpowered him. It reminded him of the casket spray of flowers at his father's funeral.

At the white-tiled morgue where his father was taken after the accident, Finlay had drawn back the sheet. He had felt the softness of Papa's brown curls, and touched his closed eyelids and icy hands. He had hailed a cab to go home and plodded down the shoveled path bordered by the twin walls of snow. He yanked his cap down over his forehead, but the flakes continued to whip his cheeks. By the porch, the boughs of the lilac tree, glazed with ice, crackled in the wind. He plodded up the steps of the gray porch and took off his parka and boots in the vestibule. He rubbed his arms and stamped his feet. In the living room, he leaned against the radiator, but could not get warm. He sank onto the couch in the living room, pulled the gray mohair spread over his head and lay in the gloom until the hospital phoned and told him his mother was ready for discharge. It was seven p.m. In the taxi on his way to the hospital to pick her up after the accident, he'd seen the skid marks where the Ford had gone off the road. She'd been driving too fast to make the curb; he was sure of it. Mum relished the feel of skidding in ice and snow, that heady sensation of being out of control and always, always getting lucky. She and Mo were alike that way, both reckless.

A thick white patch had covered Mum's right eye. They didn't speak. After they got home, she sat in her usual spot at the kitchen table. "Your father was wearing his seat belt. I wasn't. It's not fair. I should never have taken that wee drop. I'm the one who should be dead." She muttered something else, but she was talking too fast for him. He got up from his chair and stretched his arms around her to comfort her. And there it was—the whiff of whiskey.

"You better eat something." His voice sounded odd to him, low and guttural. Without quite knowing what he was doing, he put the frying pan on the stove, got butter and eggs from the refrigerator, scrambled them, put on water for coffee, and placed a slice of white bread in the toaster. Mum ate one bite of the toast and set it down. She pushed away the plate, the eggs runny white on the pink-and-yellow flowered Spode china.

"I can't eat. Pray with me? The Lord's prayer?" she said.

If he could harden himself, he'd be all right. He helped Mum up from the chair, and she knelt down on the black-and-white linoleum, the joints in her knees crackling. That jolted Finlay from his stupor. Mum was a Presbyterian, not a Catholic. She prayed in a loud voice, and he bowed his head but did not kneel. He tried to forget about the whiskey.

"Amen," she said. She repeated the line, "Forgive us our trespasses," three or four times. It wasn't a good sign.

He helped her to her feet. "What happened to your eye?" he asked.

"It's my ribs that hurt. The doctor gave me pain pills."

"Better take them." At the sink, Finlay rinsed the whiskey glass and filled it with cold water. He watched her swallow the pills. "Go to bed, Mum. Try to get some sleep," he said.

As he lay awake in bed, he kept telling himself it was an accident; it could have happened to anyone, but it was so like Mum, so drunken, reckless and irresponsible. Mo would argue he needed to take into account how hard it must have been for Mum growing up with her brute of a father. Anyone could make a mistake, and Finlay had to forgive her.

He must have fallen asleep that terrible night because Mum's sobbing awakened him in the blackness. He wanted her to be comforted, but by someone better at that kind of thing. He waited, hoping she would stop. When she didn't, he got out of the warm bed, the floor icy under his bare feet, and went to her room. He stood outside the open door. In the dark, he couldn't see her. As a child he had been scared of the dark and Papa had comforted him by saying there was nothing in the dark that wasn't there in the day. He wasn't afraid of the day, so why should he be fearful at night?

When he came in the room, Mum switched on the lamp on the bedside table. She was in her flannel nightgown, curled up on Papa's side of the bed, the pillow streaked with her tears. "It's the worst thing that's ever happened to us," Finlay said.

She wept, pitiful sounds. Her cheeks were wet. If only he could go back to bed and burrow under the familiar blanket with its green, black, and red stripes, and sleep for a very long time. She reached out and clung to him, her large breasts against his chest, making him uncomfortable. He looked up at the painting above the bed. It was of an odalisque, lying on a couch, scantily clad, with a red necklace on that bare bosom that had mortified him as a boy. Papa must have brought it back from Algeria, where he had done his French military service before coming to Canada. Finlay looked away from it. On the bedside table was the picture Mum had taken of Mo and Anouk at the crest of Mount Royal. Arms tight against their ribs, ski mitts gripped on their ski poles, they leaped, soaring through the air. Almost always, Mo came in first. He once offered to wax Anouk's skis to help her go faster, but Mo refused, saying competition was good for her.

He preferred cross-country, the snow on the trail unscarred by the steel edges of skis. In his blue cable-knit sweater and leather mitts he'd set off, skating and gliding across the powdered snow between the evergreens, their boughs bent low with snow. He wished he could be there, not here, anywhere but here. On the bottom shelf of the bookcase was Papa's precious volume of *The Arabian Nights*. He picked it up and leafed through the tales of Aladdin and the magic lamp, Ali Baba and the cave of treasures, and Sinbad the Sailor who sailed the ocean blue. Someday, if Finlay were fortunate, he too would visit that land of enchantment, Papa had often told him years ago when he was a boy.

And now, years later, here he was in Beirut. When he returned to campus after getting the flowers, Mo was in the living room doing her morning yoga. In sky blue leotard, she sat in full lotus position, hands palm up on her thighs. In the kitchen, he set the lily of the valley in a vase and made a pot of coffee. When she joined him, she had changed into a beige shirt and slacks, what she called her uniform. She bent to smell the tiny bell-shaped flowers and, standing on tiptoe, kissed him on the cheek. Anouk came in, plucked a sprig, and pinned it behind her ear, the bloom white against her dark hair. She pestered him to come see the May Day parade, but he pointed to the pile of essays on his desk.

"So give yourself a break. Don't assign so many," Anouk said.

He smiled. "Can't. Essays, that's what the course is about."

After they left for the parade, he sipped his coffee. As a child in Montreal, his father had taken him every year to the Christmas parade, propping him on his shoulders so he could see over the crowd, and Finlay had marveled at the floats, the clowns, and the reindeer pulling Santa in his sleigh. Perhaps he should have gone down to be with Anouk. He was glad they'd arranged with Zaki to watch over her. He couldn't count on Mo. She'd forget Anouk the instant she spotted a photo op.

He set his cup in the sink and sat down to read the batch of essays he'd assigned on the. He read each twice, first with pleasure in that privileged insight into his students' ideas and then a second time, after which he wrote a few comments that they rarely read and duly entered their grades in his register. He disliked grading, for who was he to sit in judgment?

He took his coffee out on the balcony. The parade had not yet begun. Six floors below, the waves crashed against the shore. In the far distance, a gray battleship headed toward the harbor. The Titanic would have been the same size. Same color anyhow. Its passengers had waltzed until icy waves crashed onto the deck and sloshed over their feet. They resembled his colleagues who made it a point of honor not to abandon ship, as they called it: Beirut had been kind to them; they'd be loyal to it. He understood that feeling, for he too had loved the vibrant city. And of course, leaving, actually getting into a car and speeding down Airport Road with its roadblocks and ambushes, held a terror all its own. He sniffed the lily of the valley in its small vase, and the scent reminded him of his papa.

He had not forgiven his mum for Papa's death, but he had spared Anouk the story. It wouldn't be fair. Mum was devoted to her, had given her a Macgregor kilt, taught her the Sword Dance, and loved to watch her small feet skipping to the skirl of the pipes. In any case, the police had said they'd allow the dust to settle before proceeding with charges; a few months later, the whole sorry incident was forgotten.

After the funeral, Mum asked him to go through the family papers. Papa had taken care of all their affairs; she knew nothing. In the second drawer of Papa's desk, Finlay found the documents: the wills, bank books, marriage contract, neatly-organized tax returns, stacks of canceled checks, life insurance policies, and the title deeds to both the home in Montreal and the one in Espérac, France. The Canadian document was one-page with a glossy red seal on the bottom; by contrast, the French record consisted of four sheets of parchment paper bound with rusty staples and festooned with stamps and flowery signatures.

"That house is yours now," Mum told him. "To have and to hold." She had never learned French and never even wanted to see the home where his father had grown up. Papa kept a black and white photograph of it on his dresser—a big old house with a steep-pitched roof, the kind that might have storks nesting on its tall chimney. In college Finlay once or twice considered going to see the house, but he had not. Now if ever was the time to go.

On the sidewalk six floors below, Anouk was hoping for floats, a marching band, and majorettes twirling batons, doing cartwheels, and spinning flags. But it didn't deserve to be called a parade; there was no music, no performers, nothing but a few ambulances and fire trucks along with militiamen tramping out of step, in uneven formation, wearing tattered uniforms with Kalashnikovs slung over their shoulders. Her cheerleading squad at school could do better. At least Zaki was there to keep her company while her mother took pictures. Mom took her time—adjusting the aperture and shutter speed—then her eyes narrowed, and she clicked the shot as a tank clanked forward on caterpillar tread. A soldier waved a Palestinian flag, red, black, white and green, fluttering in the sunshine. The contrast between the tonnage of the tank and the man's slim body must have appealed to Mom because she raced ahead and dropped to the pavement as the tank lumbered toward her. She jumped back at the very last second.

"Whew. Is she ever brave," Anouk said.

After a while, Mom came over and watched the parade, but soon ran off to take pictures of the men in the belly of the tank. "Aren't you going to translate for her?" Anouk asked Zaki.

"No, I get to stay with you." Another tank passed in front of them, and she poked him in the ribs. "See that?"

"A Sherman Firefly," he said.

"Weird. It's nothing like a firefly. More like an elephant."

After the parade, they strolled along the Corniche toward Luna Park. She sensed the passersby admiring them, the American girl and the handsome Arab wearing a red-and-white keffiyeh. She smiled, flattered by the attention, even though she didn't think about Zaki that way. A few blocks later, they passed one of the Missing posters of Danny. "Don't worry. He'll be fine," Zaki said.

"But what if he got sassy, used the F-word or something, and they shot him to shut him up?" She'd gone over a dozen awful scenarios since he'd disappeared.

"That's unlikely."

"The guy my mom used to work for, Mr. Newton, they killed him."

"That's different."

"Mr. Newton's parents set up scholarships in Europe for kids of war journalists. My mom made me apply, but I want to stay here."

Zaki gave her a quizzical look as if he didn't see the point of her loyalty. "Paris is better. London is better," he said. "Anywhere is better."

The sun felt warm on her back, and in the breeze, sailboats skimmed the sea. On the corner, an African in a dashiki roasted corn on the cob on a brazier, and the air smelled of smoke. One of Zaki's shoelaces had come undone, and she bent to tie it for him. He pushed her hand away. "I can do it," he said, but with his bad finger, it took him forever. She couldn't tear her eyes away from his stump. The size of a light switch, it jutted out. Repelled, she forced herself to look off at a pink mansion up on the hill until he finished and they began walking again. When they spotted a white-haired woman in rags squatting against a wall, Zaki pressed a coin into her hand. "I think she's a widow," he said.

"My mother says we shouldn't give to beggars."

"The Koran says we should," he said.

"Still, Mom's right about most things."

In front of Luna Amusement Park, sandbags were stacked like burlap sacks of potatoes on either side of the entrance. At the ticket booth, a few gunboys stood eating pink cotton candy. She tugged Zaki's sleeve. "Hey, let's check out the House of Horrors and the bumper cars."

"Nah, that's kid stuff."

"Not the Ferris wheel. It's like going to the top of the world."

"Going round in circles? Not for me. Know where I'm headed? Manhattan. Wall Street. Can't you see me in a pinstripe suit?"

She giggled, and they kept walking, the sea on their right and the sun on their backs. "Hey, let's stop here," she said. They leaned against the red railing and gazed out to sea.

"So, where do you want to end up?" Zaki said.

"I want to stay here. My dad keeps going on about France."

"But you're from Kansas."

She laughed. "Mom's sick of Dorothy and Toto jokes. Me too." She had to explain about tornados and how the wind could suck up people and houses and smash them into matchsticks. "It can be dangerous anywhere. That's what my dad doesn't get," she said.

"He wants to keep you safe. You should be glad."

"So what's going to stop it?" She looked at a battleship in the distance.

"It?"

"The war, I mean."

"If the US stopped arming Israel, it'd help," he said.

"Don't blame me. We're not crazy about Israel. Anyway, you have a home here. I saw my mom's pictures."

"That shack? You call that home? Never. Home is the old city of Jerusalem near the Western Wall—what the Israelis call the Wailing Wall." He pretended to bawl like some little kid having a tantrum.

"You shouldn't make fun of them. At least my mom is showing how awful the camps are, all jam-packed with electric wires every which way. Stinky too."

"I joined the militia to get away from the stench."

To cheer him up she said that he was brave.

"The way a bull is brave. We kill so we can live. It's a necessary evil."

"Danny wouldn't agree."

"You're so innocent, like a young filly."

His tone annoyed her. "You're calling me a horse?"

"I mean it as a compliment."

"Sure doesn't sound like it. Know what I wish? To be able to go into homeroom without anyone asking about Danny. Just one day without anyone in the cafeteria sneaking glances at me, or some teacher asking if I might like to talk to the counselor. Just one day when people wouldn't give me that yucky smile when they say, 'Take care,' and I'd know they're thinking of Danny."

Just one normal day and she'd be over it. Or maybe it'd take longer, a few days of him not being the first thing everyone thought of when they saw her. She hated how all the kids talked about the last time they had seen him, what he had said and done, and how great he was. Just one day and she'd be normal again. And she'd be careful, every single day for the rest of her life. She used to be so sure he'd come back, and they'd be playing Dungeons and Dragons again—his black hair slipping onto his pale cheeks, his shoulder blades sticking out as he hunched over to plot an adventure for his character. But now she wasn't at all sure.

Zaki touched her wrist. "That's a pretty bracelet."

Was everything going to remind her of him? She twisted the double chain of red and blue yarn. "Danny made it. If he'd had you looking out for him, he'd still be here."

"Did you know him a long time?"

"Forever. Since I was a kid." She had never told Zaki about the crush she'd had on Danny. Last April, right after the troubles had begun, Professor Lahoud, a big-time Maronite, had left the country and hired Danny to take care of his pigeons. When she had begged Danny to show them to her, he had asked her mom to check the radio to see if snipers were out, and since they weren't, Mom okayed it. In Mr. Lahoud's building, the electricity was out, so she and Danny trudged up the seven flights of stairs, past the kids on the landings playing Monopoly. The sound of cooing got louder the higher up they went. When they got to the roof, he showed her the pigeons cooped up in wire-mesh cages. He used their feathers for his peace wreaths. Most of the pigeons had smooth blue-gray feathers, but a few had black stripes or rainbow neck feathers. There were a few doves too, the smallest one a pure white. When Danny nestled it in her cupped palms, her fingers grazed his. The dove curled its tiny sharp claws in her palm, and she yelped. Danny said it was still a squeaker, too young to have its nails trimmed. "My pretty one," he said as he cupped a hand about its breast and put it back in the cage.

If only Danny would talk to her tenderly, like he did to that bird. He went inside and got them bottles of Coke. Afterward, he unlatched the hooks on the cages, opened the small doors, and the birds took to the skies, swirling like gray ribbons in the pink clouds. She moved closer to him, slid two fingers along his cheekbone and caressed his pale neck. He got a funny look on his face. She pressed her forehead against his shoulder; he smelled nice, sort of like nutmeg. She waited for him to kiss her, and when he didn't, she ran her thumb over his lips. "Want to be my boyfriend?" she whispered.

"I'm sorry. I don't ... well... that's not for me." She crouched on the floor, drew her knees to her chest, and crossed her arms tight around them. So, that was it. She'd never get to make love with him, never see his unique penis. It was all spoiled. And that was when he had told her, the one thing nobody else knew. At first she couldn't take it in; afterward, it had hurt so much that she wanted to cry, but asked her not to tell, and she promised she wouldn't—not to another living soul. She avoided him. Then it was summertime, and they all went off, her parents to the States and Danny and Mrs. Delacruz to his father's hometown Spain, where his dad, Juan was buried. In the fall she and Danny became close again. Just platonic, but better than nothing.

An airplane flew overhead and distracted her from the painful memory. "You've got a flower in your hair like a San Francisco girl," Zaki said.

"What? Oh." She unpinned the sprig of lily of the valley. "It's from my dad. Think I should stuff it in some guy's Kalashnikov?"

Zaki sniffed the tiny bell-like flower. "He'd get the wrong idea."

"It's a French thing for May Day."

"But you're not French."

"My dad is. Half anyway."

"He should take you there." Zaki glanced at his watch; it was time to feed the pigeons. She asked if she could come watch. Just like Danny, Zaki made her check first with her mother.

At Mr. Lahoud's, Zaki unlatched the door to the pigeon loft, and the birds strutted about, their heads bobbing back and forth. Zaki fetched a length of black cloth from a hook on the wall, and standing at the edge of the balcony, he waved the strip of cloth over his head like a lasso, the same way Danny used to do. The pigeons scattered over the sky until he whistled, and they all flew back. From a barrel, he scooped out seeds and dry corn kernels and scattered them on the tiles. Heads bobbing, the birds strutted toward the seeds. After they finished eating, Zaki shut them back in their cages, and he and Anouk went inside.

A portrait of Arafat hung where Danny's picture of a child with a white dove used to be. Instead of his green blanket on the cot, there was a velvety spread with a print of men in togas lounging on divans while half-naked women fed them grapes.

"You changed things," she said.

"Of course. It's my place now."

She fingered the sleazy covering. "You shouldn't have got rid of Danny's stuff. He'll want it when he gets back."

Zaki kept his voice low. "Sometimes they don't come back."

"Danny will. Of course he will," she shouted and rushed out the door.

When Finlay got home from his classes, he sat down with Mo. He was nervous and unsure how to tell her about his plan for them to leave. She looked blue. "You okay?" he asked.

"I didn't get a single decent shot."

"I'm sorry, of course," Finlay said.

"Sounds like you don't much care."

He blushed, her guess too accurate. "Sorry, I'm distracted." Normally, he'd have tried to soothe her by telling her that other things would turn up, and she'd feel better. Instead, he told her of his plan. "We're lucky to have the French house," he said, finishing off. "We won't have to sponge off anyone."

She dashed his hope with a sneer. "Not that we have anyone we could go to. Anyway, you know how I feel. I'm not going." She sat on the stool she'd found at some architect's Leaving Beirut sale, her hand on her jaw. "Here's what we'll do. I stay, and you take Anouk to France. She'll fuss, but she'll get over it. We've got the flat here. No point in letting it go to waste. I'll come as soon as I can."

As usual, Mo got her way, and this time, it rankled. He wouldn't let her put her life in jeopardy, he decided. He'd figure out a way.

At four-thirty the next afternoon, Finlay arrived for his appointment with Dean Sharif. The secretary asked him to wait and went on typing, red fingernails banging the keys of her IBM Selectric. Finlay felt dishonorable. He'd be breaking his contract. The correct procedure was to give six months' notice to allow enough time to plan for hiring a new professor. Less notice risked leaving his colleagues in the lurch. It was unprofessional. Then again, given the troubles, maybe the finance office would be relieved to have one fewer professor on the payroll. They could easily hire an adjunct or borrow someone from another department to fill in.

Finlay picked up the alumni magazine from the coffee table and skimmed the class notes. His former students were marrying, having children, and getting ahead, becoming doctors, lawyers, and businessmen. Had it been a mistake to get his Ph.D.? Teaching was what Papa had wanted him to do. It had seemed a brilliant choice. Finlay cherished Milton's words, carved into the wall of the library of his alma mater, McGill University: "Beholding the bright countenance of truth in the quiet and still air of delightful studies." The trouble was that teaching wasn't as enjoyable as studying. He disliked lecturing, and he loathed standing in judgment of his students.

He glanced at the filing cabinet that stood next to the secretary's desk. Juan's file would be in the bottom drawer with the label, Faculty, Deceased. The gossip was that his murder was in revenge for a failing grade, an absurd notion in ordinary times.

"Time enough to cry later. I'm going to give Juan a proper send-off," Molly had said. Finlay had helped lift the coffin into which his friend was wedged, all three hundred pounds of him, onto the Delacruzes' dining table. Molly placed a crucifix on his chest and threaded rosary beads between his cold fingers. She had dressed him in a navy suit and red-and-white striped tie. Someone had plugged his flaring nostrils with cotton batting as if he had a severe nosebleed; a few strands of the cotton had worked themselves free and curled above his upper lip. Candles flickered on the piano as a colleague from the Music Department played. Mo had forgotten her glass on the baby grand, and the water danced and sparkled in the candlelight as if in tribute to Juan. She snapped a picture of him in his coffin and later gave it to Molly. It seemed gruesome to Finlay, but Molly had been genuinely appreciative.

Finlay had done what he could for Juan's son. He'd listened to Danny's harebrained peace schemes, rolled bandages for his Red Crescent project, and included him and his mother in hikes. And he had done so gladly, for were they not like family? Expats were tight, friends substituting for family in time of need.

Finlay glanced again at the filing cabinet. His file, Fortin, Finlay, would be in the second drawer, Faculty E-F. He imagined its contents—student evaluations, letters from his departmental head, nothing brilliant. He had needed the usual seven years for tenure review, and he had worried whether he'd make the grade. At home, when he waved the letter granting him tenure in front of Mo, she pulled him onto the sofa, kissed him deliriously, and they made love, the letter creasing under their weight. With tenure, he was able to move his family from their cramped apartment to the garden campus. With tenure, he got away for conferences, away from Mo and her complaints and pugnacity. He loved her, of course he did, but she exhausted him.

A buzzer sounded.

"The Dean can see you now."

The secretary ushered him into the wood-paneled room. Dean Sharif sprang from behind the vast, uncluttered desk, hand extended. A full three inches shorter than Finlay, he wore a brown double-breasted jacket. "Come in, come in," he said, gesturing toward the semicircle of club chairs facing a wall lined with photographs of unsmiling men in frock coats, the missionaries who had founded the university. The secretary returned with the coffee tray. As she bent low to serve him, Finlay admired her ample cleavage.

A volley of gunfire ripped the silence.

Dean Sharif strolled to the window and peeked out. "Can't see a thing." He came back and sat down. "Now, you were saying."

"There's a call. It's urgent," the secretary stuck her head in the door, and the Dean excused himself to take the call in the outside office.

Alone in the spacious room, Finlay studied a painting of a cornucopia on the wall, and its abundance of purple grapes reminded him of Anouk's joke: "What do you call angry grapes? The Grapes of Wrath."

The Dean returned, his face drawn. "That phone call? It was Jones in Physics. I know you were friends. Yesterday his son was in a freak accident exploring some cave in New Mexico. Multiple fractures. He may never walk again."

Finlay thought of Mo's loathsome mantra: Either that bullet has your name on it or it doesn't. But he wouldn't let it deter him. "I've come to tender my resignation," he said, his voice resolute. "I've already spoken to my department chair."

The Dean frowned.

Finlay rushed on. Over the years he'd helped many of his colleagues, and now they were returning the favor. "Jones and Smith have agreed to fill in for me. I've set the final, and Jones is willing to invigilate. I've tallied the grades, and the chair has agreed to read late papers."

"You realize leaving before the end of the semester is a breach of contract. Unfortunate, but that's the way it is."

"Fair enough," Finlay said. He didn't say that Beirut now offered only diminishing returns, or that he had perhaps erred in ever thinking he was cut out to be a professor, or that ever since Danny had been grabbed, he had not slept a night without fear.

The Dean seemed sympathetic. "Don't be rash. The troubles can't go on forever. Maybe the worst is over. Imagine how you'd feel if you left, and the next day all this misery ended."

"I'm sorry, but—"

The Dean shifted tactics slightly. "You're a good man, an asset to all of us. I will miss you."

Finlay glanced again at the painting of the cornucopia. He felt abashed to be asking a favor, but he said Mo wanted to stay on. "It's her work. Our lease doesn't run out until August."

"Of course she can." The Dean cocked his head, showing curiosity. "I must say, you're very patient with her."

Finlay smiled. "Tell that to her. I don't think she'd agree."

At the British Bank of the Middle East, he closed his account, and with the funds he bought two one-way tickets to Paris for the next day. It took only an hour to clear out of his office—his files and books he left for his successor—and he returned home.

After supper, he and Mo told Anouk.

"You can't mean it," Anouk said, her face a fiery red.

"It's too dodgy here, Sunbeam." Mo got up from the stool to

hug her.

Anouk pulled away. "You know I can't go. Not until we find Danny. You can't make me." She fixed her mother with an accusing look. "Anyway, why should I have to leave when you don't?"

"It's my job. I can't just walk away."

"It's always your work. I hate it." She kicked the stool, and it banged on the tile floor.

Finlay picked it up. "Your mother loves this stool. You could have broken it."

"So?" Anouk fired back. "You know, we always used to talk things over, but now you treat me like I'm just a little kid. And why France? I don't know anyone there." She stormed out, slamming the door behind her.

Chapter 6

She raced across the parking lot, past the playground and the math and agriculture buildings, up the seventy-seven steps to upper campus. By the time she reached Main Gate, she was breathless. The Red Beret came out of his sentry box. "Better go home. It'll be bad tonight." As she stood panting, he squinted, sizing her up and down with gunmetal eyes. "Well, little one, you want something special? You want f—?" He grabbed his crotch and ran his tongue across his lips.

She rushed from him, turning onto Bliss Street, where the posters of the martyrs passed in a blur. At Abdul Aziz Street, she slowed down. Tires burned in the intersection and smoke clogged the air. She coughed. Slower now, she hugged the walls on the east side—the safe side—of the street. The shops were shuttered, and the street was empty. It felt like the minutes before a tornado: that eerie quiet before the dark funnel cloud swept up roof tiles, lacy black undies, soup bowls, and sofas, scattering them everywhere. She rushed on; finally, she arrived at Mr. Lahoud's building. She went in, sidestepping dead cockroaches in the vestibule. In the elevator she glanced in the mirror; her eyes were bloodshot from the smoke. At the seventh floor, she got out and ran up the steps to the roof. "Zaki," she called.

Wet-haired and barefoot, dressed in an undershirt and jeans, he came out on the landing, barring her way. In the background, someone was droning in Arabic on the radio. "I just had a big fight with my parents." She stood in front of his door and waited for him to invite her in.

"Give me a sec," he said. He didn't seem glad to see her. He reached for the white shirt on the chair, slipped it on, and buttoned it. "What are you doing here? I'm taking you home."

"It's weird outside," she said, trying to fend off that idea.

"It'll get worse."

"So let's stay here."

"Your parents will be crazy worried." He fiddled with the radio dial and got the station he wanted, where an announcer was listing the streets where there was fighting. He switched it off and grabbed her arm. "Come on. I'm taking you home."

"Don't be so bossy."

"Yallah!" Making her feel like a scolded child, he hurried her out of the building. At every corner, militiamen huddled behind piles of sandbags. Halfway to campus, an ambulance siren wailed, and bullets whistled. There was a massive crash. He pulled her to the ground, where they lay flat, face and hands on the pavement. When the firing stopped, he got to his feet. "If we make it to Bliss Street, we'll be okay. Let's go. Now!"

She sprinted behind him. They came to a crater in the street; at its edge, a man screamed, holding what remained of his foot.

"We'll never make it. Let's go back." Zaki grabbed her hand, and they tore down the street, the crackle of machine gun fire in her ears. Back at his place, she couldn't stop sobbing. He wrapped a crimson spread around her shoulders, went to the telephone and dialed her home number. The line was dead.

"Follow me," he said wearily. In the hall, she noticed a photograph taped to the wall of a beautiful, dark-haired girl in a wheelchair. He opened the bathroom door. "Wait here. It's safe. See, no windows." He left her, then came back with a tea tray, and poured her a cup of tea, very sugary, as he sat on the edge of the bathtub. "Hungry?"

"Yeah."

He pulled a Mars bar from his pocket, and she ate it at one go. As she folded the wrapper, another explosion rocked the neighborhood, and the pigeons cooed hysterically. "So why did you come here?" Zaki said.

"My dad's making me leave."

"At least you have a father." He reached into his back pocket for his wallet and slid out a snapshot of a tailor hunched over a Singer sewing machine. "That's mine. He was a tailor; his specialty was wedding dresses."

"I can sew too. My mom taught me."

Zaki kept talking as if he hadn't heard. "When my father was murdered, my mother asked me to join the militia."

"Why?"

"It's obvious. To avenge my father's death."

"You shouldn't have. The father of my friend Danny got killed too. He didn't do that," Anouk said.

"Why not? The sweetness of life was gone. I'll never again see my father smile, or hear him sing. My mother will never remarry. We'll be stuck in that camp forever."

"Someday you'll get back. To Palestine, I mean. Still, do you really care?"

"About Palestine?" He shrugged. "Not as much as I should." He laughed. "Maybe I'll get to America."

"I bet the Army would hire you. You've got all that experience."

"Forgetting something, aren't you?" He wiggled the stump of his finger.

She followed him out to the balcony. "All quiet on the western front," he said. He opened the pigeon cages. Bells tinkling, their colored beads catching the last rays of light, the birds strutted up and down.

"So what'll you do?" she asked.

"Maybe try for a work visa to Saudi Arabia. They pay the best, but it's too strict. The women veil and the men don't laugh. Or—"

"Or what?" she said.

He held a squeaker, still bald, all eyes and beak. "You saw the picture of Zeina?"

"The girl in the wheelchair?"

"She's my cousin in Ohio. My uncle is old and worries what will happen after he's dead. Now that they're citizens, he might wangle me a fiancé visa." He stroked the young bird.

"But do you love her?" Anouk was shocked by his matter-of-fact tone.

Zaki set down the squeaker. "Love comes after marriage. And in a few years, I could bring over the rest of my family."

"Marrying your cousin?" Anouk curled her lip.

"It is permitted."

She didn't want to hurt his feelings, but it wasn't just pathetic to marry for an ulterior motive. It was plain wrong. "Take me home," she said.

"When the firing stops."

She glanced at her watch—midnight. Her parents would be worried, but it served them right. Zaki opened a paperback. She sneaked a look at it. It was called *The Wretched of the Earth*. It looked dull, and sure enough, he soon put it down and took a book on how to win friends and influence people. Double boring. She lay on the foam mattress and pulled the spread over her. "Wake me when it's time to go."

"Danger, here be dragons" Finlay had once seen printed on an antique map of the Levant showing the Mediterranean. Hunched

over the turquoise railing, he gazed out to sea. From the Manara
Lighthouse, a slender white tower with black stripes, a broad line
of light swept over the dark. A bomb crashed somewhere in the
hotel zone, where a few years ago the Delacruzes had invited him
and Mo to the Phoenicia Hotel. At tables of gleaming brass set
under chandeliers, they had chatted over appetizers of eggplant
dip, pistachios, and black olives while onstage a belly dancer
rippled her bare belly to Oriental music, bells tinkling on her
ankles, slender arms raised as she sallied up to him. Juan slipped a
hundred lira bill down her bodice, and Finlay followed suit.

It brought a flush of anger to Mo's pale cheeks. "Don't encourage
her," she snapped at him as the dancer glided off. Had Mo been
jealous? She believed in free love, or so she used to say. She'd had
sex often before they met, and seemed surprised when he assumed
she was a virgin. He disliked promiscuity, especially in women,
although he knew he had no right to object. He too had had flings,
but not one of them what his papa would consider le grand amour.

Mo came out on the balcony. "Getting dark," she said. There
was another thud.

He glanced at his watch for the umpteenth time. "It's one a.m."

"Stop fretting. Anouk's okay," Mo said with a touch of worry. "I
bet she went to see Zaki. He'll take care of her." She went inside
to do her yoga. In the living room, she turned on the tape recorder
and sat on her mauve mat in full lotus position. He could hear the
canned soporific voice intone, "Inhale. Exhale. In. Out."

The waiting for Anouk made him want to smash something.
Fists clenched, he went to the kitchen, fighting for calm. He cast
about until finally, he assembled the ingredients to make bread.
He kneaded the dough, working out his anxieties, and set it to
rise. A line of the Psalms came to him: "You have fed them with
the bread of tears and given them tears to drink in full measure."

Afterward, in Anouk's room, he straightened the stack of LPs:

Bridge over Troubled Water, Let It Be, and all the others. He picked up her socks, shorts, and tees and tucked them in her drawer. A book lay on the floor, *The Scarlet Letter*. Wasn't she was too young for it? he thought idly. He set it on her bookcase. He went to the kitchen, punched down the dough and covered it with a dishtowel. The rat-a-tat-tat of machine gun fire began again. That was enough. He raced out of the kitchen and said he was going to find Anouk.

"Don't panic. Give her another hour," Mo said.

He started for the door. She followed, but he persuaded her to stay put in case Anouk came back while he was gone.

He wasn't sure where to look. On upper campus, he checked by the banyan tree, Anouk's favorite hideout when she was younger, but she wasn't there or on the benches in front of the Milk Bar. He kept walking. He barely noticed the words, "that they might have life and have it more abundantly," etched on the wall at Main Gate. He asked the Red Beret in the sentry box if he'd seen her, a teenager with a slight build and short black hair.

"Go home," the guard grunted.

Instead, Finlay kept searching for her for another hour. When he got back, Mo pressed a Valium in his hand. "Here, take this."

"Can't. It'd stick in my throat." He went to the kitchen, where he punched down the dough until his anger lessened.

That night he slept fitfully. At dawn, when he looked out the bedroom window, women were already lined up across the street in front of Bakr's Bakery. Bakeries provided a big kill at the start of the day—like the first batter up scoring a home run.

At six-thirty a.m., the doorbell rang. Anouk stood there in her pink shorts, Zaki towering over her.

Finlay's legs trembled. After the rush of relief, he wanted to throttle her. "Where were you?" he yelled.

Zaki cleared his throat while Anouk edged past them and headed off down the narrow hall. Halfway to her room, she stopped and turned. "Thank you, Zaki, for last night," she said, smiling.

"You abused my trust," Finlay raged. "After all we've done for you."

"It wasn't like that." Zaki looked insulted. "The telephones lines were dead. I tried to bring her, but—"

Finlay strode to the door and held it open. "Go. Get out of my sight."

Zaki left, not trying to protest further. Anouk stayed in her room.

That evening, Finlay drafted a letter to his classes and gave it to his chair. He made the rounds to say his goodbyes. The neighbors pressed drinks on him. At every flat, he sensed the unspoken question, "Why are you bailing out? Why now?"

"Teenagers, you know how they are..." he said, his voice trailing off.

When he got home, he felt guilty for deserting his friends. He sat on the bed and watched Mo brush her hair. The sheer curtains fluttered in the warm breeze, and he got up, closed the window, and sat down again beside her.

"You had a lot of booze," she said as if anticipating what came next.

"I'm concerned about Anouk."

"Don't worry. Anouk will bounce back." Mo rubbed the back of his neck to comfort him. "While you were gone, I asked if she wanted to talk about last night. I told her that if she loved Zaki, it was okay; she didn't need to explain."

"Mo, she's too young."

"Let's not get into that. In any case, she didn't. She looked at me as if I were out of my mind. She said she knew what I was thinking, but that they didn't do it.

Finlay remained suspicious. "Didn't you hear what she said to him? How she thanked him for 'last night'?"

"She didn't mean it that way. Or if she did, it was to get even with you. She's terrified that if she leaves here, everyone will give up the hunt, so I promised I'd never stop trying."

"Be careful," he said, even though Mo disliked his timidity. "It wasn't a fluke that Danny got picked up." Not wanting to be too severe, Finlay stroked her hair. "Come to France with us. It's not too late to change your mind."

"I'll come when the lease is up."

"For God's sake, that's the end of August. You can't abandon Anouk."

"Look, she'll be with you. She'll be fine."

Oh, how he loathed it when she talked that way. Next thing, she'd tell him how the Brits sent their kids off at age seven and didn't have hissy fits about it.

He'd settle for what he could. "Let's compromise. Come for the Fourth of July. That gives you six weeks. It'll be sweltering here; you'll be glad to get out."

She shook her head. "That's too soon."

He could not understand her logic. "At least come for Bastille Day. It's a holiday, July 14. That'll give you ten more days."

"I'll try," she allowed.

"Don't get yourself into trouble. Please."

She ran her hands down his bare arms. In the past that would have calmed him, even invited him. "I don't want to fight about it. Let's go to bed," she murmured.

He shook his head. "I'm too drunk."

"Suit yourself," she said.

Later he relented. He drew back the quilted spread with its wedding knot pattern, all yellows and greens and pinks, and slipped between the smooth sheets of their bed, the one place that was never a battle zone. After a colleague had called the University the "locus of rational discourse," Mo znicknamed their bed "the locus of love." Now, as one strap of her satiny nightgown slipped down her arm, he eased the nightie over her head and kissed her neck and eyelids. He ran his tongue across her lips, pink and sensual.

A blast shuddered, shattering the window.

He gave a shout, and they leaped out of bed and rushed to Anouk's room. She lay there, smiling in her sleep. Her linen curtains, patterned in orange and golden circles, hung in place. The window glass was intact, barred by silvery lengths of duct tape. Relief overwhelmed him. They'd been lucky again. He kissed her softly on the forehead and left.

Mo had already got a broom and was sweeping up the shards of glass in their bedroom. He got back into bed. After she had returned the broom to the hall closet, she crept in beside him and nibbled on his ear. "Don't let's stop."

Yet as much as he tried to slip back into the mood, he could not get stiff again. Ashamed, he squeezed her hand. "I'm sorry. All this stuff is crowding in on me."

"It doesn't matter," she said dismissively.

When he awakened in the morning, she was dressed. Canisters of Kodak film protruded from the deep pockets of her beige pants, and she had her camera slung over her chest. She rested both hands on his shoulders. "Bye," she said. "Take care."

He pulled her to him. "Don't go. You haven't said goodbye to Anouk. She'll be upset."

Mo eased out of his grip. "I'll give her a peck, but I don't want to wake her up. She'll cling, or she'll fight. It's easier this way," she said, as though she knew better. "I slipped a picture of me into her suitcase. See you July 14." She kissed him lightly on the lips and sprinted away, as light-footed as Anouk. She closed the door behind her casually as if it was an ordinary day.

He put out breakfast on the table on the balcony—yogurt, Arab bread, cheese, and bitter orange marmalade. More normality. Just pretend it's another day. He set the airplane tickets at Anouk's place and gazed out to the horizon. "Won't you miss the sea?" his neighbors had asked last night. When he was a boy, he had thought he'd become a fisherman. When his papa had taken him fishing, he had enjoyed the gurgle of the Outaouais River, the butterflies skimming the lily pads, and the bass biting.

"Fishing is in your blood," his mum had said. The summer he turned thirteen, she packed him off to her father, who fished for haddock off the coast of northern Scotland. That first night, as gentle waves lapped the sides of the boat, Finlay lay on the deck listening to the men singing psalms in Gaelic, their voices gentle under the blanket of stars. The next afternoon they tied him to the mast. "It's your initiation," Grandpa Angus said, laughing, as he headed below deck to enjoy a cup of tea.

The weather turned fierce. The sea heaved, and the winds blew gale force. He struggled to get free, but the rope held him fast. Three hours later when the deckhands returned, they found him with his head collapsed onto his shoulder and vomit on his gaiters.

"Brave lad," they said. They cut the rope that bound Finlay to the mast and gave him a wee dram to raise his spirits. "You're bound now to the sea. Aye, you're a seafaring man now. That ye be."

He had not become a fisherman. It had been his first significant decision. Now, when he felt others preying on his integrity, he reminded himself he could choose his destiny—although to please his papa, he had become a teacher. Perhaps that had been a mistake, for he had often felt he might like to be a librarian, hidden away from the public, cataloging books.

For the time being, he had a daughter to support. The drumbeat of questions started all over again. What could he find to do in France? Would he even like it? The house must be in ruins after the neglect of decades. The village was not much bigger than a hamlet, and he didn't know a soul.

Twice he had put off going— when his papa offered him an airplane ticket as a graduation present, and later as a wedding gift. The first time Finlay had spent the money on tuition for graduate school; the second time Mo nixed the offer, saying that she didn't speak French.

Anouk came out to the balcony, pulling him out of his reverie. "Where's Mom?"

"Taking pictures at a press conference." He kept his voice low.

Anouk picked up the envelope at her place, opened it and took out the tickets. "Paris? But school's not over yet. And why only two tickets?"

"For us, you and me."

A thread of fear entered her voice. "How about Mom?"

"She'll come in seven weeks. On July 14. That's a big holiday over there." Now that he'd begun, he talked fast. "The big flush," that's what his colleague Constant in university relations had advised: to release the bad news all at once and not in dismal drips and drabs.

"What!" Anouk screamed. "That's forever."

Never had she talked to him in that tone of voice. He disliked being the disciplinarian. That was Mo's forte. Instead of calling Anouk on her rudeness, he set out his case, keeping his voice calm: Jilly and most of her friends had already left; France was in her blood; she already knew the language; she would do just fine.

"I'm not going." She crossed her arms tightly over her chest.

"Your mother packed your things."

She opened her mouth to protest, but he finally put his foot down. "Anouk, I'm sorry, but that's the way it is."

The telephone rang. Relieved, Finlay hurried to answer it.

"Sure, Omar, we'll be right down. The bags are already there." He turned to Anouk. "Omar is down in the parking lot."

"How can you do this to me?" she cried.

"It's only for a few months." Would he have to drag her out, hauling her kicking and screaming?

"Of all the sneaky things. It's wrong, what you're doing," she whimpered. "I can't believe Mom let you do it."

In the car, a black Mercedes, Anouk slumped by the window, as far from him as she could. She didn't make a peep. She wouldn't want to lose face in front of Omar. He was a local hero; he rescued hostages and risked his life every day when he drove faculty to the airport to catch flights out of Beirut.

Finlay read the decal on the side window, "The cure for fate is patience." He stared at the turquoise beads dangling from the rearview mirror to ward off misfortune. Anouk kept her face turned away from him, but they reached the airport without incident. Omar opened the door for her, and she got out without making a scene.

The Departures Hall was half-empty. The plate glass had been blown out of the windows, leaving jagged shards of glass in the steel frames. The floor was sticky with spilled Pepsis, littered with cigarette butts. Pus-colored foam bulged out of the gray cushions in the chairs in the departure lounge.

Finlay and Anouk boarded Middle East Airlines flight 206 to Paris. They didn't speak one word during the four-hour trip. He drank cup after cup of coffee to calm his nerves. He was no longer sure he was doing this to protect his daughter. Maybe he was doing this for himself.

As the jet made its final descent, raindrops slid down the window. Finlay touched Anouk on the arm

"What now?" she snapped.

"It's going to be OK."

"Not for you," she said. "I'm getting even. Just you wait."

Chapter 7

In Paris, he checked them into a shabby hotel situated next to Notre Dame Cathedral. Given the long flight, he slept until the pealing of the matins bells awakened him at daybreak. A light rain was falling. At eight o'clock he knocked on Anouk's door. No answer. She might be still asleep, so he went downstairs and ate breakfast—applesauce compote, flaky croissants, and coffee with chicory. Afterward, he read the newspaper that someone had left on the table. In Beirut, another attack on a bakery killed fifteen and maimed fifty-five. He studied the photograph of a toddler wearing a Mickey Mouse T-shirt lying dead on the pavement. He drained his coffee, feeling vindicated. Even if Anouk did not speak to him for a very long time, he had done the right thing.

He returned to her door and knocked again. "Anouk," he called. When she didn't reply, he opened the door. She stood at the window, watching the rain slide down the glass. When she turned toward him, her eyes were puffy and red-rimmed. He tried to hug her, but she stepped aside.

"Let's not waste the day," he said cheerfully. "It's Paris. Let's see the sights. We've got time before the train leaves. We could go on a boat down the Seine. You'll see everything, the bridges, the Louvre, the Eiffel Tower. It'll be fun."

She shook her head. "It's raining."

"Just drizzling. We could stroll around the Left Bank. I'd like to see the statue of Montaigne."

"I've never heard of him."

"He was a philosopher. Students rub his foot to bring good luck on their exams. Maybe it works for other things too."

She wasn't giving him an inch. "Fat chance."

"About yesterday." Ashamed of having forced her to go, he paused. "Someday you'll understand," he finally said.

"Just leave me alone."

Frustrated, he returned to his room, where the rain pattered on the skylight. After a while, he put on his windbreaker. He knocked on Anouk's door to try again to persuade her, and when there was no answer, he opened it. The room was empty. Bile rose in his throat. When she was little, she used to creep under the bed to weep there. He got down on his hands and knees to look but saw only dust bunnies.

He raced down the staircase to the lobby. "Have you seen my daughter?" he asked the desk clerk. "She's wearing jeans and red sneakers." He grabbed his wallet from his back pocket and pulled out a snapshot.

The clerk glanced at it. "A pretty girl. She left a few minutes ago."

"Our train leaves at two p.m. She doesn't know the city. She may be lost."

"These adolescents, how they make us worry. Calm yourself, my dear friend. Your daughter will soon return."

"Runaway Child," the phrase echoed in Finlay's ears. For the next half-hour, he paced up and down the waxed floorboards of her room: from the unmade bed to the window that overlooked the alley and back again. He wanted to telephone the U.S. Consulate to say she was missing, didn't know a soul here and had no money, but some vice-consul or other would probably tell him it was too soon to worry.

At eleven a.m. Finlay splashed his way through puddles to a police station at the corner a few blocks away. The cold rain dripped on his neck. Inside, two women in hijab sat on a bench that faced flyers warning of pickpockets and the consequences of overstaying visas. Finlay explained what had happened to the policeman at the desk. The officer inserted a form and two sheets of carbon paper into his typewriter, a blue-gray Hermes. Clack, clack, clack, went the keys. After he had finished, he lamented the worry adolescents were to their parents and advised Finlay to return to the hotel and wait for her there.

On his way back, he stopped at a bank whose granite walls were darkened by the rain. He exchanged his grimy liras for a wad of French francs. In the open-air marketplace, he bought Anouk a fashion magazine and a sweater, both as a peace offering and protection from the cold.

When he got to the hotel at one-thirty, there she was, thank God. Her teeth were chattering, hair damp with rain, red sneakers splotched with it. He tried again to hug her, but she stiff-armed him. He gave her the sweater and hailed a cab to take them to the Austerlitz terminal. There he asked her to please carry her suitcase down to the platform, but she played deaf. He made two trips, and they boarded the train moments before the conductor waved the departure flag.

Finlay hoped the novelty of riding a train might ease her out of her funk. She took the window seat, and they rumbled out of the terminal. At the first stop, an elderly couple with a yappy poodle entered the compartment and sat opposite them. The woman settled the wet puppy in her lap. Anouk didn't so much as glance at them.

At the next stop, the couple got off, and a fellow in a black leather jacket entered. Finlay had to twist his legs to the side to make room as the kid took the seat facing Anouk. With acne scars on his cheeks, he looked like a juvenile delinquent. He shook his jacket, which was dripping wet, and set it on the seat next to him.

"Going far, Mademoiselle?" he asked.

"Ask my dad," Anouk muttered in French.

"To Bergerac," Finlay said, not looking up.

"Ah." The youth opened France Soir and skimmed the paper. He snickered and showed Anouk the headline, Gourmet execution in Texas. "Listen to what he had for his last supper: fruit cocktail with strawberries, raspberries, oranges, pineapple, and watermelon. And a cheeseburger and fried chicken. Pie and cake, even chocolates. They gave it to the bastard. All of it."

"Maybe he figured the more he got to eat, the longer he got to live," she said.

"A pig."

"At least it wasn't junk food. It's nice the way he got to say goodbye to his favorites." She seemed to be warming up to the conversation, and it irked Finlay.

The fellow leaned toward her. "You have a pretty little accent."

"I learned it at my grandfather's home in Quebec."

"Ah. And you, what would you choose for your last meal?" the creep asked.

Finlay gritted his teeth. The fellow had the gall to use *tu* instead of *vous*, as if they were close friends.

"I couldn't care less. I'd just like my mom to be with me," she said, glaring at Finlay, and he felt hurt. The young Frenchman winked at Anouk, but when he invited her for a glass in the bar, she refused, and the good-for-nothing slouched off. She flipped through the fashion magazine, and Finlay glanced over her shoulder at the horoscopes, summer styles, and four-page spread on Brigitte Bardot's passion for baby seals.

Annoyed by him, Anouk shut the magazine and pretended to sleep.

Beyond the rain-streaked windows, fertile fields spread out before him, wheat and barley, oats and rye. By the time the vineyards north of Bordeaux came into view, the rain had diminished to a gentle pitter-patter. Their connecting train to Bergerac was yellow and boxy, its seats upholstered in checkered turquoise. It was still cold and wet, but the fact that he could open the windows gave Finlay an overwhelming sense of freedom.

Eventually, he tired of looking at the vineyards. He opened his satchel and took out the title deed to the Espérac house. He read the accompanying letter from the notary that stated that he was entitled "from this day forward to enjoy the jouissance of the property." It seemed odd that word in this context. Previously, he had heard it used only to mean orgasm. He tucked the deed back in his satchel and reread the telegram from his father's childhood friend, Monsieur Noel. It was brief and formal, a single line to the effect that he or his daughter would meet him at the Bergerac Station.

Anouk edged past him to go to the toilet but returned shortly to report there wasn't one. She slumped against the window, head resting on the pleated orange curtains. Perhaps she was frightened. At four or five, she had been afraid of the dark. A nightlight wouldn't do; she insisted on him beside her. "Mom might leave when I'm asleep, but you won't, will you?" she'd whisper, and he'd stroke her forehead to comfort her.

At Sainte-Foy-La-Grande, two youths with bulky backpacks got on, their feet in wet socks and sandals. In guttural French—they sounded like Germans—they said they were going on retreat in a nearby Buddhist center. A passenger murmured that she could not fathom why foreigners came from all over Europe to listen to the strange notions of those Buddhist monks, who had not the least desire for pleasure. The remark reminded him of Mo. Her Buddhist pamphlets advised how to make up after a fight—to tell the other the tenderness one harbored for them, yet the words of love stuck in her throat. Like his mum, she cloaked her emotions. But sometimes she ruffled his hair and glided her hand down the side of his face. Once she told him that he had "a beautifully proportioned head."

Up the hills and down the valleys of the Périgord the little train trundled. After an hour or so, it rounded a curve, and a cemetery flashed by with its granite vaults and garish flowers. All at once, they arrived at their destination. The conductor came down the aisle. "Bergerac, Bergerac," he cried.

When they disembarked, the rain had stopped, and the sun was out. Anouk bounded off to locate a toilet. While she was gone, a short-legged hunchback in a beret bustled up, seized Finlay's hand with extraordinary power, kissed him once on each cheek, and looked around as if he expected to see a wife. It was Monsieur Noel. Finlay looked down, ashamed. If Mo loved them more, she'd be here.

Very soon Anouk came back. "That toilet was gross. Just a hole in the cement. And sh—well, you know what—everywhere."

Thank God, she was talking to him at last.

"My daughter, Anouk," Finlay said, introducing her.

"I didn't know you had a daughter. Such a pretty girl."

Monsieur Noel guided them through the station out to a parking lot and a blue-gray van. Finlay got in front while Anouk sat in the back on a green blanket, half-covered with dog hair and smelling of strawberries. Monsieur Noel drove down the narrow streets lined with stone houses to the city center with its courthouse, auction house, and war memorial of an angel bearing off a dead warrior. They crossed the bridge over the broad Dordogne River, and Monsieur Noel slowed in front of a bar with a sign in the window, "Citizens, you who love good wine. Go no farther."

"Shall we stop for a glass?" he asked.

"I'd like to reach Espérac before dark," Finlay said.

"Of course." He speeded up, all the while fiddling with the radio dial until he located a station playing Edith Piaf. "Your papa loved her, a slum girl singing for tips in bars, abandoned by all. And yet no regrets. Ah, what a woman!"

Anouk piped up from the back. "What she's singing?"

He twisted his head around. "About a streetwalker who comforts some jerk who got jilted. Piaf sings that life always gives a second chance, and that love will make him dance again."

"That sounds nice."

Finlay looked out on the yellow broom that grew thick along the hedgerows. He opened his window and breathed in their fragrance.

"Almost there now." Monsieur Noel turned left off the highway and drove up a narrow street. "Welcome to the heart of the Périgord. It's ancient, as you probably know. In Cro-Magnon times women collected strawberries here while their men hooked eel and salmon in the rivers. It's a small place, but it has a natural spring and a grove of bamboos. Ah, those bamboos, how they rustle in the wind."

They reached the village square as the sun hovered like an orange halo behind the church and eased into gauzy panels of pink and scarlet.

"Trailing clouds of glory," Finlay couldn't help himself.

"Daaaad!"

"Here we are—Espérac." Monsieur Noel parked beside the war memorial, a life-size bronze of a soldier, rifle in hand, and sporting a mustache.

Espérac was smaller than Finlay had expected: no shops on the square, only a café with a rundown hotel opposite it, a rickety bench for a bus stop, a huge cross, and a bakery called Au Bon Pain. As a college student, one summer he had worked in one, and now he yearned for the odor of just-milled flour. His heart pounded when he saw the tall chimney and the stacks of wood in the lean-to: real country bread, baked in a wood-fired oven. But when he came nearer, he saw the FOR SALE sign.

Monsieur Noel clapped a hand on Finlay's shoulder. "Find me a buyer, and you'll save my life."

Finlay sighed, acutely disappointed. Before the troubles, he bought French bread daily, one of the many small pleasures that made life in Beirut agreeable. But after the series of attacks on bakeries, targeting the civilians waiting in line, he baked their bread at home. Anouk claimed she liked it better than store bought. He glanced over at her. She had her neck craned up at the church steeple with its misshapen cross. "Weird. I'll call it the Church of the Crooked Cross." She crossed her two index fingers to make the shape of a cross. Back when she was a little tyke, she had made the hand gestures to accompany the nursery rhyme, "Here's the church and here's the steeple. Open the door and see all the people."

She glanced around the square. "Where's everybody? Looks like a ghost town."

Monsieur Noel chuckled. "Mademoiselle, they're peeking out the window and spying on us. "Eee, eee, eee," he giggled.

"We should call Mom to tell her we're here," Anouk said.

"As soon as we've seen the house," Finlay said.

"Okay."

Leaping over puddles, they followed Monsieur Noel down the street, where strands of vermicelli floated on the dirty water in the gutter. The bells tolled seven loud clangs. A young man came out of the café. Monsieur Noel introduced him as the son of the mason. Pierre wore tight jeans that showed his muscles and a red T-shirt with the crest of a whale. Anouk stared at him, fascinated by the mole, the size of a chocolate chip, to the right of his mouth. Raindrops spattered his tortoiseshell glasses as he and Monsieur Noel chatted about a contest for the best soup-maker of the village.

Pierre turned to Anouk. "Mademoiselle, you will love my nettle soup." He blew a kiss and walked off down the wet street.

Like Shakespeare's home in Stratford on Avon, their house was half-timbered, but instead of thatch, pink and orange tiles covered its steeply pitched roof. From where Finlay stood in the long, wet weeds amid chunks of fallen plaster, he saw that the wall bulged and the pointing needed repair. A grapevine, the grapes still green pips, hung from a rusty wire above the door, a weathered gray. Its ancient nails were flat-headed and crucifixion-thick.

Monsieur Noel handed the key to Finlay. Made of iron, it was as long as his hand, its bow heart-shaped. He was seized by a crazy impulse to kiss it—like Agamemnon kissing the earth on his return from the Trojan wars. Instead, he handed the key to Anouk. "You do the honors."

She shook her head. "Mom is the one who opens up."

"You're the lady of the house until July 14."

Anouk twisted the key to the left. The door creaked on iron hinges and opened to darkness.

Chapter 8

Monsieur Noel dug in his pants pocket, found the lighter, and rubbed the striker. Nothing. "Damn wheel is damp," he said. He tried again. On his fifth attempt, he struck a spark. No flame.

"Now I know why they call it the Dark Ages," Anouk said.

He grunted and kept trying— a few flickers, and finally a flame. Holding the steel lighter high, he led them through what seemed to be a narrow hallway.

"Smells weird." She crinkled her nose.

"Well, that's normal. It's been closed up for years," Monsieur Noel said.

Dad let out a cry of pain. He'd bashed his forehead against the top of the doorframe. It served him right. He never looked where he was going, just like he hadn't bothered to consider how much she hated leaving home. She pulled her sweater tighter.

"Cold?" Monsieur Noel said.

"Freezing. Aren't there any radiators?"

"Stones keep in the cold. Wait until July, and you'll be glad of it." He shuffled toward the window, opened it and unfastened the shutter. "Ah, behold the last rays of the glorious sun." Chattering in his funny accent, he told her father to be careful when he went through doors because people were shorter when the house was built. Monsieur Noel should talk—he was skinny and short as a dwarf, the opposite of what you'd expect of someone called Mr. Christmas.

"Had we known a week earlier that you were coming, we'd have had the entire house cleaned. Alas, my daughter had time only to pick some flowers, lay the fire, set the table, and get a few provisions before leaving for work." He switched on the light bulb that dangled from a wire above the table.

"So what does she do?" Anouk asked, her eye on an ant crawling on the petal of a pink peony in a vase.

"Colette? She's an entrepreneur. A hairdresser. Hers is the best of the four beauty salons in Issigeac. Everyone asks for her: brides, pensioners, and bachelors, even teenagers. Know why?" He snapped a finger, making a clicking sound. "She's got magic fingers."

Her father sure didn't. He took a match from the box on the mantel to light the kindling. The flame went out, and he had to start over. He pumped the pair of bellows a long while before he finally got the fire going. It looked pitifully small in the huge fireplace. She coughed. "Awfully smoky in here."

"Confounded birds build nests in the chimney and block the flow of air." He walked to the window and threw it open wide.

She looked around the room. Instead of being plastered, the ceiling had wooden beams, black like licorice sticks, from which dusty bunches of dried herbs hung. Pots and skillets lined the wall above a cast iron stove. Most of the orange and pink tiles on the floor were cracked, and a few were missing, with squares of packed earth in their place. Everything looked old and shabby.

Once the fire got going, he reminisced with her dad. "Your papa and I waltzed on these tiles. How we missed dear Maurice after he sailed for America and abandoned your home to the mice and their big brothers."

"You mean rats?" Anouk said, her hand at her mouth.

"Alas, yes. Luckily, Colette's cats keep their numbers down." He held out a chair for her next to her father. Before she sat down, Dad observed that the seat was made of rush. Whatever it was, it was scratchy. Dad's legs were too long to fit underneath the table, and he angled them sideways toward her. She edged away.

Monsieur Noel lit the candles, uncorked the dusty wine bottle, and filled their glasses.

"I'm not twenty-one yet," she said.

"Only sixteen you need to be, and that's for cafés or bars. At home, on a special occasion, of course, you'll want to join in the mirth and merriment."

Mom would object, but Anouk took a sip. Just as she expected, it was sour, and she made a face.

"You prefer Coca-Cola," he said.

"How did you guess?"

"My daughter suggested it. You're American, after all." He got her a Coke and filled her glass. As he raised his glass, he looked in her eyes. "Tchin, tchin. To your good health."

"'Chin Chin?' Weird." Anouk smirked and tapped her chin. She expected him to giggle, as if he found it slightly amusing, but he burst out laughing as if she'd said something hilarious. The Coke tasted normal, and the candles looked pretty. Wax dripped down the side of one of them, and she touched the warm little puddle on the table. She glanced at her watch. In Beirut, Mom would be meditating now, a white candle burning to help her concentrate.

"Agreeable, is it not, the smell of beeswax?" He turned to her. "As boys, your grandfather and I feasted on goose at this very table. You'll be perfectly happy here."

Fat chance, she thought.

"A little foie gras?" He passed her a plate in the center of which was a round of flesh-colored paste.

Fatty liver? It sounded revolting, but it had a velvety texture, and she actually liked it. Afterward, he ladled chicken noodle soup into their bowls. Her spoon was ten times heavier than normal, and her father slurped his soup in his disgusting way. After they finished, she cleared the table while Monsieur Noel cracked some eggs for an omelet, which tasted okay. He and Dad wiped their plates clean with the crusts, something Dad never did at home. She touched the pointy, sharp tines of the hefty fork, and asked if her ancestors were giants and needed huge cutlery and ultra-wide sheets, or short like Napoleon who fit comfortably beneath the little front door.

Monsieur Noel shrugged. "Who knows? Your father must have inherited his stature from his mother."

"My mom is tall too. We need to telephone her."

"After supper." Dad didn't seem in any hurry. He took a slice of bread from the basket and passed it to Anouk. Beirut baguettes were better, all golden and crusty on the outside and creamy white, soft and chewy inside.

Monsieur Noel apologized for the bread, saying it was "inferior, industrial production." He hung his head as if it was the worst thing in the world and he was responsible for it. She hesitated, unsure of what to say. It was tricky to be rude to Dad, as he deserved, while at the same time being polite to nice Monsieur Noel. She tried her best to look interested as he droned on about bread and the dense crumb and complex scent of loaves baked in a wood-fired oven. Dad looked as if he thought that little lecture was fascinating. After supper, Monsieur Noel offered to make hot chocolate. He got a pitcher of milk, which he'd got from the farmer just outside the village.

"Is that safe? I don't want to get TB or something," she said.

"Baf." He slapped the table. "I know the cow in question. She's a Charolais that grazes among the buttercups in the pasture. She'll amble up to the fence to greet you as you stroll by."

The cocoa was thick, creamy, and delicious. It was getting late, and they climbed the flight of steep and uneven stairs that led to the three bedrooms. Dad let her have first choice. She nixed the room with a scary-looking crucifix. After checking the other two, both with flowered wallpaper, she chose the one with a radio. It had what looked like a single bed, half-as-wide as her parents' double bed.

"The matrimonial bed," Monsieur Noel said.

"People then must've been midgets."

He giggled. "The smaller the bed, the greater the pleasures. Perfect for tickling."

He fetched an armload of linen from the armoire. Dad took a sheet and flung it over the bed. Twice as wide as it should be, the sheet puddled on the floor. While he made the bed, she stuffed an enormous square pillow into a cute pillowcase with lace borders and a monogram in the middle. Looking pensive, Anouk traced the inverwoven decorative letters. "Who's AF?" she asked.

"My grandmother. The linen must have been part of her trousseau. The initials stand for Anouk Fortin. She married François Fortin, and I named you after her."

"A valiant woman," Monsieur Noel said. "She suffered in the First War, but of course, so did we all." He peered at Anouk from under his pleated eyelids. "You're still shivering. We should find you a bearskin and wrap you up in it to keep you warm. Isn't that what they do in America? No bears here, but I'll get you the next best thing." He left the room and returned with a rubber hot water bottle. It was red and heart-shaped, and he tucked it between the sheets. He shook the quilt to distribute the feathers, placed it on the bed, and told her she'd sleep as soundly as a dormouse.

"We need to call Mom first."

"She won't worry," her father said.

"That's not the point. I always say good night to her."

Monsieur Noel explained that in the countryside, few people had telephones. There was a three-year waiting list, but they were in luck because he happened to be in charge of the village telephone.

"Let's go," she said.

They left right away.

On the south wall of his house was a blue enamel plate with the words "Cabine Publique." When they entered, the phone was the first thing she saw. It was on a little table below two charts, one listing the area codes for each department in France and various foreign countries, and the other a price list per minute. There was also a timer and a white saucer in which callers left the francs for their calls. Her dad dialed their number several times, but he didn't get through.

"At least you tried."

Monsieur Noel rambled on about how he kept the village telephone so as to help people in their time of trouble, but she suspected he took pleasure in eavesdropping.

They went back to their house. While her dad chatted with him, she looked for a bathroom. She really had to pee. She couldn't hold it for a minute more. When she asked where it was, Monsieur Noel looked embarrassed. "Ah, you're a city girl. You would like a 'little corner,' as we call it. Alas, modern conveniences are few in Espérac but don't fret. What is it that Montaigne says? Ah yes. 'Kings and philosophers shit: and so do ladies. Upon the highest throne in the world, we are seated, still, upon our arses.'"

"So, where is it, please?"

"Come with me." He crooked a finger, and she followed him out the back door. He handed her a flashlight, pointed his bony finger at the far end of the yard and offered to show her the way. She tossed her head, extremely embarrassed. The instant he disappeared into their house, she unzipped her jeans and squatted behind the nearest bush. Pee trickled onto her thighs. When she stood up, her bare bottom brushed against the nettles, and she whimpered. Then she gritted her teeth, pulled up her pants, and hurried inside.

Ignoring the men, she went upstairs to unpack. When she took the photo of her mom out of the suitcase, she wanted to sob. July 14 was weeks and weeks from now. Her dad had kidnapped her and brought here by brute force. In the States, you could get arrested for that. If she had to leave Beirut, her parents should have offered her the choice of returning to the States. They could have found somebody to take her in, maybe Jilly's parents.

All she wanted was a choice. Monsieur Noel was trying his best, but it just wasn't nice here.

She must have fallen asleep eventually, for she awakened in the night. The hot water bottle had turned cold and clammy, and she pushed it to the foot of the bed. Every time she turned in bed, it squeaked. Maybe her great-grandma had died in it. After a while, she got up. The icy tiles bit her feet. She turned on the flashlight and rummaged in her suitcase for a pair of socks. She pulled them on and crept back into bed.

Mom would tell her to look on the bright side. At least, unlike poor Zaki, she still had all her fingers, and she was safe here. It was nothing like what Danny might be facing. But without her in Beirut to help keep up the hunt, how could he ever hope to be rescued?

Chapter 9

The next morning, a rapping awakened him. In the pitch black of the bedroom, Finlay felt disoriented. He gradually realized the pounding came from downstairs, and he shouted, "J'arrive." Still in his pajamas, he ran down the stairs. The thumping wasn't coming from the front door, so he rushed into the kitchen and pushed open the shutter. The sunshine streamed in, and he blinked.

Two gendarmes stood outside, dressed in identical blue uniforms with a patch of an exploding grenade on their breast pockets. "We have received a complaint," one said as he swung a rat by its long pink tail. "Is it you who threw this rat on the road?"

Anouk came into the room just as he tossed the rodent into the undergrowth. She gasped, and Finlay put his arm around her and told her not to worry. "Everything is okay. The police need to check that we aren't squatters."

He fetched his satchel, opened it and presented their papers. One of the gendarmes flipped through their passports and inspected their visa stamps. The other studied the title deed to the house. They tipped their képis, apologized for disturbing them, and strutted off.

"What creeps," Anouk said.

"Yeah. Let's go out for breakfast. Coffee and croissants sound good?"

She paused, long enough to make it clear she still wasn't on speaking terms with him. "I guess. A café has to have a proper toilet."

"Your mother wouldn't mind using an outhouse."

"Well, I don't see why I should," she snapped and flounced off.

He supposed he couldn't blame her. He heated a pot of water on the stove and retrieved his shaving kit from his suitcase. If Mo were here, she'd order Anouk to come along. Mo was brusque and bossy, but she leavened things, making life with Anouk easier. He shaved, the bone handle of his father's straight razor smooth in his grip. Perhaps as a young man, he thought wistfully, Papa had used this same razor in this very kitchen. After Finlay had finished shaving and was splashing on aftershave, Anouk came up to him. "Okay, let's go. At least, it'll be warmer there."

Her words felt like a peace offering.

The Café de la Paix was empty apart from a man in blue coveralls standing at the zinc counter, a cup of coffee in hand. The owner, a gray-haired woman in a navy dress, was grumbling to him how Monsieur Noel still hadn't found a replacement baker and how could anyone expect her to run a café without a reliable source of decent bread.

Finlay and Anouk sat down at a table by the window next to an antique parlor stove, a Godin. Anouk touched it with one finger. "Stone cold," she pointed out. "It's not even turned on."

"You'll feel better with something to eat."

Finlay called over the woman at the bar and ordered a coffee for himself, cocoa for Anouk, and toast and jam for both of them.

"No bread," the woman snarled. "All we've got are yesterday's croissants."

"We'll take them."

After the owner went off, Finlay asked Anouk if she was hungry.

"I guess." She wasn't even trying to be civil.

"Thirsty?"

"Yeah."

"I'm sorry it's cold in here."

"Figures. It's all crappy in this place."

Neither of them spoke until their beverages arrived. Finlay asked if her hot chocolate was okay.

"So-so." To avoid him, she looked up at a menu chalked on a slate on the wall.

He took a sip of coffee.

"Don't," she said.

"Don't what?"

"Slurp. It's gross. Anyway, who ever heard of drinking coffee from a bowl?"

He set down his bowl. He had relished the warmth of it in his hands. If that friend of hers, Jilly, were here, Anouk would giggle and say what fun to sip it out of a bowl. His croissant tasted doughy, not flaky in the least. He turned it over— instead of a beautiful brown, the bottom was whitish.

Anouk took one bite of hers and put it down. "Why can't they make them properly like they do at home?"

What to do about Anouk's funk? If Mo were here, she wouldn't even notice it, so intently would she be concentrating on the surroundings: the light glinting on the bottles of Pastis and Johnny Walker; the owner's scowl; the stars-and-moons print on her navy dress; and the wall poster that forbade public drunkenness. She would pull out her Canon, frame each picture, and click, oblivious to Anouk.

Monsieur Noel arrived, surprising them. Finlay ordered him a coffee and Anouk chattered about the police and how they had black mustaches like the detectives Thomson and Thompson in Tintin.

"Don't let their visit alarm you," Monsieur Noel said. "There are informants roundabout, always have been. I bet it's that Madame Jabert at the Hotel du Dragon. Or gypsies." He leaned forward and put a finger to his lips. "One whisper the gypsies are near, and everybody rushes home to lock up tight. In fact, any stranger is cause for alarm. Already, everyone in the village knows you're here. They're talking."

"I wish they wouldn't," Finlay said.

"Baf. We all need a bit of excitement. Whenever we hear something, a footstep or the rumble of a car, we like to find out who it is. This is how we do it." He drew the edge of the lace curtain and peeked out. "Sometimes we only think we hear someone, and we say, 'Oh, nobody there.'"

"But who put the rat in front of our door?" Anouk asked.

He tugged his earlobe. "Eh? Speak up."

When the owner of the café brought his coffee, she tapped him on the shoulder. "All those years we championed you. Will you condemn us to live without bread the rest of our lives? Do something, I beg of you."

He rose to his feet. "Madame, with all due respect, I am sixty-five. I am retired. Is that not the law? As I have told you many times, a good baker is hard to find."

"You must know somebody," the owner said.

"Most bakers prefer city life." He shrugged and sat down.

"Word of mouth, that's the way. Tell them it's pleasant in Espérac. Who better to speak for us than you?"

"I am doing my best," he said.

"You must try harder." The woman scowled and went back to the bar.

As Anouk fretted about the rat at their door, Monsieur Noel droned on about the packs of them that roamed the village at night. "Vicious creatures. When I saw one climbing the wall, I worried it might bite your darling daughter."

"What?" Anouk shrieked.

"Oh yes, it's possible. At dawn, when I saw that filthy rat making for your window, I shot it."

"I guess . . . um, that was nice of you," Anouk said.

As if to make amends, he got up from the table and ambled toward a glass-fronted player piano and slipped a coin into the slot.

As the "Marseillaise" began to play, Anouk tapped her finger to the melody. "The tune is soft. It doesn't match the words about bloody banners and throat-cutting soldiers."

"The martyrs of the Resistance sang it as they fell to the Vichy firing squads. Vive la France, those were their last words."

Anouk thought of Danny. "I bet someone told them to do it. All they did was obey," she snapped.

"It was a brave act of defiance." Finlay bristled at what Monsieur Noel would see as her insolence.

"Believe it possible, Mademoiselle, that you may be mistaken in your opinion." He put a finger to his lips. "Now, shh. Listen."

Anouk waited quietly, but when the tune finished, she gestured toward a narrow door with a brass sign with the letters W.C. "Same one for men and women?"

While she was gone, Monsieur Noel chatted about Espérac. He made it sound like a sad little borough, its hundred inhabitants retired or unemployed, on the dole one way or another. Many of its derelict homes had been passed down from generation to generation, the legacy going in equal shares to all the offspring. If any one of the heirs declined to sell, well, the house couldn't be sold. In the first years after the deaths of the parents, all the adult children would arrive in the summer to vacation together. Gradually, fewer would return. Eventually, there would be just one, usually the poorest sibling, who in mid-July would open up the house and kill off the rats. Every year a roof tile or two would slip.

With no one around in winter to mop the leaks or shore up the sagging roof, at some point, a wall would bulge, and some years later, blocks of dressed stone would tumble to the ground. The mayor's office would dispatch a warning with a date scheduled for the demolition.

Anouk returned from the toilet in a foul mood. "What's the matter with the French? Why can't they be like the Lebanese, where the cafés have nice sit-down toilets, and you can stay as long as you like?"

Monsieur Noel acted as if he hadn't heard a word. "Your house is the oldest one here, which makes it worthy of rescue. If the house is only for holidays or for an investment property, that's one thing. If you intend it to be your home sweet home, that's something else altogether."

Finlay turned to Anouk. "Shall we give it a try?"

"Get a toilet," she snapped.

Finlay wanted to slap her. Monsieur Noel pretended he had not heard, but she'd given him reason to believe what people said about ill-bred American children. The instant they got home, Finlay called Anouk on her behavior.

"I don't want to be here, and you know it. So maybe I was rude, but the toilet was just a hole in the ground, bad as the one in the station. The light went off, and there I was in the pitch black. I yanked the chain, and water splashed everywhere, even over my feet."

"You were disrespectful."

"Okay, I'm sorry. But we need a toilet." Her voice came out squeaky as it did when she was worked up.

"That's no excuse. You'll need to apologize to Monsieur Noel."

Finlay left her to her own devices and set about cleaning the place. First, he threw open all the windows to air out the house, closed up for some thirty years. He yanked the dustsheets, stained by decades of rat urine, off the furniture and piled them in a corner to deal with later. Broom in hand, he went from room to room to sweep off the dead flies from the windowsills and knock down the spider webs in the corners. He scrubbed the grime off the stovetop. He took down the calendar that patched a cracked window in the kitchen. The calendar, a pinup of a blonde in a red dress, was dated 1947, likely the year his aunt died, when he was already in Montreal.

Anouk came in to show him one of her finds, a large board. Finlay ran his hand along the curved ridges and brushed off the spider webs at the corners. "An old-fashioned washboard? Maybe your great-grandmother scrubbed clothes on it."

Later in the morning, Monsieur Noel dropped by. He advised Finlay to dump the filthy dust cloths in the washing basin, the cold freshwater pool fed by the spring that ran beneath Espérac, and after they'd soaked, to drape them over the bushes, where the sun would bleach them, and they'd be good as new. Monsieur Noel reminisced about the days when all the women of the village would gather by the spring to do the family laundry. He was saying what a jolly spot it used to be when Anouk came in holding what looked like a painting in her arms. "Look what I found in the attic. Bet you can't guess what it is." She shifted from foot to foot with excitement.

"Don't you have something to say to our neighbor?" Finlay murmured.

She dropped her gaze to her feet. "I'm sorry I was rude. Actually, it was nice of you to shoot that rat for us."

Monsieur Noel beamed. "The apology is all mine. I should have hidden it. I overlooked the fact you're a city girl. And such a pretty one. Now show us your find."

It was a square of embroidered muslin in a gold frame. Below the entwined flags of Germany and France were the words, "SOUVENIR OF MY CAPTIVITY," stitched in blue yarn, along with the date 23 August 1914 and a spray of blue forget-me-nots. Set in two ovals were black-and-white photographs of a man with a handlebar mustache and a woman in a high-necked blouse pinned with a cameo. The names, François Fortin and Anna Klein, in gold thread, identified them.

"Who are these guys?" Anouk asked.

"François was your great-grandfather," Finlay said.

"But who's Anna Klein? Didn't you say my great-grandma's name was Anouk?"

"It was." Finlay turned to Monsieur Noel. "I've never heard of any Anna Klein."

"Let me take a look." He took the embroidery in both his hands and brought it close to his eyes. "Ah yes, I see the family resemblance." He turned to Finlay. "You and François have the same nose." He touched Anouk's chin. "And you, my dear, have François' strong jaw."

"My mom says I get that from her."

"What do you know about my grandfather and the German woman?" Finlay asked.

Monsieur Noel put down his glass of nut wine. "I never met her, but I heard the gossip. It happened after the Germans deported François to Alsace along with thousands of other Frenchmen."

"How awful." Anouk traced the embroidered blue flowers with her finger.

"It was wartime, after all. The enemy grabbed our men and sent them to do hard labor in Germany. François was billeted on the farm of a widow in Alsace—Anna Klein. At least, I believe she was a widow. A merry widow," he giggled. "Don't feel sorry for François. He was one of the lucky ones. He feasted on thick slabs of beef and pork while our soldiers had nothing to eat but cats and broth."

"I'd never eat a cat," Anouk exclaimed. "Never, not even if I were starving."

"My Colette would say the same, but neither of you has ever been hungry." He rubbed his stomach. "Euh, the hunger pangs. You have no idea."

"Tell me about Anna Klein," Finlay said.

"All right, if you insist. After the Armistice, instead of hurrying home to the arms of his good wife, your great-grandfather François lingered with the fräulein."

"I bet they fell in love." Anouk's cheeks were pink with excitement.

Monsieur Noel scratched his chin. "Who knows? She was likely older. A widow, after all. Perhaps she fancied him. And why not? He was handsome like your papa. Virile, too, I should imagine— probably liked a roll in the hay." Monsieur Noel leaned back in his chair and took another sip of wine. "At any rate, François milked the widow's cows and plowed her fields until the moment destiny stepped in. One day while scything a meadow, he sliced off his middle finger. Because he'd be no use as a farmer, the Germans sent him off. And home he came to Espérac, one digit short."

"That happened to Zaki, a friend of mine back in Beirut. He got his trigger finger blown off, and he has a mustache too."

"Always in style." Monsieur Noel took the embroidery to the window. "We can see better here. See how this branch of the rose bush is brown—dead—while the other is a vivid green? I interpret that to mean Anna Klein feared she would surely die of lovesickness."

"How about my great-grandma? She must have been jealous."

"Most likely. You say you found this hidden away. Maybe François hid it. Ah, such a lucky fellow. Compared to the others, he —"

"He should have been faithful," Anouk said.

"Who knows? Montaigne wrote that any man smitten with his wife was a man so dull no one else could love him. It was the time of arranged marriages, and love didn't enter into it."

"That's wrong," she said.

Monsieur Noel handed the embroidery to her. "You've seen the war memorial? Count the names on it. Seventeen gallant men. Each left a sweetheart. Oh yes, they were the unlucky ones, not your great-grandfather. After all, when François returned from Alsace, he made a name for himself. That he, lacking a finger, should become a master baker, well, it defies the imagination, does it not? And yet it was he who taught the craft and art of baking to your great-uncle Jacques, who later taught it to me."

After Monsieur Noel had left, Finlay gathered the dustsheets and dumped them in a wheelbarrow. They overflowed the edges of the barrow, and he struggled to keep it upright as he wheeled it down the hill to the pool. In the late morning sun, a blue-tailed damselfly, darting after a dragonfly, looped around the oval basin. White butterflies flitted by the gray stone edge of the pool. As he set down the wheelbarrow, he stooped to unlace his shoes and took them off as it felt like holy ground. A few feet from the pool, he noticed a limestone outcropping, covered with shaggy vegetation. As he approached it, he realized it was the spring, its water so transparent he could see a few stones on its sandy bottom. He cupped his hand, dipped it in the water, and drank. Refreshed, he turned to the oval basin. In the sunshine, the water shimmered like moiré silk.

One by one, he hurled in the sheets. With a long stick, he swirled each in the pool, hauled it out, and spread it on the bushes to dry. He went home and ate lunch with Anouk, after which he spent the afternoon cleaning.

At nine p.m., shortly before sunset, he returned to the spring.

Now bone dry, the sheets smelled sweet. He folded them as best he could by himself and stacked them in the wheelbarrow. Reluctant to leave this lovely spot, he sat on the grass. Perhaps his papa had lingered here to look down over the valley, and his grandmère too. Likely every one of the Fortins whose tombstones he'd seen in the cemetery had come here. This place was home to them. Like Monsieur Noel, they likely never traveled even as far as Bordeaux, let alone Paris. What must that be like, to be so rooted to a place that you never left it? And where was the place that felt like home? For his Palestinian students, it was the country loved and lost, a land most of them had never seen. For Anouk, it was Beirut. And for Mo? Not her birthplace, the Flint Hills of Kansas. Beautiful though they were, she liked to say she came from nowhere. She didn't share his need for a place to call home.

He slipped off his shoes, the grass moist and cool on the soles of his feet. He sat in the shade of the chestnut tree on the gnarled bench and ran his hand over the soft moss and poked a finger in its knotholes. High in the branches of an oak tree, a nightingale sang. Attracted by the reflection of the church steeple in the pond, he drew near to it, dipped in his hand, and trickled water onto his neck. He gasped from the cold. After he washed the dirt from his face, he took off his shirt and jeans, set them under the tree, waded in to his shins, and splashed the frigid water on his chest and over his shoulders.

He heard the woman's voice before he saw her. She was strolling down the daisy-speckled path singing "A La Claire Fontaine," a love song he had thought only French-Canadians knew. Startled, with his hands he covered his bare chest and loins, mortified at being seen in his skivvies. She looked at him a long while; she smiled, an enigmatic, ironic smile.

She was young and attractive, with a red Cupid's bow mouth. People here were slight and dark-haired, but this woman had fair hair that fell in luxurious ringlets to her shoulders.

"Bonjour, Madame." He blushed.

"You found the water so beautiful you took a bath? Like in the song I was singing?" Her voice was soft and teasing. She came closer. He nodded, his throat so dry he was unable to speak. She had full arms and a lovely throat and bosom. "Few brave such cold water," she said.

He could think of nothing to say. He was very conscious of the water dripping off his bare skin. She turned toward the spring, a few feet above the pool. Kneeling on the stone ledge, she bent over and dipped in the pitcher. She wore red patent leather heels. Such tiny feet she had. She turned, and he met her gaze. She smiled again, that beguiling complicated smile; her eyes locked on his as if she had all the time in the world. Then she waved at him as she left.

Who was she?

As he got out of the water and put on his clothes, a literary reference came to him. She was Nausicaa, come to rescue him, like naked Odysseus, from the shipwreck of his life. He headed up the hill to the village, shaking his head. No, nothing as dramatic as that.

Chapter 10

One morning in early June, the mailman delivered a registered letter from the American University of Beirut. It included a check for Finlay's severance pay, a month's pay for each year of service. That same afternoon he deposited the check in the bank in Issigeac. With the knowledge he could now afford to make improvements, he decided to ask the mason, Pierre's father, for advice.

Finlay's main worry, however, was the rats. Sometimes he awakened at night to the sound of gunfire, and he was never sure whether it was a bad dream or Monsieur Noel shooting rats. Anouk screamed every time she saw a rat or mouse, but when Finlay suggested poison pellets, she rejected that as too cruel.

Monsieur Noel touted the benefits of the ultrasound. Last week he had bought one, a black box no bigger than a box of candy, which emitted a squeak that repelled vermin. After he had installed it in his garden, the moles decamped from their holes and fled, leaving his dahlias to flourish. Because it was supposed to work on rats and mice, too, he lent it to Finlay, who placed it in the attic. For the first four days, it had no effect. The following evening while he and Anouk were playing Scrabble at the kitchen table—she had just formed the triple point word "die,"—an alarming racket startled them. Alarmed, they looked up. At the south corner of the room where the wall joined the ceiling, a legion of mice scampered down the wall and disappeared as if lured by an invisible Pied Piper.

The next morning, Monsieur Lebon arrived with his son, who helped out during the summer holidays. Anouk recognized Pierre right away. In his jeans, he was tall like her dad. Pierre's father had brawny arms and wore a beret and bright blue overalls. The men stood outside and stared up at the walls. "Sound for the time being—but vulnerable," the mason said. He glared at the wisteria and predicted it would creep in between the joints and cause cracks. In winter, frost would cause the cracks to widen and endanger the wall. He reached into his pocket for a cigarette and stuck the Gauloise between his lips. "Dig the wisteria up. Right now, I tell you."

"But it's got such cute purple flowers," Anouk said. "Let's keep it for now. We can get rid of it when we go home in August."

"Won't cost a franc to dig it up," Monsieur Lebon harrumphed.

"We'll think about it." Finlay led them into the kitchen, where Monsieur Lebon looked askance at the cracked and broken tiles. He got the poker from the hearth and banged it on the floor. "Know what's underneath? Clay. It'll give you no end of trouble. You should chuck out your tiles, put in a layer of cement and start fresh."

"But I like those tiles," Anouk said. "Yesterday when it rained they glistened."

"Rising damp, Mademoiselle. Bad for the health. Make a note," he said to Pierre. Next, the men studied the ceiling beams. Pierre leaned a wooden ladder against the wall and climbed until he was high enough to prod the massive beams with the tip of his knife.

"Hard as iron. No woodworm here." Pierre grinned. "No matter how hard the poor beetle tries to bore his way in, he can't."

Anouk hooted as if he'd said something hilarious. Monsieur

Lebon rambled on about how the beams had been carved from centuries-old chestnut, soaked in the river a year or so, and burned to harden further. Pierre didn't interrupt the long-winded speech. Finlay wryly hoped Anouk would notice the boy's deference to his father.

The lad hoisted the ladder on his shoulder, and they went from room to room to continue their inspection. The good news was that they found no woodworm. In Anouk's bedroom, Finlay showed them the beam five feet directly above her bed. He worried it might fall on her.

"I can live touch-and-go," she said.

"Oh, but we want to keep you safe, Mademoiselle," Pierre said. He suggested they hire the blacksmith to forge a clamp to undergird the beam and hold it fast to the wall.

"Excellent idea." Finlay jotted a note.

"Look at those cracks in the wall. That's what needs fixing," Anouk said.

Monsieur Lebon recommended repointing the joints so as to expose the stone. "It won't cost much and that look is all the rage," he said.

"We should cover it. Stone looks gloomy and gray," she said.

"Mademoiselle likes things to be pretty." Pierre winked at her, and Finlay wished the boy would stop his flirting.

In the attic, they inspected the dormer windows, one of which leaked. Monsieur Lebon recommended a roofer who could advise them on whether a patch job would do, or if they needed to replace the entire roof. Anouk stuck her hand out the window and felt the moss on the wavy tiles. "It's like a fairy tale roof," she said. "We should leave it alone."

Finlay felt a sudden pang: she saw the roof with her mother's eyes. But Monsieur Lebon looked at him with dismay. "Damp, Monsieur Fortin. You must beware of damp. Moss encourages it and will shorten the lifespan of your roof."

"I doubt we have sufficient funds to do all that needs doing," Finlay said. "Perhaps the roof can wait."

Monsieur Lebon smiled. "It's very well that Mademoiselle likes her roof, for with summer upon us, every roofer for kilometers around will already be booked."

Anouk tugged Finlay's arm. "What can't wait is a toilet."

Monsieur Lebon measured the yard. To determine where best to install a grease pit and septic tank, he struck the ground here and there with a pick. He grunted with the effort. It was bedrock— no simple matter to excavate. Finlay listened with growing distress as he learned about the cost of pipes, drywall, plaster and tiles for a bathroom. "And don't forget the fixtures—the sink, toilet, tub, and bidet," he said.

"Bidet?" Anouk said, confused. "We can do without one of those."

They walked over to the outhouse, a roofed structure of weathered planks. The gray door squeaked on its hinges as Finlay pulled it open. Monsieur Lebon sniffed. "Doesn't stink. You could make do. As you know, a bathroom is an expensive proposition."

"It's not just me. Mom couldn't stand that outhouse either."

Pierre touched her arm. "Don't be upset, Mademoiselle. A hundred million francs can't buy what you now possess: this peaceful, sunny spot on the square." He nudged his father, and Monsieur Lebon suggested they wait before undertaking major repairs. "That way you will come to know the pleasantest parts of the house, the ones you and your daughter will desire to keep."

In the night, a crash of thunder awakened Finlay. He went up to the attic to check the basins were properly positioned to catch the leaks. Afterward, on his way downstairs, he overheard Anouk crying and went to her. "It's going to be okay," he said, putting his arms around her. "We'll take it a day at a time."

"Forget it," she snapped and pushed him away. "You act as if we're going to be here forever. And you know how I feel about a nice bathroom, yet you act as if it doesn't matter two hoots. And you kidnapped me. There's no way I can get over that."

"It was to keep you safe."

"Ha." With tears continuing to stream down her face, she fiddled with Danny's bracelet. "It's awful here. I want to go home."

He wasn't sure what to say. He wanted to hold Anouk close, but that wasn't possible with her being so antagonistic. "Sunbeam, I'm very sorry you're so unhappy."

She sniffed, not mollified in the slightest. "You still don't get it, do you, why I needed to stay in Beirut? All the kids at school were already forgetting Danny. Most of those posters we pinned on the telephone poles got ripped off. No one seemed to care about him anymore except Mom and me. I could —"

A thunderbolt crashed, and lightning forked across the black sky. As a lame way to make her feel better, Finlay closed the shutters. As the rain pelted, the raindrops dripped into the buckets he'd set in the attic. Anouk pulled the sheet tight around her. "Know what Danny once told me? 'When it rains, the dead are jealous of the living.' Their Armenian maid said so."

Finlay took a deep breath. "Anouk, you have to know Danny's not coming back."

"You're wrong," she yelled, sitting up straight in bed. "Danny's okay. I just know it. When a person really truly wants something, it comes true. He'll escape. I'm sure of it."

She was wrong, of course, but he wouldn't rub her face in the horrible truth. Instead, he told her what he meant to discuss earlier. "You need to go to school," he said.

She was outraged. "That's not fair. School back home ends in a couple of weeks. I won't miss a thing."

At least, he had distracted her from Danny. "I don't want you falling behind," he said. "The lycée in Bergerac will take you.

There's a bus."

"No way."

"You'll meet kids your age."

"Me hang around a bunch of hicks? Anyway, you know I get carsick. I'll throw up over everyone."

"You need to go," he said patiently. "It's the law."

"Nobody will find out."

"But you like school. You even applied for that scholarship your mother wanted you to."

"That's different."

Mo would soon be here to straighten things out, so he decided to be lenient. "All right, for the time being, no school. In return, why don't you try to make the best of things?"

The following day, Finlay informed Monsieur Lebon that he had decided to delay work on the house. Anouk did what he asked. She spent her free time listening to her tapes and the French hit parade on the radio. One day she discovered a sewing machine and settled down to make curtains for her bedroom. Finlay listened to her happily outlining her new project. She bought packets of green dye at the market and soaked a set of her great-grandma's sheets in an enormous copper jam basin until the linen turned the color of lettuce. Seated at the treadle sewing machine, a Singer, she threaded the bobbin, dropped the needle, and pressed the fabric bit by bit under the foot as she worked the pedal the way her mother had taught her. It took her a week to stitch and hem the curtains, but they looked pretty at her bedroom window.

He kept himself busy too. From time to time, he would think of the singing woman he'd met at the spring. He went there often to fetch water and to do the laundry. Not once did he see her. He spent most of his time working on the house. He scrubbed the floor in the kitchen, but since the tiles were set directly on beaten dirt, all he succeeded in doing was to move the dirt around. He was nervous about cleaning the ceiling because he was afraid of heights. He had worked as a roofer summers during college, and it would take long minutes of sitting on the roof to get his legs to stop trembling. He had learned not to let his fear deter him. Perched on a stepladder, he pushed the wire brush back and forth a linear foot at a time. Soot coated his cheeks, and Anouk joked he looked like a miner. Once the beams in the kitchen were clean, he prepared a batch of sour-smelling whitewash, and together they slopped it on the beams and the walls. Afterward, he threw open the windows, and a fresh breeze blew through.

"Lighter now. Mom will like it," Anouk said. To match the new mood, she picked wildflowers from the meadow outside the village, filled the green vase with cornflowers and Queen Anne's lace and placed it on the dining table. She bought pots of geranium from the market and set them on the south-facing windowsill.

"Little by little, that's what Zaki used to say."

It was the first time she had mentioned him since leaving, and Finlay asked if she missed him.

"Not much. I bet Zaki's gone off to marry his cousin in the States and become a millionaire. You know what I say? Tough Twinkies," she said as she went off laughing.

Chapter 11

Anouk was threading the bobbin of the sewing machine, preparing
to work on her bedroom curtains, when Monsieur Noel banged
on the front door with an invitation to go escargot hunting. "We
meet at midnight in the cemetery," he said.

"Midnight?" she said, puzzled.

"That's when the snails come out. They're tasty with garlic.
Nothing better." He smacked his lips.

"But from a cemetery? It doesn't sound sanitary."

"Best place there is. No pesticides. Should you see a snail in the
garden, beware. Look and make sure no blue pellets lurk near.
That's slug bait; it does in our little friends. And don't you go
collecting them from the fields. Nasty chemicals there too."

Her mom would have liked the idea, but not her dad. "Going
out in the dead of night to chase —of all things—snails?" he said.
"You've got better things to do."

"Okay, we won't go. No big deal."

"But we should—to be neighborly," he said, reconsidering.

"Sounds like fun."

"You go. You might meet some kids your age."

"You don't have friends either, just old Monsieur Noel. Mom
better hurry up and get here, for your sake." Anouk had spoken

to her only twice, and both times the telephone connection was awful. When they tried to call yesterday, they couldn't get through, and her dad didn't seem the least bit bothered; he said she had to be patient.

At ten p.m., it was still light, another thing wrong about this place. In Beirut, at this time of year, the sun set before eight, just the way it should. She tuned in to the hit parade on the radio as she hemmed a curtain. She was bored. She missed the nights in the shelter with the machine guns going rat-a-tat-tat, and all the kids scarfing popcorn and pizza in their cozy hideaway basement. The snail hunt was the first exciting thing to happen since she arrived. Toward midnight, she glanced at the mound of linen and decided she was sick of sewing. "Dad, I'm off," she said.

In the square, old women were milling about, chatting with the men, who wore their berets pulled low over their wrinkled foreheads. Nobody her age. It was just as well she hadn't bothered to change out of her jeans. She recognized some of the villagers by sight, although she didn't know their names. Luckily, here that didn't matter. Hardly anybody used first names. Just saying Monsieur or Madame was enough. Still, she was nervous about the kissing. Which cheek got kissed first? Was it right-left-right, or left-right-left? It'd be dreadful to end up kissing some stranger on the lips by accident. She made the rounds, shaking hands with the men and managing to kiss the women in the correct way. Eventually, she located Monsieur Noel. Wearing mud-caked boots, he was sitting at the bus stop beside a Marilyn Monroe lookalike in a red miniskirt and spangles in her hair. He stood up and introduced them.

The woman, whose name was Madame Labelle, pressed her cheek to Anouk's and made birdie-sounding smooches. She looked about her mom's age, but had curly hair, platinum blonde, and wore bright red lipstick and a ton of mascara. She smelled like lily of the valley. She brushed away a silk flower that had drifted down from the graveyard onto the bench and made space for Anouk. Anouk read the postings on the bulletin board behind them. There were official memos from the mayor, tattered notices of fetes and horse races, and a notice of a funeral mass for a Daniel Dupuis. That reminded her of her Danny, and she felt the familiar pang of longing and guilt.

"Think the Vamps will come?" Madame Labelle said.

"What? Who are they?" Anouk said, intrigued.

"That's Papa's nickname for Madame Vaubon and her sister. Poor dearies, they like a bit of fun. And right they are. Who wants the dull life of dinner at eight, television at nine, and then to bed?"

An old man with a paunch and an accordion slung round his chest came up to them. He told Anouk he'd known her great-grandfather François, whose reputation as a baker was so fine that people would travel to Espérac all the way from Bergerac to buy his bread. And not only was he a maître boulanger, but a handsome fellow too. The accordionist winked at Madame Labelle. "And young M. Fortin, with those lucky genes he'll be good-looking too."

"Well, let the Vamps have him." Madame Labelle chuckled and went off.

Anouk needed to tell everybody her father was married, but more villagers were arriving, and no one was paying attention to her. They couldn't stop grumbling about having to eat soup with no bread and how they needed a baker— tout de suite.

Unable to get a word in edgewise, she ran ahead and caught up with Monsieur Noel and his daughter, already on their way to the cemetery. At the house with the green shutters, he stopped on the road. "Do you hear what I hear? Listen." He cupped his hand to his left ear. "Those moans?"

"Papa! Stop imagining things. It's the television," his daughter said, laughing.

Moments later, leaning on his furled umbrella and skirting puddles, he rushed off toward a thicket.

"Poor Papa. It's his bladder." She took Anouk's arm. "Let's go on ahead."

At least, she wouldn't have to see him fiddling with his fly, but she wondered what to say to his daughter. Since Jilly once said everyone liked a compliment, Anouk said her skirt was pretty.

Madame Labelle smiled. "I wear red when it's my period."

That was the way the French were— not the least bit shy about their bodies. At the cemetery, Anouk's feet sank into the squishy grass and her toes got wet. She shouldn't have worn sandals. If there were snails, there were bound to be yucky slugs too. She shone her flashlight over the cemetery, but she couldn't see much, only crosses aligned in rows below the church steeple and its crooked cross. Then she noticed a burial vault that looked like the one where Juliet kissed poor dead Romeo. She cracked a joke about how people were dying to get into the cemetery, but Madame Labelle didn't get it.

A few minutes later Monsieur Noel came up.

"Here comes the Master of the Mollusks," said a woman with lipstick smeared over her upper lip. He lectured them about the thousands of species of snail, how their slime protected them, and how the animals in Noah's ark had to practice patience while they waited for the snails to embark.

"Easy to catch, they are. Not like butterflies." The woman swung her cane in spirals as if it were a butterfly flitting about. She had to be one of the Vamps.

After Monsieur Noel finished his speech, the dozen or so villagers cheered and scattered. Anouk followed Madame Labelle, who drifted from grave to grave, lifting each flowerpot and checking around the pebbles, weeds, and leaf litter for snails, grabbing them when she spotted them and depositing them in her red cloth bag. Anouk, who had spotted only two snails, caught up with Madame Labelle, who was hovering over one, its tiny horns glistening in the moonlight as it edged forward. She plucked it between her thumb and forefinger and got a good look at it before setting it on the ground.

"Don't you want it?" Anouk asked.

"Not that one." Monsieur Noel's daughter shook her head. "Those who set forth boldly deserve to live."

Brave like Danny, Anouk thought, wishing she knew the Frenchwoman well enough to tell her about him.

A couple of rows over, Monsieur Noel was kicking a granite vault with the name Jabert engraved in gold on it. "Asshole. I hope you burn forever. May you enjoy cutting hair in hell."

His daughter rushed up to him as if he'd gone berserk. "Papa. Stop. He's dead. There's no point."

Her father spat on the vault.

"Come along now." She swung her lantern toward the far end of the cemetery. "Look, your friends are waiting for you."

"Stop bothering me. I'll go after I get these." With both hands, he grabbed the snails clinging to the Jabert vault and dropped them in the wire basket he held gripped between his teeth.

"Hurry up," one of his pals yelled. "Let's get them before it starts pouring."

Monsieur Noel held onto the edge of the vault and pulled himself upright. "Oh, my aching back," he moaned as, leaning on his black umbrella, he headed off toward his friends.

"Who's Monsieur Jabert?" Anouk asked.

"A toad. He mistreated my maman when I was still a baby," Madame Labelle said.

"But that must have been ages ago."

"Of course it was."

Kicking and spitting on a grave. It was disgusting, At least her father never acted like that. Anouk returned to collecting snails. Now she spotted hundreds—it was as if they were calling, "Here I am. Pick me." Each slightly resisted as she plucked it and stuffed it with the others. When her bag bulged so it couldn't hold one more snail, Madame Labelle offered to lend her a basket she had in her car.

On their way out of the cemetery, Madame Labelle stopped at a grave enclosed by a wrought iron fence with a rose bush that rambled along it. Pink petals lay on the ground. She unlatched the gate and showed Anouk the headstone with the name, MARIE LAFORET NOEL, and a black-and-white photo under glass of a pretty dark-haired woman. Chiseled into the marble were the dates 1924-1953. "That's my maman," Colette said. "She died when I was ten."

"She didn't get to live long. That's so sad."

The rain got going, and they raced out of the graveyard and across the square to Madame Labelle's Peugeot, by the war memorial. It was cozy inside the car, the rain pelting on the red roof. Madame Labelle got the hamper she used for house calls and turned it upside down. Out tumbled combs and brushes, scissors, rollers, and bottles of peroxide, hairspray, shampoo and hair color. It seemed unsanitary to put snails in it, but that wouldn't bother the French. As Anouk arranged the scissors, she said she was thinking of letting her hair grow out.

"You'll need to be patient. Most people give up after a few weeks. Still, you'll feel more sensual with long hair." She ran her fingers through Anouk's damp hair. "American hair. Shiny, healthy, thick. So long as you keep the part on the right, it'll look beautiful." She took a bag of bonbons from the glove compartment. "Here, take one. I hope my father wasn't boring you. It's his cataracts. He can't tell when our eyes glaze over. He wants you to think he's fascinating, but old people tend to ramble. If that happens, change the subject. Ask whatever you like. He's always glad to chat."

Anouk sucked the red-and-white striped peppermint. The string of turquoise beads dangling from the rearview mirror reminded her of the donkey beads in Cinderella's Coach, fat as marbles and the same blue as Madame Labelle's eyes. Danny called them worry beads and said they were supposed to work against the evil eye. It occurred to her that maybe Goldfingers and Fathead had grabbed him because they thought he came from a wealthy family who could pay a huge ransom.

"Rain should end soon," Madame Labelle said.

Anouk fiddled with the bracelet Danny had given her, feeling comfortable with this woman. "Was Victor your first love? You look young. To be a widow, I mean."

Madame Labelle smiled. "And you, my flea, have you ever been in love?"

Anouk bit her lip. She was scared she'd bawl if she talked about Danny, so instead she asked about Victor. Madame Labelle had met him in Bordeaux, where he was studying medicine, and they fell in love. His family had been in Algeria forever. On their estate near Algiers, they had a thousand workers who grew oranges and lemons for export. When Victor was a teenager, he would stitch up their cuts, set their broken limbs, and pass out pills. Even then he knew he wanted to be a doctor. After they married, he took her to Algeria with him and they lived in Algiers in the French Quarter, where the skyscrapers glistened in the sunshine. Sometimes she visited the old city where the Arabs lived, the women in white robes and the kids running around barefoot on the narrow lanes. She loved the tramway, the bandstand, the palm trees, the Café du Vieux Grenadier, the hospital where Victor worked, and her beautiful church, Notre Dame d'Afrique.

"Sounds like you miss it," Anouk said. At that moment, lightning zigzagged across the sky and thunder rumbled. "It's nice and dry in here. The others must be sopping wet."

"Won't hurt them."

"So why did you and Victor leave when you liked it so much?"

"We had to. After the Arabs won the war, their slogan was 'The suitcase or the coffin.' Do you understand?"

Anouk had to think a moment before she got it. "That's awful," she said.

"Death or exile. So we evacuated with all the others that July 1962. When we got to Marseille, all the French were at the beach, tanning. Nothing was organized. I left Victor and came here to Espérac."

Anouk wanted to know more about why she had left Victor, but her new friend was done talking.

When the rain let up, they clambered out of the car. Anouk shone her lantern on the war memorial. There was a plaque with the names of those who had died in World War I, World War II, and the war in North Africa. She counted them: "Seventeen men, almost all from the First World War."

"Even more died than are listed here," Madame Labelle said. "You know Pierre Lebon?"

Anouk nodded. "The mason's son. He's nice."

"The names of those executed for so-called 'cowardice' are not inscribed. Pierre's grandfather was one of them."

"Executed because they were pacifists? That's wrong." Anouk touched Danny's bracelet. The villagers would have shot him too. She didn't want to think about it. "Let's catch up with the others," she said. Baskets banging against their hips, leaping over puddles, they raced hand in hand across the square and up to the cemetery. And then not a thing in the world counted but snatching snails, dozens, hundreds of them.

When the snail hunt was over, she glanced at her watch. It was three a.m. in Beirut. She moved the hour hand back an hour. Now she was on French time.

Chapter 12

In the third week of June, the sulky weather shifted, turning torrid with the oppressive heat that precedes storms. Finlay bought a pair of shorts, something he had not worn since he was a boy. The blond fuzz stood out against his tanned legs. He felt comfortable in the shorts, free and easy, like a younger version of himself.

Still no word from Mo. At least Anouk had settled down. Instead of snarling, giving him the silent treatment, or flicking her head and doing whatever she wanted, she argued with him now that they were on speaking terms again. She chatted about Monsieur Noel's daughter, whom she'd met on the snail hunt and who had given Anouk her old bicycle, a pink one, which she used to explore the countryside. Could this Madame Labelle be the woman who had spied him frisking in the pond? The memory embarrassed Finlay. Whenever he caught a glimpse of her through Monsieur Noel's window, he averted his gaze. The French were quick to accuse others of what they called indiscreet glances.

Now that the snails had purged themselves of grit, Monsieur Noel invited Finlay and Anouk to an escargot feast, after which they would attend the annual bonfire honoring the feast of Saint John. Finlay hesitated. He sensed the alluring woman from the spring would be there. He reminded himself that he was a married man and should stay clear of her.

When Monsieur Noel opened the door, the dog lunged at Anouk and pawed the turquoise mini-skirt that barely covered her thighs.

"Merde!" Monsieur Noel shouted. He raised his cane and Saucisse slunk off to a corner to gnaw at a bone. In the salon, the grandfather clocks in all four corners of the room chimed, and a bird popped out of a cuckoo clock on the mantel. "Tempus fugit," he said. "Time flies." The golden-haired woman entered, and he introduced her. "My daughter, Colette Labelle."

Finlay stood up. She had on a different dress, not red but green, but she was indeed the woman from the spring. She smelled of perfume. Maybe like Marilyn Monroe, she wore nothing but a few drops of Chanel No. 5 to bed. She looked him over in a leisurely way with her soft brown eyes, and as she smiled, her left cheek dimpled. Her hand felt soft in his; she wore a ring on each of her fingers. He smoothed back his hair and straightened his tie; his heart was thumping. They sat in comfortable chairs around a mahogany table set on a Persian rug, and he took surreptitious peeks at her reflection in the gilt mirror.

Oblivious to his subterfuge, Anouk gestured at the trophy on the wall. The beast had short tusks, a pronounced snout, pointed ears, yellowed teeth, and dull gray fur. She nudged her father. "Disgusting, huh?"

"Sus scrofa." Monsieur Noel puffed out his chest with pride. "Wild boar."

"I can't bear to look at it," Colette agreed. "Still, my papa is an exceptional marksman. He keeps us in stews and sausage all winter long."

It was a wonder the old fellow could shoot at all, so terribly did he shake. Once Finlay had met a painter in Beirut who trembled all the time—when he chatted, ate, and maybe even when he dreamed—but the moment he grasped his palette in one hand and a paintbrush in the other, he was utterly self-possessed. Perhaps Monsieur Noel was like that and enjoyed a firm grip once he had a rifle in hand. Apparently, the woods teemed with boar, partridge, hare, and deer, so hunting was more a matter of patience than skill.

When it was time for apéritifs, Anouk took one look at the bottles of Ricard, Campari, and Johnny Walker, and asked for a glass of soda. Madame Labelle sashayed off. She had shapely ankles even though everything else about her was ample. Finlay forced his gaze away, down at the Oriental carpet, the edges of which had unraveled.

Monsieur Noel went to the window. "Looks like a squall is coming."

Anouk kept on flipping through the pages of his thick red dictionary, a Petit Larousse. It had exactly 1,789 pages.

"Was that in honor of your revolution?" she said.

"Such a smart girl. And do you know why we stormed the Bastille?"

"To set the prisoners free?" She looked wistful, and it occurred to Finlay that she was thinking of Danny languishing somewhere in Beirut.

Monsieur Noel said the revolutionaries needed the Bastille to get access to the wheat stored there.

"Oh." She turned to the charts at the back of the book, found the map for the Périgord and touched the dot for Bergerac. Monsieur Noel said the town got its name from Cyrano de Bergerac, who had been baptized there.

"So who was he?"

"A lover, long of nose, brave in battle but shy in love." That got him going. He pontificated about the correlation between the size of a man's nose and his penis, and how fortune favored the man with an extraordinary proboscis until Colette came in and scolded him. "Enough of that, Papa." She uncorked the wine, the bottle so cold that drops of moisture beaded the neck. "Monsieur Fortin, a bit of nut wine?"

"Why so formal?" her father said. "You're both the same age. Call the man by his first name."

"Finlay, then." She smiled, testing that out. With her accent, she made his name sound like Feen-lee. She handed Anouk a minty green drink and poured nut wine for the adults. As Monsieur Noel served them hors d'oeuvres, he pointed out the bits of truffle in the foie gras. On the half-hour, the clocks chimed, and Colette led them to the table spread with a blue-checked cloth. The table, made of oak, hailed from centuries ago when people were shorter, and Finlay had to twist sideways for his legs to fit. An inch closer and he'd touch Colette's bare calf. The thought made him lightheaded.

The meal began with artichokes. Monsieur Noel tucked his napkin into his shirt collar, and Colette demonstrated how to tug off the leaves, dip them in melted butter and nibble the soft flesh. When she'd finished with the leaves, she gouged out the bristly choke and put it to the side of her plate, cut the artichoke bottom into pieces, dipped each in the melted butter, and one by one, popped them into her mouth. Finlay couldn't keep his eyes off her.

Anouk asked about John the Baptist, and Colette leaned close to her. "No one ever told you how he wore animal skins and ate grasshoppers and honey?"

Anouk shot an accusing look at Finlay. "I'm behind when it comes to religion."

Colette looked upset. "Surely, a child needs to know God loves her."

Anouk sprang to his defense. "I'm not so far behind as all that. My father taught me that God was love. Not the ordinary kind, but big-time love, 'love that moves the sun and other stars.'"

"That's true," Colette said.

"It's from Dante," Finlay said.

"Yes. And Dad told me about Daniel, that hero in the Old Testament."

Monsieur Noel cleared his throat. "Well, they weren't all such fine fellows. Let me tell you about that jerk John. When he spurned the affections of the sexpot Salome, she vowed to get even. Later, Salome danced for King Herod, and he promised her whatever her heart desired. Know what that bitch wanted? John's head on a platter. He had hurt her vanity." Monsieur Noel slashed his knife through the air. "Ah, yes, women can be brutal."

A bit of melted butter glistened on Colette's lips, and Finlay yearned to wipe it off, but he didn't dare. "Do you celebrate June 24 in Canada too?" she asked.

"Only in Quebec. Thousands march, waving their little blue flags with the Fleur de Lys."

"At midnight, they shoot off fireworks, which are as loud as the shelling in Beirut," Anouk chimed in.

Colette frowned at that. "When do you think the war will stop?"

"It's not a war. It's the troubles," Anouk clarified.

Finlay had a sudden image of Mo at a roadblock, her camera at the ready, Zaki hulking beside her.

"Finlay, are you all right?" Colette's long eyelashes fluttered in concern.

He rubbed his eyes and murmured that he was.

As Colette cleared the table, her father apologized for the lack of fresh bread. Finlay reminisced about how he had once shaped the dough for Lebanese mountain bread, tossed it from hand to hand, but had not been able to make it thin enough.

"Nothing to be ashamed of," Monsieur Noel said.

Colette carried in a platter of escargots, and her papa put one to his lips and made kissing noises. Curious, Anouk picked up the two-pronged fork at her place, pried a snail from its shell, and balanced it on the tip of the little fork. "Here goes," she said. She popped in the snail.

"Well?" Monsieur Noel said.

"Chewy. Mmm. Garlicky."

"Even on a diet, you can have them," Colette said. "Twenty snails weigh less than a hundred grams—you can devour dozens and never get fat."

Her papa turned to Finlay. "An excellent aphrodisiac. I'm sure our good King Henry ate many. A most manly man. They say he indulged in a liaison with a local woman. Still, he wasn't in league with Louis XV, who proved his love to Madame de Pompadour seven times their first night."

"Good God!" Colette exclaimed though she must have heard the tale many times.

Anouk extracted another snail from its twirly shell. "It tastes good." She smiled at Colette. "When my mom comes, she should make an exception for snails. She's a vegetarian, you know."

Colette flushed. As she got up from her chair, it scraped against the tiles. She left the room abruptly. "You never told us you had a wife," Monsieur Noel snapped. "Why didn't Madame Fortin come long ago? Is there some problem?"

Finlay pressed a hand to his eyes and bowed his head. The answer was simple enough: Mo hadn't come because she didn't love him. Not enough. Not as much as her work. There was no way he could tell them that and keep his pride. She wouldn't come until she was ready.

Monsieur Noel offered Finlay another glass, but he refused because he was already tipsy.

"I'll have some," Anouk said.

"Anouk shouldn't—"

"But, Dad, I like it."

The remainder of the meal was gloomy. Saucisse began barking, and although Monsieur Noel tied him to the leg of a chair, he kept up a high-pitched whine for a long time, until he rested his chin on his paws and lay still.

Colette returned with the cheese plate: little pats of creamy Cabeçou, a round of goat cheese wrapped in grape leaves, and triangles of Brie and Cantal. Finlay cut himself a wedge of Brie, so overripe that it oozed and smelled. "It's a shame that we've only got crackers to put it on, no bread." She tucked a strand of her blond hair behind her ear and helped herself to the cheeses. "Alas, they're all fattening. Worse than foie gras."

They had barely sampled the cheeses when all the clocks struck ten. "Let's go. We don't want to miss the bonfire." As Anouk pestered them to hurry up, Colette brewed coffee to sober up the men so they wouldn't fall into the fire. Then she kissed Anouk and left for her home on the far side of the square.

Without Colette, the bonfire wouldn't be much fun. Finlay wanted to leave except it wasn't fair to disappoint Anouk. So they clambered in the car with Monsieur Noel, who drove the five kilometers to the site. Crosses woven from yellow broom adorned the country lane, their scent so strong it felt like walking through a tunnel of fragrance. As they neared the pasture, the night darkened, and a few stars pricked the sky of midnight blue.

"Don't expect too much," Monsieur Noel said. "It's nothing as grand as when I was a boy and the priests were kingpins. Baf, charlatans every one of them. There I was—hands folded over a lace-edged blouson, standing behind some no-good in a cassock who waved his shiny cross and mouthed some mumbo-jumbo before he torched the fire."

Finlay strained to hear the accordionist, who played the melodies of the Auvergne, while Colette's father stopped every

few minutes to introduce him to some geezer in a beret. "This is
Finlay Fortin, the son of dear Maurice and grandson of François,
Maître Boulanger, who traipsed off to Canada. And this is his
lovely daughter."

"My dad is Canadian, but I'm half and half. My mom is
American."

Although she carried an American passport—Mo had seen to
that— Anouk had been born in Montreal. Luckily, she spoke
French with a Québeçois, not an American accent—"like Donald
Duck," as Monsieur Noel would say.

A crowd had already assembled on the field. When people
greeted Monsieur Noel, they grumbled about being deprived of
their daily bread, but he prattled about the heat wave, his liver
troubles, and the chicaneries of the president, that jerk as bad
as DeGaulle. A pile of six-foot long branches— winter pruning
from the vine shoots —lay by the fire pit. The sight worried Finlay.
"Perhaps jumping the flames should be forbidden. I doubt it would
be allowed in Canada or the States."

Monsieur Noel jabbed his cane in the air. "It's a test of courage.
The boys leap through the fire, and afterward, they kiss the girls.
That's how it was in my day. Now they go hand-in-hand."

In the distance, a long-legged boy twisted sheets of newspaper
into torpedoes, which he pushed under the kindling. He lit a
match to the heap, and flames shot up three and six feet high.
Once the ends caught fire, he forked them over so fire burned
all along the length. The lad looked familiar, but at first Finlay
couldn't place him. When the boy turned to load another stack of
vine shoots on the fire, Anouk shouted. "Hey, Pierre."

Finlay recognized the mason's son.

"Let's go closer," Anouk yelled.

"We're too close already," Finlay tugged her back from the curls
of red-orange wood shavings that lay burning on the ground.

"Da-a-a-d. I can look after myself."

He stayed by her side until the shoots had burned to embers. He watched as Pierre took her hand, and they skipped around the fire while the red-cheeked accordionist played, arms pumping in-and-out as his fingers danced over the black and white keys.

"Now let the leaping begin," Monsieur Noel yelled.

Everyone cheered. Three youths, bare arms flung high, were first. Next, a fellow with a Santa Claus beard swaggered up, took a bow, jumped, and made it, but his beard caught fire. Finlay clenched his hands. The scorched smell drew him back to a January dawn in Beirut. He was on the balcony staring east toward the refugee camp of Karantina, the sky above it lit a dull orange. Mo had already left, telephoto lens packed in her camera bag, to seize the photograph that would bring her fame or alter people's attitudes toward the war; Finlay had never been sure which was uppermost for her. Now, unhappy and afraid, he worried about the refugees in Karantina, their homes on fire like those of the Trojans. He thought of the old story of how after the Greeks had set Troy on fire, Aeneas hoisted his blind father onto his broad shoulders, took his young son by the hand, and told his wife Creusa to follow close behind. When Aeneas looked back, she had vanished. But Mo wasn't the type to walk behind; she'd be right beside him or a few steps ahead of him. He tried to remember the rest of the story, something about how when Aeneas went back to look for her, he encountered her ghost, who told him he was destined to marry again after reaching his new homeland.

It started to rain. Where was Anouk? He searched the crowd and spotted Pierre standing in front of her, his hand outstretched. Finlay's mouth went dry, but she must have refused Pierre because the boy leaped alone over the fire, black hair flying, right arm punching the dark sky, the fire sizzling as raindrops beat down on it.

Monsieur Noel jabbed a thumb upward. "It'll get worse. We better go."

Anouk begged to stay. "Please, Dad, just a little longer."

"You're sopping wet."

"Who cares? Look who's coming."

Pierre made his way around the firepit toward them. Raindrops splattered his tortoiseshell glasses and plastered his rugby T-shirt with the whale mascot to his chest. He held out his hand to Anouk. This time she took it, and they rocketed, shrieking, toward the fire. A bolt of lightning forked, followed by a thunderbolt.

Sweat trickled down Finlay's sides as the dark silhouettes raced toward the orange flame. As the rain pelted down, his chest tightened with terror as hand in hand they leaped over the fire. And then he saw his darling girl laughing with Pierre, safe on the far side of the firepit.

Chapter 13

On the afternoon of July 1, Monsieur Noel unlocked the door of Pain Toujours and pushed open the shutters. Glorious sunlight streamed in, dappling the pink floor tiles in the clean room.

Finlay looked around. It was a pleasant sight. Against a side wall, a cart stood, stacked with wood, while overhead, hanging from a rack suspended from the ceiling, were the flat wooden peels used to position the loaves in the oven. A scale rested on the long table, below which sat several large bags of flour. It took a while to spot the oven, but when he did, it took his breath away. The oven was set in the ivory-colored brick wall, and its ornamental curves reminded him of those of a wide-hipped woman. A tremor passed through him, not the usual twitch of his eyelid, but a clenching in his chest. He spread wide his arms and turned to Monsieur Noel. "Won't you miss it? All this?"

"Baf. If our government in its wisdom and providence offers me a free retirement, who am I to refuse?"

Finlay nodded. On the oven's frontispiece, above a plaque of a sheaf of wheat bound by a flowing ribbon, he made out the date 1857. He traced the inscription as he recalled his high school Latin. "*Labor omnia vincit improbus.* Work overcomes all'—I get that— but what's *improbus?*"

"Improbus? Ah, that's the key." He stood so close Finlay could smell the wine on his breath. "It's not a craze to work that a baker requires. Oh, no, he is not demented. On the contrary, he is focused, dedicated, and deliberate in the manner in which he works. Otherwise, he could not consistently produce excellent bread. I, alas, no longer have the necessary zeal. That's what they do not comprehend, those who pester me." He tugged on Finlay's shirtsleeve. "Dear friend, find me someone to run it before my clients drive me to distraction."

"Your daughter maybe?"

"Can you imagine Colette in her high heels, shouldering sacks of flour?" He laughed. "Not possible. Alas, I was getting on when I married my darling Marie, and maybe my sperm wasn't potent enough for sons. Not good to be a geezer." He shot Finlay a keen gaze. "I would like my Colette to have something in the oven. You understand?"

Finlay blushed, afraid Monsieur Noel had caught him staring at his daughter.

"About the bakery." Monsieur Noel looked down at his hands. Age spots speckled the crepey skin. "Like claws, they've become. Goddamn arthritis. But here come my golden days, my few precious years to play Bingo and pétanque and to join my pals in the hunt. My sight is good—but who knows for how long— and the woods teem with rabbits, boar, and deer." He dipped his thick-knuckled fingers into a sack of flour and scooped out a handful. "See these flakes of bran? Beautiful, aren't they? When the Nazis seized the harvest and carted our wheat off to Germany, many dreamed of baguettes. Not me. Squishy inside and the next day no damn good except to feed chickens. Give me real bread made with wheat flour and fermented with leaven."

He opened the door of the baking chamber and Finlay, stooping low, breathed in the vestigial aroma of thousands upon thousands of loaves of country bread.

"A baker is the most honorable of professions." Monsieur Noel directed a tungsten light deep inside the oven. "Did not Proust wish to be a baker? And as my Colette is sure to tell you, did not Jesus teach us to pray for bread?" He shone the light from one end of the oven to the other. To Finlay, it seemed like a landscape at dusk seen from afar.

He stammered, overcome with emotion, "I-I would like to be of service."

"Eh? What's that?" Monsieur Noel pulled on an earlobe, surprised and delighted by the offer. "Well, of course. The blood of a baker runs in your veins."

"My father was an accountant," Finlay corrected him.

"Sometimes the gift skips a generation," he said easily. "In any case, Maurice was in the New World, where no one knows the métier. Think of your grandfather, François, my predecessor, the most renowned baker of the Périgord."

Finlay closed his eyes and breathed in the faint odor. It was so different from that of the bread factory where he had worked the summer of his sophomore year in college—pushing buttons, taking thermostat readings, and moving trays onto a conveyor belt, where a machine sliced the loaves and wrapped them in plastic.

"Baf. Industrial bread. Pallid, good only for toast."

"Agreed. But I don't know how to make artisanal bread."

"Eh?" Monsieur Noel tugged on his good ear. "Speak up, dear friend."

"I would like to be of service, but I—"

Monsieur Noel clapped him on the back. "It's not complicated. All you need is flour, water, starter, salt, and time—eight hours for sourdough." He took a white handkerchief from his breast pocket. "And dough requires a tender touch, for like all living things it needs care. Not for us the assembly line, to be slaves ruled by the clock." He unfolded the kerchief, shook it, and after blowing his nose stuffed it into his pocket and turned to Finlay. "You are a man of few words. Such a man makes a competent baker."

The sight of the oven made Finlay go weak at the knees. He put his hand in his pocket and felt his wallet. He had already run up too many bills, and if they were to make a home here, there would be more to come. Cautiously, he pursued the subject. "Can a baker in such a small place earn a decent living?" he asked.

"If you're careful. It's hard to predict how many loaves you can sell. You have to fill the oven, or it's not worth the effort. Over in Cadouin, the baker went bankrupt. But pay no attention to that cautionary tale. Let the desire of the heart rule the quibbles of the mind."

Dare he use his severance pay for a down payment? Mo would balk at that, and with reason. He shook his head. "I'm sorry, but I can't afford to buy it."

Monsieur Noel dismissed that objection. "Baf. Money—even the dog won't eat it—but I could not endure watching Au Bon Pain die, to think that never again might dough rise in this oven. So I have a proposition for you. Come get to know the oven. Come as often as you like, and I will teach you the craft. You can rent the shop. A very modest rent, I assure you. And when the bakery is a grand success, I will sell it to you." He threw his arms in the air, showing his months of frustrations, which Finlay had come to know very well. "Anything to get Madame Blanchard, Madame Picard, the accordionist, the Vamps, the whole lot of them off my back."

"At night I need to be home for Anouk," Finlay said.

"Ah, that's a problem." Monsieur Noel waggled his finger. "Bread should be born in the dark—like worms rising from the ground. Everybody knows that."

Like a child entranced, Finlay watched a thousand specks of

flour dust dancing in the light. Meanwhile, Monsieur Noel rummaged through the drawer of the worktable for what he needed. "Voilà. Here you'll find all you need to know." He handed Finlay a soft-covered book, a baker's manual. "Study it, and one day, dear confrère, you too will be a master baker."

Late that same afternoon, Finlay settled himself toward the rear of the Café de la Paix and watched the local boys play billiards. When they left, he ordered a Heineken, but they were out of it, and the owner suggested a Belgian beer, Mort Subite, Sudden Death. Light amber in color, it smelled and tasted of apples, although slightly sour and yeasty. As he sipped, he mulled over Monsieur Noel's offer. He pictured the villagers, all smiles as they tucked the warm loaves into their string bags. So long as they had their daily bread, they might not object if it came later in the day. Finlay had not been able to tamp down his excitement at the prospect of becoming the village baker. It was powerful magic— that from flour, water, salt, and fire, he could create sustenance.

He glanced out the window. Deaf Madame Jabert and another crone were making their way across the street from the Hotel du Dragon. They strained under the weight of the wicker basket. He had reason to dislike Madame Jabert because Monsieur Noel had claimed that she was the one who had called the police on him that first morning in Espérac. Now Finlay looked at her warily as she passed his table, her breasts jabbing forward under a dark housedress. Her companion had wattles, a double chin, and frizzy white hair.

Neither paid him any attention. At the billiard table, Madame Jabert yanked a sheet from the hamper. "Give me a hand," she yelled. "Here, catch." She flung it across the expanse of green felt to the woman on the other side of the billiard table. Together they spread the sheet across it, tugging until the linen was flat and taut.

"See any stains?" Madame Jabert asked.

"Thank God, no."

"Menstruators, masturbators, babies making pipi. Revolting! In my prayers I thank God for bleach." Madame Jabert's voice rang clear and loud through the café.

Amused, Finlay glanced at her, but she seemed oblivious to his presence.

"Remember Madame Labelle in the old days? The beautiful Colette. That minx. Pu—tain," Madame Jabert spat out. Finlay colored at the word for prostitute. How dare she!

"Thank God she's calmed down," Madame Jabert continued. "My God, those first months after she arrived. What a slut! Those young men she brought to the hotel. It didn't surprise me. Not in the least. Don't forget that her maman was the Nazi's whore, and as the proverb teaches us, the apple doesn't fall far from the tree."

Finlay clenched his fists. How dare she vilify Colette? If the old witch were a man, he'd slug her. He pulled some coins from his pocket, pushed them under his saucer, shot a baleful look at the two hags, and strode out of the café.

At breakfast the next morning, he told Anouk of his plan to rent the bakery and learn the secrets of artisanal baking.

"That's cool," she said, delighted by the idea. A moment later, she set down her slice of toast. "Mom wouldn't like you being a baker."

"It's only for a trial period. We can see how it goes before we come to a final decision."

In the days that followed, Monsieur Noel introduced Finlay to the miller from whom he would buy flour and the forester who would deliver fagots of chestnut and pine. For six days Finlay shadowed the old baker. He swept the tile floor a half-dozen times a day. He weighed and cut the dough, and slid the unbaked loaves from the long-handled wooden peels onto the oven floor. Occasionally he would think about Colette. In the evenings, Monsieur Noel coached him on the fine points of bread making and how to remedy the inevitable catastrophes. For the inauguration, as his parting gift to the village, Monsieur Noel paid the cost of the wood and flour necessary to bake sixty one-kilo loaves, one for each family in the village.

Finlay arrived at the bakery early on the day of the ceremonial opening. Dressed in white shorts and a sleeveless undershirt, he stretched on the red gloves with the leather palms, opened the oven door and stacked three rows of four logs each, a mix of chestnut and fast-burning pine topped with a branch of juniper for fragrance. One match, and the fire caught. Five minutes later, it had turned to embers, and he began again.

"Little by little," Monsieur Noel counseled. "Too large a fire smokes."

Finlay wiped the sweat from his forehead, took a swig of water from a bottle and started yet another new fire. While the oven heated up, he poured flour, salt, leaven, and spring water into the mixing trough. He pressed the switch, and the blades kneaded the mix.

"Progress, that's what your great-grandfather François preached." Monsieur Noel placed a hand on Finlay's shoulder. "In the 1920s, he bought one of the first electric mixers. It saved many hours of hand kneading. I'm not against progress, not at all. But I honor the earth. Never buy flour made from wheat grown on land treated with pesticides or chemical fertilizer. No matter how good the deal, never buy flour from those jerks who sell it."

Finlay promised that he wouldn't. He covered the dough for its first rising, closed the shutters to keep out the heat of the sun, and continued to fire the oven while Monsieur Noel left to buy provisions. An hour later, when he returned with sausages, a good base of coals glowed in the hearth. After they had eaten the sausages, hot and spicy, and drunk the cold ale, he left Finlay to study the baker's manual and watch over the dough.

On his return, Monsieur Noel poked a finger into the oozing mass and bent over it to sniff the sourish smell. "It's moving fast," he said. "Mustn't let it ferment overlong." He wound the strings of his white apron behind his back and brought them around to the front, where he tied them. Hands white with flour, he stretched and folded the dough, and once it was smooth and silky, he slapped it down. He cut off a hunk and placed it on the scales. Exactly a kilo. He weighed three or four more loaves, taking no more than thirty seconds each.

"Got the idea?"

Finlay nodded. Frequently he had to add or remove a bit of dough until it weighed a kilo—not a gram more or less. Then he put the loaf to rise along with the others on the bolts of linen on the trolley.

After the second proofing, Monsieur Noel set a clay jug of water on the hearth to steam. He slapped two loaves on a peel, sprinkled flour on them, grabbed a razor from between his teeth, and slashed each loaf with three quick strokes. The iron door squeaked when he pulled it open. As he slid in the long-handled wooden shovel, he angled it so that each loaf slid off onto the tile hearth. He handed the peel to Finlay. "Here, you finish up. Takes practice, that's all."

Finlay kept at it. After he had loaded the oven, he scraped the flour off the worktable and swept the floor yet again. Monsieur Noel fetched a couple of beers from the refrigerator, and the two men settled down in an alcove in the adjoining room. "Ah, the good old days when I drank beer with your dear papa."

Finlay watched the beer head die down and took his first sip. It tasted sour. He glanced at the label, Mort Subite.

"Excellent beer," Monsieur Noel said as he drained the bottle.

Finlay nodded but then remembered Danny, who was perhaps dead. "Take mine," he said and poured a glass of spring water from the pitcher in the refrigerator. He came and sat beside the old man.

Monsieur Noel took off his beret and stretched out his short legs. He was bald, his scalp pink as a billiard ball. "Feels good here," he said. "Hot, but not too bad. So what did your mother's people do for a living?"

"They were fishermen in Scotland. As a boy, I did a bit of that, too, but I didn't care for it. In college, I took a pottery course. At first I ran to the sink every few minutes to wash the clay off my hands, but I became comfortable with the sensation of it and began to dream of becoming a potter. My father objected. He wanted me to be something respectable, and he was glad when I became a teacher."

"Ah, your dear papa. How I wish he'd stayed here in Espérac to make bread like his father before him."

"He liked being an accountant."

"Numbers. Baf. A dry and austere profession. At least, he wanted you to be secure. Nothing wrong with that. But the baker's life is the one for you. Gives you time to read." He set down his beer, opened the drawer and pulled out a copy of an old book, the crimson leather binding worn at the corners. "I often read Montaigne's *Essays* while I waited for the dough to rise."

Finlay laughed, thinking he might as well be a professor again. "That's not possible when you're making—what did you call it—industrial bread."

"Eh, eh? What's that? Pottery, you say?" He put his hand to his bad ear. "Maybe I'll take it up in my retirement." He cackled.

"Your experience in handling the dough would stand you in good stead. The potter in Cadouin would probably let you use his kiln. He's a generous fellow," Finlay said.

"Baf. He's as poor as a church mouse. Better to be a baker."

Finlay peeked in the oven and smelled the bit of flour that had caramelized on the hearth. The bread had a warm brown crust, and he breathed in the aroma, that of mushrooms and the forest after rain. When it was time, he unloaded the oven, left the loaves to cool, and strolled home, his heart at peace.

Two hours later, the two men climbed the rickety stairs to the church tower and rang the bells to announce the Vin d'Honneur to celebrate the grand re-opening of Pain Toujours. Dozens of villagers milled around the square and crowded into the *Salle des Fêtes*. The mayor, a tricolor sash over his suit, threw open the doors and beckoned them toward a long table with platters of canapés lined up the middle of the white tablecloth. A photographer from the Bergerac paper took Finlay's picture and proclaimed this the happiest of days, because M. Fortin, like his great-grandfather François, had now undertaken to bake their daily bread. After this the mayor called Monsieur Noel and Finlay to the front.

"Honor to our former baker. Best wishes to his successor." After the mayor had shaken Finlay's hand, he presented Monsieur Noel with a certificate of appreciation for his years of service. There was a round of applause.

"I thank you all for your fidelity over these many years," Monsieur Noel said. "Now is the time for new beginnings. Now on a winter's night, I'll snuggle with a hot water bottle under my feather tick. And on summer days like today, I'll laze in the shade of the chestnut tree down by the spring and remember the pleasures of my youth. But I am not done for yet. Oh, not by a long shot." Monsieur Noel called on Monsieur Zazie, a handsome white-haired man, to come up as he made a shameless plug for their new venture. "Do you have any grandfather clocks, extra chairs, or worm-eaten tables? If so, come see us, and we will exchange them for new, giving your homes a grand facelift."

Then Monsieur Noel handed the mayor the first loaf of fragrant bread, after which each resident of Espérac received a free loaf of bread that Monsieur Noel hoped they would eat with glad hearts and due reverence. Finally, he called for Finlay. "Dear confrère, kindly bow your head."

As Monsieur Noel spoke the solemn words, he fitted a baker's cap on Finlay. It felt to Finlay as if he were being anointed. The onlookers cheered, and the photographer from the Bordeaux paper took a picture of the glorious event. The town councilors uncorked a dozen bottles of wine and poured glasses of chilled white and rosé for all. While the crones in their print dresses sat on the sidelines and sipped their wine, the others crowded near the buffet table and gorged on walnuts, thin slices of saucisson, and canapés of foie gras.

Anouk and Pierre slipped out of the *Salle des Fêtes*. Through the open window, Finlay watched them saunter off. He was glad that she had Pierre to take her mind off Danny. But where was Colette?

Only after almost everyone had left did she arrive. They strolled down the path to the spring, where they sat on the gnarled bench under the spreading chestnut tree and talked quietly of their families. "I should have realized you were married," she said. "A cute guy like you."

Finlay invited her to go for a walk, but she refused, saying she already had an engagement.

When he got home, Anouk was eating warm bread spread with chocolate shavings. "France is super," she said brightly. "Mom better like it."

Chapter 14

Anouk awakened in the night needing to pee. When she couldn't hold it a second longer, she groped her way out of her room past the shadows cast by the armoire down the rickety stairs. She hurried along the path, swinging her flashlight to alert her to puddles, slugs, and stinging nettles. In the outhouse, she brushed against a cobweb as she climbed onto the cracked wooden seat and perched over the black hole. She looked about for toilet paper, but there wasn't any, only squares of yellowed newspaper in a tin can. Above her, a giant black spider hung suspended from its web. She was quick, in case a rat nipped her bum. She wiped herself and rushed out, the door swinging shut behind her.

Back in the house, she stretched out on her bed and daydreamed about Pierre and how warm his hand felt in hers as they leaped over the fire. He was the one cute boy she'd met here. She'd goofed in refusing to go to school. It would have been okay. The kids would check her out at recess and in the halls, and the teacher would assign her a buddy, someone like Jilly, to show her around— far more fun than helping her father fix the place, although he paid her for her work. It looked good now. She'd even whitewashed the outhouse and tacked up a picture of sunflowers, her mom's favorite flowers.

She must have fallen asleep because the next thing she knew, the sporty yellow mail car crunched on the gravel. She bolted to the window and drew the curtain. She was becoming a peeker—like everybody else. The mailman left, and she ran downstairs to pick up the envelopes he'd left under the front door: a letter for her from Jilly in London and one addressed to Dad and her. Elated by the handwriting, she ran to find him in the kitchen. "Here." She thrust the envelope toward him. "It's from Mom."

He opened it to reveal a tiny slip of paper inside and a bunch of photos.

"Oh. It's not even a real letter," Anouk said crossly.

"It's hard for your mother to write. You know that."

Anouk did not hide her disappointment.

"Here, take a look." He handed her the photos.

She flipped through them, stopping at one of a long-haired girl hanging off an armored car, two fingers raised in the victory sign. The other pictures showed kids tanning themselves on the university beach while gunboys with Kalashnikovs stood guard. Having been away so long, she realized she was sick of war pictures. If only Mom would write a real letter just for her, one with fat, juicy paragraphs, the sort Mrs. Delacruz would write Danny if only she had an address, with something nice at the end like, "I miss you."

"The note is for you." Dad passed her the slip of paper. "Goodpye and pe a good girl for your father." Her mom couldn't spell worth beans. Grandma Beulah had taken her to a doctor when she was a kid to see what the matter was, but no one could figure it out. Still, Mom was never lazy. Her being barely able to read was one of those weird things. Ansel Adams had whatever it was she had, and he'd succeeded, so she could, too, she'd once said. Mom kept it a secret so people wouldn't think she was stupid. Still, she hated long letters, which were hard for her to read. "I ate snails. Can't wait until July 14," Anouk wrote last time and left it at that.

Upstairs, she sprawled on her bed and opened Jilly's letter, scrawled on Wonder Woman stationery. She wrote about her new, ever-so-cute boyfriend Malcolm—who was also going to board in the fall at the American Community School in London. Anouk couldn't help feeling jealous. She wrote back about the snail hunt, the pastries, funny Monsieur Noel, and Colette; and about how when she held your ear against the oak beams she could hear the deathwatch beetles gnawing; and how kids drank wine and it was no big deal. She was about to write about Pierre when she looked up and saw her dad standing in the doorway. His shirt was freshly pressed, and he had shined his loafers. It irritated her.

"Still in your pajamas? Didn't you hear the church bells? It's noon, time to go," he said.

"I don't want to," Anouk grumbled.

"Come on. Let's not keep Monsieur Noel waiting. He's making this Fourth of July dinner especially for you."

"It won't be any fun without Mom."

"Only ten days now." He squeezed Anouk's shoulder. "And today's the Glorious Fourth, my petite américaine. Be happy."

She pushed off his hand. "No hot dogs. No band. No fireworks. Bo-ring. In Beirut they'll be roasting marshmallows. And what have we got? Another ten-course meal that'll drag on forever."

"I'm sorry you're homesick."

"Sorry, schmorry," she muttered under her breath. As he went downstairs, she wondered if he'd bang his head against the frame of the kitchen door. He'd hit it four times already. Why didn't he duck?

She brushed her hair and changed into her shorts, the green-striped ones she'd been wearing when the kidnappers grabbed Danny. Any day now, Goldfingers and Fathead would let him go, and if it took a bit longer, he'd use the time chatting with them to get his Arabic down pat. Danny was like that. He wasn't one to mope.

"Anouk," her father called up. "Time to go."

"Okay. I'm coming." When she checked herself in the mirror, she frowned. She'd forgotten: girls here didn't wear short shorts.

Dad yelled up from the foot of the stairs. "What's keeping you?"

"I heard you the first time. I can't find my sundress."

"It's in the spare room on the ironing board."

"Okay."

Ten minutes later, she came down in her white dress with the blue polka dots.

"At last." He stopped pacing. "Let's go."

When they arrived, Finlay knocked on Monsieur Noel's door. Colette opened it, her bell earrings jingling, and as she leaned toward him, he breathed in a whiff of fragrance. Finlay kissed her once on each cheek, and they joined her father in the garden, where he was reclining in a white iron chair in the shade of the oak tree. As Finlay sat down, Colette plumped a cushion and tucked it behind his back. Her father lifted the Veuve Clicquot from an ice bucket and untwisted the wire around the neck of the bottle.

"Did you know that during the First World War, Churchill declared it wasn't only for France the English were fighting but also for champagne?" Monsieur Noel said as he wedged out the cork.

It popped, loud as a pistol shot. "Vive l'Amerique," he cried. He took a flute, and as he filled it, he spilled the champagne. "Zut, I'm so goddamn decrepit."

"Allow me," Finlay said.

Monsieur Noel raised his flute. "A toast to Franco-American friendship."

They all clinked glasses.

Monsieur Noel tapped Finlay on the hand. "Tsk-tsk. You must gaze into the eyes of the person with whom you toast. You omitted to do so with Colette. Seven years' bad sex—that's what you get."

"Papa, stop," Colette said, laughing.

"Give me another chance," Finlay said. This time, as they touched glasses, his heart hammering, he looked deep into her warm eyes.

"Ah, Finlay, that's better. Much better," her father said.

She passed a plate of cheese puffs, walnut-sized, light and airy, while her father suggested another round of champagne. And then another. Anouk was the first to burp and giggle; Monsieur Noel cackled, eee, eee, and soon they were all hiccupping and laughing.

Monsieur Noel turned to Finlay. "Perhaps, you know me well enough to use my first name. You may call me Jean-Baptiste," he said.

Finlay demurred, saying that out of respect—he meant for the man's venerable age—he and Anouk would continue to address him as Monsieur Noel.

When they had finished the apéritifs, they seated themselves at a long table covered with a simple white cloth and nibbled steaming asparagus stalks. Afterward, Colette set a platter of duck roasted in a blood orange sauce in front of Finlay for him to carve. "It's a shame Madame Fortin isn't here to taste it," she said.

"My wife is a vegetarian," he said.

"She sure is," Anouk said. "She'd lecture you about the poor little ducky that never did anybody any harm."

"But this duck had a pleasant life paddling in our neighbor's pond," Colette protested.

"*Quin. Quin,*" her father laughed, imitating the sound of their quacking, but then he turned serious. "Death comes to all, humans as well as ducks. Still, it's good you left Beirut. That infernal war is on the news every single night."

Anouk took exception. "It's not that bad. It's just the troubles."

Colette leaned forward, chin resting in her hand, eyes riveted on Finlay as he carved a slice of breast meat and placed it on her plate. As she forked a carrot, her shiny bangles clinked against each other, and a wave of golden hair fell over her cheek. "Tell me all about it," she said.

Finlay set the bone-handled carving knife down on the table. "It began one Saturday last April. We were heading home after spending the day hiking in the mountains when armed men stopped some cars at a roadblock— "

"Not ours," Anouk interrupted. "But there was machine gunfire too. My mom jumped out to take pictures, but Dad made her get back in. When we got home, I turned on the radio and started my homework. I was trying to figure out the Pythagorean theorem when the deejay interrupted the program to say that gunmen had fired on a bus in East Beirut."

"Good God," Colette exclaimed. "It's dangerous. You should have come here long ago."

"Oh, the militiamen just like trying out their new machine guns. They like grenades, too. 'Pomegranates,' they call them. That's what my mom's fixer told me. Funny, huh?"

"Fixer?" Colette frowned.

"Yes. That's Zaki. He drives my mom around, translates for her, and acts as her bodyguard."

Colette shuddered.

"It was okay," Anouk said. "We have safe places—the basement, the hall with bookcases on both sides and the bathroom. Dad crisscrossed all our windows with silvery duct tape—big Xs— so if the glass broke, it wouldn't shatter."

Colette seemed shocked at such precautions. "My poor flea. I can't bear to think of it."

She got up to clear the table, and Finlay followed. In the kitchen, he scraped the dishes, putting the leavings aside for the dog, while she made vinaigrette and poured it into a flask. She asked why he hadn't taken Anouk out earlier.

"All last summer I tried to find a teaching position in the States. At the beginning of the fall semester, things seemed calm enough in Beirut, so we returned. But the troubles returned again, off and on. In December, things got terrible. For a long time I managed to convince myself it hadn't affected Anouk. Once a bullet shot through the elevator shaft and landed in the bathtub. She joked about it. She never complained about water shortages, or the gunboys, checkpoints and the tires burning on the street. Nothing seemed to bother her. I think it was because she never saw a dead body. It was all make-believe to her."

"Hush." Colette smoothed the lines on his forehead, and after a while they rejoined the others. Anouk stopped playing with Saucisse and came back to the table. Monsieur Noel put down his wedge of Brie de Meaux and told them how General Lafayette wanted both the tricolor and the Star-Spangled Banner flown over his grave. After they had finished the salad and cheese, Finlay collected the plates, took them inside and stacked them by the sink, where Colette was hulling the strawberries, her hair falling loosely down her back.

Dare he touch it? She turned, as if called, her body brushing against his. She asked him to get the wire whisk from the top shelf, as she wasn't tall enough. He handed it to her.

Her fingers were stained red with berry juice. "A little reward," she said. "Open up." She set a strawberry on the tip of his tongue.

She poured the cream into a bowl. He offered to whip it for her and beat it— ferociously— until it formed stiff peaks.

Once again out in the sunshine, he sensed Anouk staring at him. "You were gone a long time," she said, her voice hostile.

He blushed.

After they had eaten the berries, Monsieur Noel went inside and hunted about in his liquor cabinet for a prized bottle of Armagnac. The telephone rang. A few minutes later, he came out. "Baf. Some woman. Can't understand a word. It must be for you, Finlay."

He raced inside, Anouk following. "Mo," he said as he grabbed the receiver.

"What happened?" Anouk tugged his shirtsleeve until he jabbed the speakerphone button.

"Relax. Everything's cool." Mo chatted about her assignments, how the AP photo editor had taken to calling her "Calamity Jane" and how Zaki was arranging for her to cover an interrogation. Finlay pictured goons pushing some poor lad against a wall, the pee of fear darkening the crotch of his pants. "Mo, don't. Anouk shouldn't—"

"She's not a kid."

His stomach contorted. "Can't you understand? We're worried about you."

"Well, don't be. I know it's hard for you and Anouk, but I'm fine. And if I make it through this, and I will, I'll have my pick of jobs."

"Hi, Mom." Anouk grabbed the telephone.

"Hi, Sunbeam, I miss you. I wish I could be in two places at the same time. Listen, stay away from all that whipped cream. It'll make you fat. And your father shouldn't let you touch snails. Disgusting. Just because French girls eat anything doesn't mean you should."

"But Mom —" Anouk cupped her hand around the receiver. "Aren't you lonely without us?"

"For you, yes. So much I can barely stand it. Look, be good for your father."

"I will." Anouk paused, afraid of the answer, before she asked, "Is there any news about Danny?"

"Still no word. If I can find him, and I will, that'll be the icing on the cake. Look. There's something I've got to tell your father. Put him back on, okay?"

Anouk passed him the receiver.

"Mo?"

"Well, the thing is…. Don't get all upset, but AP offered me a chunk of money now that Bill's gone."

"For the love of God, Mo."

"It's my lucky break. If I do well, I'll make staff reporter."

"But you said you were —"

"I wish I could. I hate letting Anouk down, so I asked AP for a month off for family leave, but they refused." A roar muffled her voice.

Finlay yelled, "What's that?"

"Don't you remember? The seven p.m. mortar."

In Beirut, he barely registered it, but hearing the boom over the telephone wire from thousands of miles away made him flinch. He was so glad to have left that madness behind.

Anouk grabbed the phone from him. "You've got to come. You promised," she cried. "I've been cleaning like a maniac getting everything ready for you. I made curtains too, and I took care with the seams like you taught me. And I bought an African violet for you and put it in the kitchen, and—"

"Sunbeam, I'll be there soon as I can."

"No, you won't," she wailed. "There'll always be some sick photo you've just gotta shoot."

"It's not for long. I promise."

"Your promises suck." Anouk thrust the receiver in her father's hand and fled.

"Come to me, chérie," Colette said, her arms open wide.

Anouk burst past her and out the door.

Chapter 15

On the following Monday, Finlay was kneading dough as he listened to the classical station on the radio. Anouk was still angry about her mother's not coming, but she'd come around in time. As for himself, he didn't mind not having her with them. It was pleasant in the clean, well-lighted bakery, its scent of fresh-milled flour sweet and sensual. On the radio, a tenor sang a Mozart aria about a heart nourished by the hope of love. It was Colette's day off and he pictured her weeding in her garden, her hands in flowered gardening gloves. As he swept the ashes from the hearth, it occurred to him that she might like to have them for fertilizer. He filled the metal pail with them and set off. When he didn't find her at home, he wandered around the village looking for her. The vamps in their usual spot on the bench at the bus stop said they'd seen her at the cemetery, so he headed there.

He opened the south gate and entered, his feet crunching on the gravel of the alleys lined with vaults. He recognized a few names—DeLorme, Bornat, Lescure, Delpech—but time had obliterated most of the others. It was a charming little cemetery, and he wondered what Mo would make of it. He thought of her photographs of shrouded bodies being lowered from stretchers into a mass grave. Like him, she didn't believe in an afterlife, but her mother did. Not heaven, but something, Beulah wasn't sure exactly what. He and Mo had scattered her ashes over the prairie where the roots of bluestem grass penetrated six feet deep. Beulah was born on the prairie in a sod house, and death had held no fear for her because she ached to return whence she had come.

In the cemetery, a woman was singing the same melody he'd heard almost six weeks ago now when he'd frolicked half-naked in the pond by the spring.

"*Il y a longtemps que je t'aime. Jamais je ne t'oublierai,*" she sang. I've loved you a long time. Never will I forget you.

The woman knelt on a grassy plot, her back to him. She was half-hidden by pink roses that rambled over an iron fence that enclosed the gravesite. His heart raced as he hurried toward her. "Colette," he called.

She stood up, a tangle of bindweed dangling from hand. She was in a lime-green halter-top dress, her hair tucked under a kerchief. He gave her the bucket of ashes to use to fertilize her garden.

"Ashes keep slugs away too," she said as she thanked him. What was that pungent smell? An open bottle of Javel water stood propped against a wire brush, and he realized she'd been scrubbing the tombstone. Whose was it? When he made out the name chiseled on the granite, he breathed a sigh of relief that it was not Victor's.

She grinned and raised an arm to the heavens. "Maman, see what a good job I'm doing."

Finlay traced the dates 1925-1953 incised on the headstone. "Your mother died young."

"It was cancer. I was ten, but I still miss her."

He murmured a few sympathetic words and asked if she'd like to go for a walk.

The trail started a few hundred meters beyond the village

square. Riders from the stable nearby used this path, and Finlay and Colette skirted occasional clumps of rounded manure. After a few minutes, the trail narrowed and a fresh breeze blew through the canopy. He liked the way they walked at the same pace, neither having to slow down or to wait for the other to catch up. They came to a rocky ledge beneath a scrub oak where they sat and gazed out across a field of sunflowers. When he had first arrived in Espérac, they had been seedlings sticking out of the pebbly field; by the Feast of St. John, a multitude of seeds spiraled on each flower head. Now the blooms were the size of soup bowls, their petals the same gold as Colette's hair.

"It's peaceful here," he said.

She smiled and asked if he'd heard from his wife. He shifted uneasily on the ledge and said Mo had sent a note saying the fighting was continuing.

"That's all?"

"Reading and writing are hard for her. That's why she became a photographer." He pictured her, Canon slung about her neck, hand feeling in her pocket for the appropriate lens, fastening it to the camera body and angling it to get the best shot. She took her time, adjusting the focus, aperture, and shutter speed. She could sense the instant things changed, feel it in her belly, so she said. Her heart stopped, her breathing too as she pressed the shutter. Of course, none of this would interest Colette. He stood up and ran his hand over the raspy bark of the scrub oak. A metal wire pierced its trunk and came out through the other side of the tree. "That's like Mo," he said. "She forges ahead, pushing her way through, never letting anything stop her."

"Let's go." Colette got up, and they walked alongside each other. She told him how once, on this very path, she'd heard the pounding of hooves. Seconds later, a black stallion neighed and reared in front of her. "I screamed. Your wife wouldn't have."

He smiled. "No, she'd get out her camera instead."

"She'd be right. The rider wore a scallop shell on his chest. That's the pilgrim's sign. Lots of pilgrims pass this way because we're on one of the routes to Santiago de Compostella."

Finlay remembered how poor Molly and Danny had followed the pilgrimage route south through France and into Spain all the way to Juan's family home so they could bury his ashes there.

"You look sad," Colette said.

He shook his head as if it were nothing. It would take too long to explain.

Colette continued her story. "So after the rider had calmed his horse, I asked why he was undertaking this journey, and if he believed in heaven—"

"Do you?"

"Of course. But that pilgrim had no time for me. He spurred his horse and off he galloped toward Cadouin. Never a moment to waste when you're a pilgrim, or there's no bed for you at the end of the day," Colette said.

"Your father wants to show me Cadouin."

"Papa has an ulterior motive." She made a face. "Cadouin makes Catholics look like fools. Even after the so-called shroud of Christ was proved to be a fake, the 'greedy bastards,' as Papa calls the priests, kept the pilgrims coming so as to fill their coffers."

"So how was it?" Finlay asked.

"Pilgrimage? Hard. The straps of my backpack rubbed my shoulders raw. I wish I'd hired a donkey to carry my pack. He would have been good company too."

Farther on she showed him the spot under an oak tree where Saucisse would help her find cepes after a shower. She asked if he thought Anouk might like helping her in the hunt.

"Maybe with you," he said. "She's moody. She doesn't like to spend time with me."

"This is all new for her, and she's missing her maman." Colette stopped walking and ran her hand through his hair. "I wish you hadn't cut it. Few men have such thick hair."

He delighted in the feel of her fingers but defended himself. "It's cooler short."

"Once it grows back, leave it alone," she grinned. "That's my professional advice."

As the path narrowed, she led the way, and he followed, his eyes fixed on her red espadrilles. Her dress swished, and all along the hedgerow, bumblebees buzzed, balancing on flowers. She stooped to pick a snail and placed it on his palm. Not knowing what to do with it, after a moment he set it back on the path, and it launched itself forward, glistening horns quivering. "See how brave it is," she said.

They walked, only birdsong breaking the silence, and passed under a spider web, the sun shining through its filaments. He plucked a blackberry from the hedgerow and put it to her lips. They were drifting closer to something with all this touching, and he wanted to see what it was.

"Not ripe yet, still hard and bitter." She let the blackberry fall to the ground.

They strolled on beneath the scrub oaks that lined the wire fencing that separated the path from a field of wheat. She gestured to the woods beyond, where wild boars lived. They kept on, pausing at a heap of rusted-out pails and empty tin cans half-hidden in the undergrowth. A hermit had once lived in a cave down there. "It's an ordinary cave, nothing like the ones at Lascaux," she said. "Want to see it?"

He took her hand, small, soft and warm, and they dipped under the wire of the electric fence and scrambled down the hill, bordered by gray limestone. She pointed to an opening in the cliff. "There it is. See, over on the left, that oval slit in the rock? It lets in fresh air and a bit of light."

She ventured inside. He followed, feeling his way in the semi-dark with his hands along the clammy walls, his feet unsteady on the uneven dirt.

"See that long ledge? That's the hermit's bed." She gave a little laugh. "Why anyone would choose to live like that I cannot understand."

She brushed against Finlay, and he swallowed. He imagined tearing off her dress and burying his head in her breasts. Without quite realizing what he was doing, he lunged at her.

She gave a cry and darted off. Ashamed, he stumbled after her through the gloom into the bright light of day. She held her hand to her chest as if to calm its rising and falling.

"I'm sorry," he said, his cheeks blazing. "I don't know what got into me."

She smiled. "You startled me. That's all. And now the sun blinds us. And maybe something else." She looked at him with infinite attention. It seemed the purest, most wicked look. The sun dappled her bare shoulders, and he placed his hands on them and gently drew her to him. He buried his face in her hair, which smelled of almonds. He kissed the inside of her arm and the hollow at the base of her throat. "You are beautiful," he said, in a voice that sounded odd in his ears. "Come with me?"

She followed him to a honeysuckle-scented grove. There, in the shade, he unbuttoned her blouse, and they lay on the grass. Her brassiere was red, made of lace, and she trembled under his touch as he touched her lips and breasts. Never had he gone so slowly with a woman. Then he realized what he lacked. "I'm sorry," he said. "I forgot a —."

"*Une lettre anglaise?*"

Clouds moved above the trees. He heard the cry of a wren. "I'm sorry," he said a second time.

They lay in silence a long while, not touching, until she reached for his hand and stroked his fingers, putting each in turn to her lips. In a clear voice she said, "You are married, but you wear no ring."

"My wife doesn't wear one, either. She says it's a symbol of captivity."

Colette sat up, disapproval written all over her face. "Really? With a handsome husband like you? Your wife's an idiot." Her voice hardened. She twisted the gold band on her finger. "A ring is a politeness, a way of showing one's heart is taken."

He was glad to hear her defend the practice. He touched her ring. "You're a widow. Why do you still wear it?"

"To keep the men away." She giggled and pushed off his hand. "Come on, let's go back."

They retraced their steps to the village, taking the shortcut through the cemetery, where she stopped to pick up a crucifix lying on the ground and set it against a headstone. They passed the Jaberts' marble vault. Finlay pointed at the yellow streak that marred the headstone. "It's peculiar, the marble discolored like that."

"It's Papa. His bladder. Can't help himself, so he says." She leaned toward Finlay. "But's that's not the only reason. Promise you won't tell?"

He shook his head. "No, of course not."

"Sometimes Papa lets Saucisse pee there."

"What! Why on earth—?"

"It's a long story. I better tell you now before I change my mind. Come." She beckoned, and he followed her out of the cemetery to her house on the square. "I want to show you the portrait of Maman, and it's in my bedroom. Don't get any ideas," she said as she led him upstairs.

Yellow and white striped curtains fluttered in the breeze in the small room where Minou was asleep on a sleigh bed covered with a white crochet spread. Colette took Finlay by the hand and led him to her dresser, above which hung a gold-framed portrait of a young woman with dark curls and laughing eyes. "That's Maman."

"She's pretty," Finlay said.

"Still, she had a hard life." Colette bent and drew open the bottom drawer, took out a midnight blue velvet pouch and placed it in his hands. "Open it."

He untied the gold cord and put his hand inside. He felt as if he were back in first grade, playing a touchy-feely game, and Colette was the teacher who asked, "Hard or soft? Rough or smooth?" It felt like hair, and for a moment he thought her mother had kept Colette's baby curls. But when he pulled out his hand, he saw that he held lank black hair. Revolted by the touch, he asked if it was cancer that caused her mother's hair to fall out.

"Smell it," she said.

He put the dark curls to his nose, and there it was, the undeniable scorched stink. Disgusted by the touch of the dead woman's hair, he stuffed it back into the blue pouch. He was breathing fast.

"Listen carefully," Colette said. "I couldn't bear to tell you twice." She paled and her eyes darkened to sapphire. "I was born in 1945, about the time the Nazis fled. My maman was only eighteen. She was a good girl who did her homework and helped around the house, a laughing, dark-haired girl who liked to flirt and dance." Colette hesitated.

"Go on," he said.

In a hesitant voice, she told him about the German officers who would come to the Sunday market in Issigeac. That was how her maman met Rainer Hardt, a lieutenant billeted at the Hotel du Dragon. "Good God, how can I say it?" Colette clasped her hands so tightly that her knuckles turned white, and she blurted out the hard words. "Some nights Maman joined Rainer at the hotel. I was their bad seed."

"What?" Finlay said. "What's that—?"

"Rainer Hardt was my papa."

"But Monsieur Noel—?"

Colette shook her head. "Not my flesh and blood."

It took Finlay a few moments to take it in. It should make no difference who her father was, but somehow it did.

"Tell me everything," he said. Colette went and sat beside Minou on the bed and petted her as if the long steady strokes would calm her too. "After the Americans landed on the beaches of Normandy, it was the Libération. A terrible time for Maman." Colette looked at her hands and paused.

"Go on."

"The Widow Jabert at the Hotel du Dragon? You know who I mean— the ugly one, skinny as a nail? Her husband, the barber, was still alive then, head over heels in love with Maman. Madame Jabert was crazy jealous, and she took it out on Maman." Colette fingered the velvet pouch.

He sat beside her on the bed and put his arm around her shoulders, but she edged away. "The day the Germans ran away, Madame Jabert denounced Maman for horizontal collaboration."

"What?"

"Slang for sleeping with the enemy, the Boches." Colette unloosed the gold cord, slipped her hand into the pale blue pouch and pulled out a curl. "See, Maman's hair is like everybody's, dark brown like everyone in the village except me." Colette gave a bitter laugh as she ran her fingers through her mass of blond curls, lifted it and let it fall onto her shoulders. "Aryan hair, Madame Jabert used to call it. As any fool could see, it wasn't Papa's. In his youth, he had a head of thick dark hair."

Finlay reached for her hand and held it tight, afraid she might let go and run off before she had unburdened herself of her secret.

It was in late September before the vendange, right after the war turned in favor of the Allies and the Germans ran away. Madame Jabert got her husband and some thugs to round up the girls who were rumored to have slept with the German soldiers. They pushed the girls into the back of a truck, and as Monsieur Jabert drove them to the courthouse, the villagers lining the streets jeered and hurled rotten tomatoes at them. When they arrived at the courthouse in Bergerac, Marie Laforet cuddled Colette as she waited on its curved marble steps for Monsieur Jabert in his white barber's coat, scissors in his pudgy hands, to finish with the other girls. When it was her turn, he showed her no mercy.

"Of course, I was too young to remember, but I imagine he yelled, 'Boche whore,' as he sheared her as if she were an animal."

"How brutal."

"And that's not the end of it." Colette's voice rose. "The day I dressed my maman for her funeral, I saw the thick white scar." She paused, and fearful of what she might say next, Finlay drew in his breath. "That devil Jabert ripped Maman's blouse and carved a swastika onto her right breast."

Finlay's gaze darted around the room; if Colette could nestle Minou in her arms, it would comfort her. But the cat had darted off. He held Colette close. "I'm sorry for what you and your maman suffered," he murmured. "But it's over now."

Her blue eyes sparked, and she pulled away. "I'll never forget it. Maman was no collaborator. She knew where the Maquis hid in the woods, but she never squealed. And she shared the ham hocks and the cheese that Rainer gave her with the neighbors who were half-starved. She loved him. She learned German songs so she could sing them to him when he felt homesick." Colette went to her desk, drew out a manila folder, and put a crumpled newspaper clipping in his hands.

He glanced at the date, September 25, 1944. Below the banner headline, "Collaborators punished," were photographs of the women sitting stone-faced on the steps of Bergerac's courthouse, the marble columns towering above them, dark hair littering the steps. He imagined Mo taking these pictures, feeling proud when they got published. He wanted to retch.

"That's you, isn't it, the baby in her arms?"

Colette nodded. "Now comes the good part. After the townspeople had swept the girls' hair in huge piles and burned it, Papa persuaded Monsieur Jabert to give him some to spread over his lettuces to keep the slugs out. It was a trick, but he got Maman's hair. Clever of Papa, wasn't it? He had been in love with Maman for years, but he couldn't have her. She was the cute girl with dimples in her cheeks, the one all the boys adored, and she wasn't interested in Papa any more than she had been in Monsieur Jabert." Colette lowered her voice. "You know the way poor Papa looks and how cruel people joke he should stick himself back in the oven to get baked again, this time correctly, so he'll come out tall and straight? I know it's odd, but Papa believed that if he rescued her hair and gave it to her, she would see it as a proof of his devotion and feel less humiliated."

Finlay nodded even though it didn't make much sense.

"Two weeks later, Papa spotted her at the Sunday market. She was wearing a blue turban on which she'd embroidered a Fleur de Lys."

"To show she wasn't ashamed? That she retained her pride," he said.

Colette's eyes widened. "How did you guess?"

"A woman in a novel I like did the same thing."

"And did she marry her love?"

"No. The man was a coward."

"Well, Papa's not. He courted Maman, and when her hair was still spiky, no bigger than this—Colette drew her thumb and index finger a half-inch apart— he married her. People made fun of Papa because Maman never stopped loving Rainer. She'd take me to see the stone on which he'd carved their initials. It's not far. Want to see it?"

She seemed eager to show him, but he hesitated until it occurred to him this might help her purge herself of the memory. They set off right away. Halfway to Issigeac, right after they passed a cottage with pink hollyhocks in its front garden, Colette turned down a path and made for a cluster of pine trees. She counted them to get her bearings and headed downhill toward a creek. Halfway down, she stopped at a boulder, knelt and yanked the bindweed from around its base, all the while humming a tune.

He recognized it. "That's 'Lili Marlene.'"

"It's about a girl waiting for her lover to return from battle. My maman used to sing it sometimes when she came here." Colette scratched the coating of scabby lichen on the boulder, pushing her thumb upward against it until it came off. "See? That's where they carved their initials, M.L. for Marie Laforet, and R.H. for him, Rainer Hardt." Colette lowered her voice to a whisper, as if she were reciting a prayer. "Maman and Rainer had it—the grand amour—before he abandoned her."

"The scoundrel."

"Don't be so harsh. Remember, Rainer had little choice—all his battalion fled." Colette traced his initials, curiously like a child. "Maman never blamed him, not once."

"And Monsieur Noel?"

"She loved him too because he was kind and good. After she died, he sent me to the convent in Périgueux, where nobody knew about Maman's past. My life became easier there. Here, the good women of Espérac"—a note of sarcasm entered her voice — "wouldn't allow their children to play with me. They used to run after me, screaming, 'Goldilocks, Goldilocks' because of my yellow hair. They'd yell that I was like her, a thief who broke and stole things and made messes. But Papa comforted me, saying that I was adventurous, smart and brave, and that those stupid kids would panic if they got lost or in trouble, but I would know how to take care of myself."

With thickness in his throat, Finlay touched her cheek. "Yet you married. It didn't stand in your way."

"So now you're asking about my marriage?" She tossed her hair.

Abashed, he looked at the ground at his feet. "I'm interested in it."

Colette smiled. "I'd never even kissed a boy when I left the convent. I met Victor right after high school. I married him within three weeks. We sailed to Algeria, where the Arabs were fighting for independence."

"Nothing's safe from war."

She shook her head. "That wasn't the problem with our marriage. Victor seduced young girls by the dozen."

Finlay squeezed her hand. So she hadn't yet had the grand amour. He felt exhilarated, his blood rushing.

"I detested Victor's playing around. I couldn't sleep at night, not one wink, so I left him when our boat docked in Marseille and I took the train home to Papa. That November, Victor was killed in a freak accident. He had a blowout, lost control of his car, and it overturned. The girl with him died too. Victor left me his fortune. That was when I changed my life. I had no need to work, but I learned hairdressing to redeem what Monsieur Jabert had done to my maman. And there's something else you should know." She withdrew her hand from Finlay's. "That summer I had a few flings."

Finlay flushed, the sense of ease gone. "What do you mean?"

"I vowed to take any man who pleased me as long as he was single and of age. Men seduce girls all the time. So why can't a young widow take comfort where she finds it?"

Finlay twitched at the thought of sharing her. "How many?"

She looked him in the eye. "Some had not been with a woman before. It's something a youth must learn."

"But—"

"Don't criticize. I never made another woman miserable the way Victor made me. No vows were broken. I never once had sex with a married man. And even though Victor hadn't loved me, not as he should, I respected his memory. I didn't want his ring to graze other lips, bellies, and zizis, so I took it off. In any case, I soon grew weary of men. After I made the pilgrimage to Compostella, I put Victor's ring back on."

"Why?"

"To keep away the flirts." She made a gesture of shooing flies away.

"And now?"

"I'm older. I doubt I will ever remarry."

On their return to Espérac, they passed the cottage with the hollyhocks. The dark green paint on its shutters was peeling, a large crack ran up the front wall, and the wood at the base of the door had rotted. She told him that the couple who lived there were old and frail now, but forty years earlier the girl's parents, who lived in a magnificent chateau, had objected to their marriage because the boy was the son of their hired hand. "Everyone said it was impossible, but they married and lived happily in poverty." Colette smiled, her teeth white against her red lips. And then she surprised him. She tugged the gold band on her ring finger. "There. It's off." She slipped the ring into her pocket. "I'm free. I always have been."

Finlay was still puzzling through what she meant when she switched the subject. "Why is your wife staying on in Beirut, anyway?"

"For her job."

"What?"

"Impossible to explain." He put his arms around Colette to regain what they'd shared, but she pulled away.

"If only you were free," she said, her voice mournful.

At five o'clock that same afternoon, Pierre rose to his feet when Anouk arrived at the Café de la Paix. He tucked a lock of hair behind her ear and kissed her on the forehead, which seemed more intimate than the routine cheek kisses. She smoothed her dress that she had ironed for this first date—if she could call it that. In the other room, a soccer match was playing on the television. The French must have scored a goal because the men jumped out of their chairs and cheered.

"Wouldn't you rather watch the game?"

Pierre smiled and shook his head. He got her a Coke, sat close beside her. He was playful with her, telling her to hurry and finish making the curtains to stop people from peeking in. She twirled the straw in her Coca-Cola and teased him back. After a while, she turned serious and asked if he would work with his father now that he had graduated.

"Papa hopes I'll become a mason. I like pointing stone—it's in my blood—but rendering and concrete work bore me. I'd prefer to study engineering." Cheers erupted from the other room; the soccer match was over, and France had beaten Germany.

The eight p.m. news followed the game; the lead item was the fighting in Beirut. Anouk moved closer to the television. On the screen, a crowd of men rushed, holding aloft a coffin draped with the Palestinian flag. "God is great," they shouted. For a moment she thought she saw Goldfingers and Fathead.

Pierre called for the bill.

"Don't let's go. Not until the news is over. Maybe I'll see my mom. She'll be somewhere high up where she can get a good shot."

"Don't you worry about her?"

Sooner or later, people always asked her that. Mostly she pretended everything was fine, but it seemed wrong not to be honest with Pierre, especially when he looked at her in that way of his, but she didn't feel up to a heart-to-heart and only said that her mom was okay. "Let's go."

Pierre left a few coins for a tip, and as they left the café, they spotted the propeller plane on the daily Bergerac-to-Paris run. "Your father should go and get her," he said.

"She wouldn't like that," Anouk said.

"It'd be for her own good."

Hand in hand they walked to their cycles, parked in the lane behind the café. They took the long way to Espérac, past Cow Hill, the Roundabout, and the pond where he fished for carp. Instead of turning in the driveway to his house, Pierre kept cycling so as to keep her company all the way to Espérac, and when they got there, they talked for a long time. Perhaps he did like her.

Later, when the seven o'clock bells rang, she set the table for supper. Her father ladled out the soup. It was chicken noodle, her favorite, but she had no appetite. It took her dad forever to finish his, and in his disgusting way, he slurped it. Why couldn't he learn not to? He cleared the table and brought in the plate of charcuterie, slabs of cured ham and rounds of salami with a few pickles. "Want some?" he asked.

She shook her head.

"Something's bothering you."

"Yeah."

"Are you missing Zaki?"

"What? Of course not. I never cared about him. Mom thought I did. Know what I think? You should force her to leave, the way you did with me."

"Like that would work." He speared a slice of ham and spread mustard on it. Nettled by his attitude—and wondering if Colette had anything to do with it—Anouk left the table.

Upstairs in her room, she put on her tape of the Beatles, lay down on her bed, and tried to figure out what to do. She gazed at the SOUVENIR OF MY CAPTIVITY embroidery that hung above the mantel. She tried to recall that night her father and Colette stayed so long in the kitchen. Was he attracted to Colette? She didn't want him falling for Colette the way her great-grandpa François had with Anna Klein. She hoped Dad was just worried about money for the tickets. They probably cost an arm and a leg.

She looked around her bedroom, crammed with furniture: the seventeenth-century armoire stuffed with her great-grandma's linen sheets, the upholstered Louis-this-and-that chairs, the andirons in the fireplace, the Persian carpets on the tile floor. She got an idea, a brilliant one, and ran to check out the other bedrooms. Again, too much furniture: beds, oil paintings, wardrobes, and marble-topped chests of drawers. She hated it all. Downstairs, it was the same thing: ten chairs with rush seats, far more than they needed, a cabinet to store jam, four oil paintings, more andirons.

Once she had thought through her plan, she went out to the garden, where Monsieur Noel was sipping a glass of Chateau Carignan red as he listened to her dad. She waited until they were finished. "I know where we can get some money," she said.

"Really?" Dad smiled at her.

"Easy peasy. We've got a ton of antiques, and I bet they're worth a lot. We should take them to auction. There's an auction house here. I saw it the day we arrived. It's before the bridge, right after the courthouse and the statue of the angel carrying a dead soldier. So, let's put all this stuff up for the highest bidder. Mom won't care. This way we'll get a ton of money, and you can buy plane tickets to go and get her."

"What?" Monsieur Noel tapped his head and yelled at her. "Have you gone berserk? To sell your inheritance —the vestiges of your ancestors—to fly back to that hellhole? Finlay, talk sense to that girl of yours."

She paid no attention to Monsieur Noel but worked on convincing her father that once they auctioned off all the old stuff, they'd get a fresh start. Dad promised to think about it, and Monsieur Noel went off in a huff.

Knowing her dad hated being pestered, she managed not to talk about the auction. Three days later he brought up the subject himself. "Are you sure? Won't you miss these things?"

"Only the tapestry. Let's keep it, and when Danny gets free, we can give it to him."

Her father looked sad. "He may not get out, Sunbeam."

"Of course he will," she cried. "And we need to get Mom here."

"I know," he said.

"So let's get the money for her ticket."

"All right."

Going from room to room around the house, Anouk tied a yellow ribbon on every household item and piece of furniture she disliked. She beat and aired the carpets and helped Dad load them in the truck. She took down the portraits of their ancestors. She picked three gilded Louis-this-or-that chairs to sacrifice. She unwired the crystals from the chandelier in the salon and dusted and packed each one in its bit of newspaper. The dozen pricey Galle glasses she wrapped in tissue paper. She pulled bundles of dry lavender from the shelves of the Louis XIV armoire someone had put there to keep away mice and moths. She whipped out the neat stacks of linen, keeping only four sets for themselves. She polished the wardrobe until it smelled of beeswax; afterward, she and Dad disassembled it, carried out its doors, sides, and shelves, and loaded them on the truck that would take them to the auction house.

To make amends for shouting at her, Monsieur Noel bought their eighteenth-century grandfather clock— a smiling moon painted on the white enamel clock face—to add to his collection. He promised to sell it back to them at the same price if ever they changed their mind.

The auction took place that Saturday, at two p.m. sharp. The rear of the vast hall was crowded with long tables stacked with boxes. Up front, the auctioneer, a red-cheeked heavyset fellow with horn-rimmed glasses, stood at a podium facing the dealers, collectors, and bargain hunters. Anouk and her father found seats in the cheap folding chairs toward the back. First up was a World War One war uniform and a helmet; it was sold to a lady in the row in front of them. The auctioneer spoke quickly and lots went at a fast pace: a walking stick and a Napoleon-style hat, a collection of mended sheets; boxes stuffed with wire wine carriers, eggbeaters; a set of cast-iron pots. Anouk wished she'd cleared out the kitchen cabinets.

She couldn't always figure out who was bidding for what, but every time the auctioneer banged his gavel three times, workers carried off the lots that had sold— pistols, jewelry, old maps, cases of wine, a violin, and even a suit of armor.

Finally, their turn came. Everything sold and by six p.m. they were home. She swept up the dust bunnies that had been hidden under the furniture. "Place smells better now that the musty sofa and armchairs are gone," she said.

"Place looks bare," Dad said.

"That's just temporary. We have the money for Mom's ticket, and there's space now for all our stuff from Beirut. She can bring it when she comes."

"Be prepared," he cautioned. "Heads she'll come, tails she won't."

"Dad, can we be done talking about this? Of course she'll come."

Her father didn't want her staying on her own. It was just a long weekend, so she didn't see why she shouldn't. But Dad gave her his no-nonsense look, and she agreed to go to Colette's. It was the least she could do. Once her mother came, everything would get better. Mom would be safe, and her father would no longer look that way at Colette.

Chapter 16

The day after her father left for Lebanon, Anouk was antsy waiting for Colette to come back from work. She missed Jilly and decided to write her.

"It's different in France—here 'little' means pleasant—little cups of coffee, little glasses of wine, little shops, and little kisses. No bear hugs here. Everyone calls me la petite américaine, the little American girl, and when I luck out—and I know I will—they'll call Pierre, this boy I like, my little friend. People talk about food all the time and eat tons of garlic. Unluckily, they've not heard of deodorant." Anouk remembered that a kid in school once said that Jilly stank, so she crossed out the line about deodorant and continued.

"And are they ever picky here! You can't just say Bonjour. Oh no, you have to say Bonjour, Monsieur or Bonjour, Madame." She chewed the cap of her ballpoint pen. Jilly would want to know about Danny, but no news was good news. "Get this— kids here kiss their teachers when they bump into them in town. Imagine kissing Mrs. Pollock or Marcus Porcus. I never know which cheek gets kissed first, and it'd be easy to kiss someone on the lips— accidentally on purpose!"

She stuck a stamp—Joan of Arc in armor—on the envelope and

went to drop it in the mailbox on the square. On her way back, she met Colette, who had a funny-looking bandage on her middle finger. She seemed in a bad mood.

"What happened to your finger?" Anouk said.

"A little boy turned his head while I was trimming his hair, and the scissors slipped and cut my middle finger. I didn't want it in peroxide and perm solution, so I asked myself what stayed put and kept liquids out, and it came to me in a flash. The préservatif!"

"What? Oh yeah," She wanted Colette to assume she knew all about condoms, even though she'd never seen, let alone touched one.

"The pharmacist wanted to know if I preferred Manix or Durex, and I said it didn't matter just so long as it was small. You should have seen the look on his face."

Anouk tittered.

"They don't come in size small, so I had to take a medium. It's much too big. It looks ridiculous."

On the side of the road, a clump of Queen Anne's lace was waving in the breeze, and Anouk ran to pick some for Colette to cheer her up. Colette didn't even thank her. When they got to her house, Anouk ran and got her Minou, but the cat darted out of Colette's arms. "Cat doesn't like me," she said gloomily.

At suppertime, she ladled the steaming soup. It tasted like spinach. The next course was an omelet. "There, take that!" Colette cried as she cracked each of the five eggs on the edge of a bowl. It should have been a lovely supper, the golden omelet creamy and the peaches for dessert were delicious, but Colette fussed they weren't ripe, as if that were the worst thing in the world.

Mom liked to be alone when she was in a bad mood, and maybe Colette was the same, so after supper Anouk went into the garden by herself. Above, pink fluffy clouds drifted in the west. In Beirut, it would be an hour later, the sky midnight blue. She wished she could be out on their balcony listening to the sea. "Roll on, thou deep and dark blue ocean, roll on!" her dad might say, quoting somebody, but she wouldn't mind. She missed the sea and the towering palm trees—Danny was the only kid who'd ever dared to climb one—and the bustling streets with peddlers and fancy shops, and Zaki and all her friends, especially Jilly. But everybody had left. She hadn't realized how dangerous it was until she'd watched the television news in the café with Pierre.

But Mom would be here soon. She'd bring their stuff too. Their house here looked half-empty without the pictures, carpets, and furniture. Still, she comforted herself; Mom would have hated them, and they needed the money for the airplane tickets. Dad would fly to Paris, where he would transfer to a flight to Beirut.

Wanting to be alone, when she heard the kitchen door click shut Anouk retreated behind the plum tree at the far end of the garden. She watched as Colette heaved the wilted sorrel leaves, peach pits, and egg shells into the compost heap, threw down the pitchfork, buried her face in her hands, and sobbed. Her mom never cried. Anouk stood there, unsure what to do, and then she raced to Colette and flung her arms around her. "Don't. Don't cry," she begged. "Please don't."

Colette took a hanky from her pocket and blew her nose. "I've been on my feet all day," she sniffed. "Look at my ankles, all swollen. And my finger hurts. What if it's infected?"

"Let me take a look." Gently Anouk tugged the condom off. Rubbery, flat and lifeless, it made her feel funny. She unwrapped the gauze underneath it. "Where do you keep the disinfectant?"

"Third shelf in the cupboard by the sink."

Anouk found it and dribbled Mercurochrome on the cut.

"Aiyee. It stings," Colette cried.

"We should let the sun and air get to it. That's what my mother says."

"Does she now?" Colette's voice was grumpy.

"Yes. And when Mom has a bad day, she does yoga. See, like this." Anouk made claws of her hands, bared her teeth, and stuck out her tongue. "That's Lion Pose." She dropped to the floor and arched her neck and back with her chin lifted high. "That's Cobra. Know what my mom says? That you should be grateful for pain because you know you're not dead."

"Grateful?" Colette shook her head at such an idea. "When I feel like this, only one thing works. I slip into the church and see my ladies. Anyway, the priest is coming to say Mass this Sunday, so I better go clean it."

"I'll come help," Anouk said.

The church looked pretty, its doors still garlanded with pink and white paper flowers from a wedding. Inside, it felt cool and smelled nice too. Colette pressed a switch that lit up the chandeliers; in the hush, she dipped her fingers into a stone basin and made the sign of the cross with the holy water. She went to the altar and spread a lace-edged cloth on it and placed the bouquet of Queen Anne's lace there. She whisked the pulpit with her feather duster and gazed down at the rows of straight-back chairs in the sanctuary. "See how sloppy the rows are. Shocking. Nothing wrong with borrowing the chairs, but people should put them back correctly. I bet it was that Madame Jabert. What an asshole. Oh!" Colette put her hand to her mouth. "Bad language in church: it's a sin. But I won't go to confession, not until there's a woman I can confess to."

Confession sounded icky, and Anouk asked her one question after another about it. Colette pointed to a tall, narrow box at the rear of the church. "That's where you do it. First, you say, 'Bless me, my father, for I have sinned.' Father indeed! He's so young that he has pimples on his face. All he's interested in is our sins, not our good deeds. But who am I to criticize Holy Mother Church? Hardly anyone goes these days. It's not like when I was a little girl, and people would line up outside the confessional on Saturday afternoons. Sometimes I feel sorry for the priest. Well, let's fix those chairs. You take that side of the aisle while I do this one."

Down the rows they went, giving a slight push here and there, until each row was perfectly straight.

"Now, let's take care of our ladies." She took Anouk's arm and led her toward the north wall. "First, the blessed Virgin." Colette flicked the duster between two folds of Mary's blue robe. "Oh! God! There's candle wax on it." She licked the tip of a finger and pried the wax out with her fingernail. "Now, let's do Saint Joan. See, there she is, over there."

The saint was slim and carried a silver sword. Pink cheeked, with large breasts and shoulder-length hair, the same ginger color as her mom's, she wore a grimy blue tunic with tiny silver fleurs de lys. Colette dragged a chair over, climbed up on it, and dusted Joan's tunic and cheeks.

"Do her eyes too. They're cobwebby."

"That's the least of our Joan's problems. Last year, a pervert penciled a mustache on her upper lip. Believe me, I saw it with my own eyes. It was the devil to get rid of."

Anouk hesitated. "Your papa said the soldiers followed her because she was a virgin. In Lebanon, people think virginity is a big deal."

Colette looked down at Anouk from the chair. "Virginity is all very well, but ... it's true love that counts." She twisted an end of the dust cloth to a point, dug it in each of Joan's ears, and studied the bit of dirt with satisfaction. "There! Now she will hear us when we ask for help." She climbed down from the chair, tucked the duster into her string bag, and was walking toward Anouk when

what looked like a black ribbon floated up toward the blue ceiling.
Another streak of black. And another. And yet another.

"Bats," Anouk shrieked. Her heart pounded.

"There, there." Colette hurried to her and put an arm around her.
"See how they swoop and loop. They're hunting insects to nourish
their little ones."

Anouk pressed her hand to her mouth to squelch a scream.
"That one's coming right at us. What if it's got rabies?"

"The one above the baptismal font? Cute, isn't it? It's come for
a little drink. It must be thirsty. Let me tell you about bats. Very
curious, they are. Watch this. It's a game I played when I was a girl."
She put her hand in her pocket, pulled out a coin, wrapped it in
her handkerchief, knotted the ends, and flung it up. Three or four
bats swooped about it. When it fell to the ground, she ran and
picked it up. "Want a try?" she offered it to Anouk.

To please Colette, she took it and aimed it at the pulpit about
ten feet from them. Nervousness threw off her aim, and she winced
as the hankie ricocheted off a pillar a few feet away. Five or six bats
glided toward her. She screamed.

"There. There." Colette patted her on the arm as if she was
upset over nothing. Probably Colette didn't realize you could die a
horrible death from a single bite of a rabid bat, but Colette would
hate to be lectured, so Anouk only said that she didn't like their
squeaking.

"But that's what bats do. Maybe it's a male serenading a female,
or a mother calling for a lost pup."

"I still don't like them." Anouk hurried toward the back of the
church. When she went through the door, she glanced up and saw
a couple of bats fly out too, and she trembled.

Back at Colette's, Anouk lounged on a pile of turquoise-and-gold
cushions on the daybed in the living room. On the mantel was a

statue of the Madonna in a red robe. It seemed like a nice room until she noticed the painting of a dove, its head down, and its feet scarlet, dead as could be. It reminded her of Danny and the time she had spent with him feeding Professor Lahoud's pigeons. Now that Mom was leaving Beirut, Danny would have less chance of getting free.

Colette came in with a tray on which stood a bottle of cognac, a sugar bowl, and two thimble-sized glasses. "Why so sad?"

"Nothing. Does your finger still hurt?"

"That's why I'm having cognac." Colette poured a half-inch into each of the crystal glasses. Anouk took a sip, and it burned her throat.

"Wait, it's too strong that way. Try it like this." With her good hand, Colette dipped a sugar cube into the cognac and sucked on it. Anouk did the same, feeling very grown up. She actually liked the taste of the cognac. Colette smiled at her. "Do you have a boyfriend?"

"You're always asking that. No, I don't."

Minou slunk into the room, and Colette gathered the cat in her lap and stroked her. "Of course, you're young and you need to be careful not to get pregnant, but a boyfriend would make your life more pleasant. Your papa told me about the boy who was kidnapped. I thought maybe he was your little friend."

Anouk shook her head, too hard to be convincing.

"Tonight when I say my prayers, I'll ask our Joan to help him, so you won't have to worry about him anymore. Here, have another." Colette passed her the sugar bowl and Anouk picked a cube from it, dipped it in the glass and sucked. As long as they were talking about boys, she broached a subject she really wanted to learn about although she felt uncomfortable asking. "Once you said you'd tell me the etiquette of love."

Colette stopped scratching Minou behind the ear and leaned

forward. "The savoir-faire of love is simple. Use the bidet and wash your privates. Take off your socks. Never go to sleep right afterward. Don't talk—let silence do its work. That's it, my flea." She dipped another sugar cube in the cognac.

"What if you break up?"

"The one who wants to end the affair has to give reasons. It helps the other to bounce back. As for the love letters, you must return them. To burn them isn't fair play. I returned Victor's the minute I found out about his playing around."

"Did your mother keep Rainer's letters?"

"What? You know about Rainer?"

"My father told me."

"He shouldn't have."

Colette sounded upset, so Anouk asked what foods Minou liked and how often she went to the vet. Later, still curious, she wondered aloud in a roundabout way if Colette wouldn't like to meet her real dad.

Colette took a sip of cognac. "He likely made a new life for himself in Germany. I doubt he ever wrote Maman. Maybe he has other children. When I was little, sometimes I played imaginary games with Hans and Heidi and Ludwig. Those were my names for them."

"I had an imaginary friend when I was little. Then in Beirut I got to know Danny. I think you should go find Rainer—if he's still alive, I mean."

"Rainer doesn't even know my maman is dead. Or that I exist."

"But wouldn't you like to meet him?"

"No. Everyone has forgotten about Rainer or they pretend they have. All except for Madame Jabert." Colette patted Anouk's cheek. "Chérie, don't let love pass you by, not when you're young."

In the night, Anouk awakened to the sound of someone crying. She lay in bed waiting for it to be over. When she couldn't stand it a minute longer, she tiptoed down the hall to Colette's bedroom. "Is it your finger? Does it still hurt?"

Colette sniffed. "No."

Anouk sat on the bed beside her. "Did I hurt your feelings by asking if you wanted to meet your real father?"

"No, chérie, nothing like that."

"So what's bothering you?"

"A little thing, nothing to cry over."

"Tell me."

"It's my birthday, and I'm an old maid."

Anouk was annoyed with Monsieur Noel. Even though Colette had Rainer's genes and not his, he should treat her better. "If my dad were here, he would have baked you a birthday cake."

"He has a tender heart, your papa. Please don't tell him I cried."

Anouk bit her lip. Dad? A tender heart? What was that about? Did Colette have a crush on him?

He liked her, maybe even in that way, but it was wrong and anyway they were too old for falling in love. Poor Colette, she didn't stand a chance when Mom got here.

Chapter 17

By morning, Colette's cut had still not healed, and she let Anouk come help out in the salon. They walked down the main street past the florist, the shoe store, and the Café de la Paix. As they passed the Hotel du Dragon, Anouk glanced inside. Madame Jabert sat at the front desk.

"I hear she's mean," Anouk said.

"She doesn't like me. Never has." At the Coif Magique, Colette fished a key from her yellow handbag and unlocked the door. She opened the Venetian blinds, switched on the chandelier and ran a feather duster along the gold frame that held her diploma, the coveted brevet which had earned the shop its license. The salon smelled of coconut. Anouk studied the pictures of movie stars that decorated the walls and watched Colette arrange her combs, scissors, brushes, bobby pins, rollers and clips on the counter. Afterward, Colette taught her how to give a shampoo. "Keep their head back. Don't worry about getting shampoo in their eyes. It doesn't happen. Rinse twice. Let the grumpy ones complain. But no gossip. They'll say 'tu' to you, but be sure to reply with 'vous.'"

"Why?"

"Because you're young. As my assistant, you must use 'vous' with me today."

A toddler arrived for his first haircut. When Anouk lifted him
onto a booster seat, he kicked and squirmed. "Cute little rascal,"
Colette said.

"Hold still." Anouk tilted back his head. When she was little, her
mom shampooed her hair, twirling it into a pointy cone white
with lather. Now she did the same and teased the child, saying he
looked like a unicorn.

Afterward, Madame Vaubon, one of the Vamps, arrived for
her weekly appointment. Anouk draped a flimsy black cape
over her thin shoulders and escorted her to the shampoo chair.
Once the water was lukewarm, Anouk rinsed her hair, applied a
purple shampoo, and massaged her scalp. Madame Vaubon made
appreciative little noises. After Anouk rinsed and towel-dried her,
she escorted the old lady to Colette and went off to make her a cup
of coffee. When she returned, Madame Vaubon was talking about
some stranger who had come to Espérac, passed a bad check and
fled in the night.

That was gossip, Anouk was sure of it. It was fascinating, but
Colette put a stop to it by changing the subject. She told Madame
Vaubon about the bats in the church.

"Bats! Disgusting creatures. They suck out the insides of mice."
Madame Vaubon took a sip of coffee.

"Well, bats need to eat, too," Colette said mildly. "How would
you like your hair today?"

"My usual." She set down her coffee cup. "Are my roots showing?"

Colette parted the jet-black hair. "Only a centimeter or so. We'll
do them next time. Or you might consider a return to your natural
color. Silvery gray is most elegant. But a Marcel cut? Maybe
something more up-to-date?"

"The Marcel cut is perfect."

As Colette combed her hair, Madame Vaubon struck up a
conversation with Anouk. "You're American, aren't you? So you've

heard of Joséphine Baker, the most beautiful woman in all of France? Oh, you haven't? No one told you about her dance in a skirt of banana skins? Oh, yes. Not a stitch more. She resembled you, petite with shiny black hair, but with skin the color of café au lait. A singer too, and so cute with her Marcel waves." She pointed to Anouk. "Your little assistant wears her hair short too."

Feeling self-conscious, Anouk touched the nape of her neck. "I'm trying to grow it out."

"That's an error. Short is good. La Baker, how the men adored her." The old lady turned to Colette. "Like her, I need a man, a handsome one," she cackled.

Colette laughed easily. "You could find a lover. A new hairstyle might help."

"If the Marcel Wave was good enough for La Baker, it's good enough for me. Another thing," she scolded. "You shouldn't be taking care of dirty old M. Dupuis. Not for free."

Colette smiled. "If Jesus could wash his disciples' feet, I can wash and shave M. Dupuis."

Madame Vaubon looked scandalized, but she quickly recovered and chatted about the wedding to take place that evening. "If you ask me, all the groom wants is a woman to cook and clean for him."

"Maybe he wants a family," Colette said.

"Men tend to be selfish. Have lovers, but don't marry. That's what I say. If you must, let your lover get you pregnant. If he turns out to be a good father, you can regularize the situation."

"They don't do that in Beirut," Anouk blurted out.

"Every place is different," Colette said. "As for me, I'd like a baby. If she cries, I'll run to her. If she's poopy, I'll change her."

"Yuck," Anouk said.

"Hush. It's part of being a maman. If she fusses in her crib, I'll sing her lullabies." She turned to Anouk. "But you're young. For now, forget boys. Revel in your freedom. Take time to read, to listen to music, to cultivate yourself and the force of your beauty."

"As they say, a girl must suffer to be beautiful," Madame Vaubon put in.

Colette shook her head. "All it takes is time. Never say you don't have enough time. Say instead, 'I am alive.'" She pinned one last spit curl and had Anouk escort Madame Vaubon to the dryer.

"Would you like a magazine?" Anouk said politely.

"A Lucky Luke," Madame Vaubon said.

Anouk found the comic in the stack of fashion magazines. "I've never heard of him," she said as she gave it to her.

"No?" Madame Vaubon raised her eyebrows. "The lonesome cowboy and his horse Jolly Jumper? The one in love with Calamity Jane?"

"I know all about her. She fought the Indians and sent her daughter away to keep her safe."

After Anouk lowered the hood and set the timer, she wondered if Calamity Jane sometimes visited her child. When the old lady's hair was dry, she escorted her back to Colette, who combed her out, shaved the coarse hairs on her neck, and showed her the back of her do in a hand mirror.

Madame Vaubon patted the spit curls by her ears. "Ah yes, nothing better than a Marcel cut." She was smiling as she wrote out her check. For a half-hour, there were no customers and Anouk daydreamed about Pierre. After that, things got busy. Colette, who seemed to have forgotten about her sore finger, worked away while Anouk shampooed the clients. After each haircut, she swept the floor.

Finally, it was closing time, but they had to wait for a bride who was due to arrive later. Colette gave Anouk a cosmetics bag to thank her for helping out, and she excitedly tried out the mascara, eye shadow, and raspberry-red lipstick. She studied herself in the kit's small mirror. "I hope my mother won't mind."

Colette gave her a strange look. "Why ever would she?"

"Mom never wears makeup. She never gets her hair done. She thinks getting ahead is what counts, not how you look."

"To each her own," Colette said, still slightly bewildered. To pass the time while waiting for the bride, she gave Anouk a manicure.

As she sat there, her hand in the scented water, Anouk imagined herself the owner of a beauty parlor, the dryers humming, the hit parade on but barely audible above the women's chatter. "I might want to become a hairdresser," she said.

"It's a young person's profession, fine for a short while but dangerous in the long run. You inhale fumes from perms and dye. And being on your feet all day long, your ankles swell. You look old before your time."

Colette did, in fact, have wrinkles under her eyes. "At least, your customers appreciate you," Anouk said.

"Oh, yes. Beauty makes for pleasure all round."

"So what's the key?" Anouk blew on her nails, pearly pink and perfect.

"To love your clients."

"What if they're pathetic? That Madame Vaubon shouldn't wear short skirts. She's got thick blue veins on the back of her legs. I feel sorry for her."

Colette wagged a finger. "Don't. Right now she'll be remembering how marvelous she felt when you massaged her scalp. She'll look at herself in the mirror, pat her curls, and admire herself."

Finally, the bride arrived with a long, narrow box containing her wedding gown. After Colette had worked her magic, creating the perfect chignon, she buttoned the long row of buttons down the back of the dress, tucked a dozen stephanotis blooms, white and fragrant, into the edges of the chignon, and arranged the veil of Spanish lace. "Ah, the bride walks in beauty like the night," Colette said as she spirited her off through the back door.

It sounded suspiciously like one of her dad's quotations. He better not be spouting them off to Colette.

Chapter 18

In Paris, at Colette's request, Finlay lit a candle for Anouk in Notre Dame. He did not kneel. It did not take long. He left the gray hulk of the cathedral, crossed the vast, wet square, and took the bridge across the Seine, pausing halfway to gaze at the river, swollen by the rain. On the Left Bank, he visited the statue of Montaigne as Monsieur Noel had requested. Rain pounded down on the head of the philosopher, who smiled serenely, a ruff at his neck, his knees crossed under a short bouffant skirt. Finlay touched Montaigne's shoe, caressed to gold by devotees. It was naive to make a wish, but he didn't let that stop him. He closed his eyes: May Mo survive. May she relinquish me from my vows.

On the Boulevard St. Michel, a boy and girl kissed under a dripping umbrella. Behind them on a gray wall, sleek with rain, a bouquet of dead flowers hung from a marble plaque. He read the letters incised in gold:

"Dead for France. For glory. Age seventeen." He winced.

He arrived at Roissy Airport at five p.m. and waited for his flight in the departure lounge. Two salesmen—one selling sheet glass and the other electric generators—gloated about their anticipated cash killings. As Finlay boarded the Middle East Airlines plane, he noticed the Cedar of Lebanon painted on the jet's tail wing. No women or children were aboard. A stewardess came down the aisle passing out newspapers in Arabic, French, and English. She had glossy raven hair and the confidence of an attractive Arab woman.

After the ailerons of the Boeing 707 had retracted, he skimmed an article in the *Daily Star* about bodies of kidnap victims discovered on the shoreline. His thoughts turned to Molly. Which would be worse for her: the certitude that Danny was dead, or to live the rest of her life never knowing? Mo would prefer to know a bitter truth. She had told him so the third day after Danny was gone. He should have confided in her about Colette a long time ago. It wasn't a subject he could put in a letter, though, what with Mo's difficulty reading. But his reluctance wasn't only due to that. He hadn't wanted to burn his bridges. Now he did. He had a chance with Colette, but only if he were unencumbered. That was a funny word to use. He pulled down the shade, pressed the small pillow against the cold window, and burrowed his face into the softness.

The jet continued east through cloud cover over Italy and Greece. The only passenger in his row, he had the window seat. When he traveled with Mo, she took it. It made sense; she used her eyes more than he did. Even cloud formations pleased her. That led him to think: Why had he married Mo Arnold? It was simple. She had opened his eyes to beauty—the play of shadows on the pavement, the supple stretch of an alley cat, the wavering of telephone lines in the breeze. "Look at that. Oh, see that," she'd say, hazel eyes alight. And he too came to see what she did.

They had met at a cocktail party in Kansas City on a dreary November night. As he stood at the drinks table, he felt her staring at him from across the room. She reminded him of someone, and after a few minutes he realized it was his mum. Both tall and slim, they had the same eyes, broad shoulders and angular cheeks. Mo asked if he would pose for her. Flattered, he accepted. The next day,

standing behind a tripod she told him to turn his face toward the
window. "That's good. Now move your eyes back to the camera.
Now look away. Now look back," she ordered in her decisive voice.
Afterward, he invited her for coffee.

She was nineteen. At seventeen, she had run away from home
to become a photographer. While she expanded her portfolio,
she slept nights at homeless shelters, clutching her camera to her.
Her specialty, he came to realize, was sadness: portraits of failed
athletes, mothers of stillborn children, and those she met in the
food lines of the Sally Ann where she ate. Perhaps she wanted to
photograph him because she had seen some distress in his face
that others did not. She was saving her money to go to Vietnam,
where her only brother, Freddy, had been one of the first casualties.
When Finlay worried that war photography was a risky career, she
avoided answering directly by saying she had hope, which made
her success more likely. After they'd dated for a month, she wanted
to lose her virginity. "Just an adventure," she had said, laughing.
She became pregnant straight off. She wrung her hands and paced
the floor as she told him that a baby would jeopardize her career.
"Help me find a find a way out," she pleaded.

The thought of abortion sickened him; he could not countenance
it. They dilly-dallied, and six months into the pregnancy, when her
belly bulged taut and round, they married because of pressure from
their mothers. At their May wedding, she carried a bouquet of lily
of the valley, her mother was her one witness, and the minister
read Gibran's words on marriage.

Stand together, yet not too near together
For the pillars of the temple stand apart.

They made their vows: his, the traditional one from the Church
of Scotland prayer book, and hers, a pledge to look for the best in

him, always. She kept her maiden name, Arnold. On their wedding night, she told him that he was free, always, to love whomever he wished, that fidelity was a gift, and that passion for another might seize him at any moment. If that happened, he must not deny himself, for that would be denying life itself. "What? What?" he'd said. She had spoken in a whisper, her soft hand on his heart, her luminous eyes fixed on his.

"No epidural for me," she insisted when the baby was due. With each contraction, her grip tightened on the steel rails of the hospital bed, and he stroked her forehead, beaded with sweat. As the rain beat upon the window, fear gripped him that she would die in childbirth like the woman in Hemingway's *A Farewell to Arms.*

They were lucky, for Anouk was born healthy. Under the blue Kansas sky, he watched her in her crib as Mo took pictures of cowboys in Stetsons herding cattle, Black Angus, in the amber fields of wheat. He taught at a college in the Flint Hills. After his classes, he watched Anouk in the sandbox and listened as the freight trains came roaring past, loud as tornadoes. Mo became a storm spotter and several times managed to be on the spot the moment a tornado touched down. The *Kansas City Star* published two of her pictures of twisters. She still regretted not having gone to Vietnam. She could have made a difference with her photos and a name for herself. "It was a mistake, not having an abortion," she once said.

"It! What do you mean by it?" he shouted. "That's Anouk we're talking about."

After the Six Day War in June 1967, she seized her chance. Sure the Arabs would attack to regain the territory the Israelis had grabbed, she yearned to document that struggle. She persuaded him to apply to the American University of Beirut. Normally, he would not have had a chance. Although he had completed the coursework for a Ph.D., he hadn't written a thesis. It made no sense to him—that extravagant effort to explore some hidden corner of English literature. A few weeks later while he was doing the dishes, his hands in the suds, the doorbell rang. A courier held out the blue telegram. Finlay wiped his hands on his pants and opened it. "They're offering me an assistant professorship."

She'd hugged him tight. "You'll take it, won't you?"

He thought of the biblical verses about Lebanon, its cold flowing streams and the scent of its cedars lofty and lifted up.

"Let's go. What have we got to lose?" she said.

That first year, nine years ago now when Anouk started first grade, the Arabs were mired in depression, humiliated by the war with the Israelis. Afterward came a period of relative peace with only a few sonic booms to remind Beirutis who was top gun. Mo was restless, but she took what photos she could. Last April, she accompanied his Arab-American literature class to The Cedars to see the poet Gibran's birthplace. The bus snaked its way up the mountain road, bordered by cherry trees in bloom. At The Cedars, she coaxed the students to join hands around a massive Cedar of Lebanon. She sold the photograph to the *Chicago Tribune.* Later, when Egypt's President Gamal Abdul Nasser died, a thousand men paraded down the Corniche and chanted to the beat of drums, "Nasser, Beloved of God." After AP bought the photo, Bill Newton took her under his wing. The journalists at the Commodore Hotel helped her get her name out. She seemed happiest when she was with them, which happened more and more frequently.

When the plane touched down in Beirut, the dusk-to-dawn curfew was in effect. In the terminal, shards of glass littered the floor. He thought of colleagues who yearned to leave but were too fearful of the drive along Airport Road to risk it. He hurried through the silent, cavernous arrivals hall into the muggy heat.

"Hey! You—" The cabby honked his horn.

Finlay leaned into the front passenger window. "How much for the university?"

The cabby gave him a price triple the usual fee.

Finlay walked away.

"Wait. I have connections," The cabby rubbed his thumb and forefinger.

Finlay named a figure. The cabby nodded, and Finlay got in for the short drive to campus. On Airport Road, the taxi swerved to avoid a crater near the refugee camp where Zaki's family lived. They passed a jeep and militiamen patrolling the water spigots. A car backfired, and Finlay jumped.

"Welcome to Beirut." The cabby snickered.

When they passed Pigeon Rocks, Finlay relaxed. At the university, a gunboy swung open the gate and Finlay got out, exultant that he had made it.

It was eleven p.m. when he slipped his key in the lock of Apartment 602. Mo's photographer's bag lay on her desk in the entryway. Music played—Theodorakis' "Songs for Andreas"—about a prisoner knocking Tak! Tak! on his cell wall, hoping for a tap in return. She wasn't in the kitchen or on the balcony. In the hall, the photos of Anouk were gone: as a toddler feeding peanuts to an elephant in the zoo; at twelve, on the Ferris Wheel; last year turning a cartwheel in her cheerleading outfit; and only a few months ago, singing in the chorus line for *West Side Story*. In their place were her tear sheets: a man, ankles bound, roped to the back fender of a car being dragged through the streets; a woman embracing a crying child; residents clearing debris from a collapsed building; U.S. Marines bearing a casket as they marched toward a helicopter.

Finlay rapped on the bathroom door. "It's me."

She came out, barefoot in her white terrycloth robe. Her wet hair looked skimpy. "Finlay? What are you doing here? Is Sunbeam okay?"

He registered the panic in her voice. "She's fine."

"Whew. I'll make some tea."

He kissed her on the cheek, instead of the lips, and she shot him an odd look. In the kitchen, she put the kettle on, got the brown teapot and measured tea leaves from the caddy. When the kettle whistled, he jumped.

"Nervous, huh?" She took the teapot to the balcony and set it on the table to steep, Theodorakis's song of protest in the background. She looked drawn, with new lines around her mouth, but she was still Mo, pretty, abstract, and aloof.

"If everything's fine, why are you here?" she asked.

He set down the teacup. "Anouk wanted me to come." He thought of saying, "Sunbeam needs you," but Mo scorned melodrama. He pulled the one-way Beirut-Paris ticket from his breast pocket and set it in front of her.

She snatched it, took one glance at it, and slammed it back down on the table. She crossed her arms in front of her, the same as his mum when she got feisty. "So that's it. I should have guessed."

He watched the beam from the lighthouse sweep across the city. Interrogation time, he thought. Start with the least significant evidence and continue in a logical path to the most important— that was what he taught his students. But the reasons why she should leave jumbled in his mind. He wouldn't talk about the danger—that would annoy her. Instead, he said she might like how variable the sky was in the Dordogne, which was picturesque and not yet photographed to death; how his old neighbor still wore a beret; how the house was an ancient beauty; and how Anouk was settling in nicely.

Mo looked at her watch. "How long is this going to take?"

"I'm almost done. Anouk wants you to bring the Aalto stool when you come. She says to tell you we sold the old furniture, so you can furnish the house the way you like, with sleek modern stuff."

She shrugged. "Who cares about furniture?"

That was it: nothing had changed. "Any news on Danny?" he asked.

The lines in her forehead deepened. "Zaki got a tipoff about Cinderella's Coach. It was sighted a couple of days ago, but by the time we got there, poof! It vanished."

Finlay flexed his hands. "Poor Danny, poor lamb." He couldn't think of anything else to say, so he asked about her work.

"It's great. Zaki got me access to photograph an interrogation. I felt bad taking the shots—the poor kid cringing, a gun pushed in his cheek—but I sold it to the *Herald Tribune*." She rushed on. "They want to see more of my shots. I'm finally getting somewhere. See, I told you I would."

"Mo—"

"Don't look at me like that. It's my job. In any case, nobody was going to shoot the kid, not with me there."

Finlay felt a familiar giving in. "So you're going gangbusters."

"Yeah. The Brits say I'm good to have around in a pickle."

He walked to the railing and watched the shaft of light from the Manara Lighthouse move slowly, shining on the inky water. He decided to try again. That's why he had come. "Anouk needs you. Others are covering the story here. They're funded. They're protected."

She came and stood beside him. "I'll be okay. Zaki's the best. He's got contacts, and we work fast. If we go somewhere iffy, he knows the exact moment we need to hightail it out."

"But for a good shot, something bad has to happen. Right? Someone has to die."

"Not always. Look, I don't need to justify what I'm doing." She tightened her lips, and he too felt the exhaustion of these old arguments.

He was getting nowhere, all over again. "What am I supposed to tell Anouk if something happens?"

"Zilch. Nothing's going to happen." She touched his wrist. "Please, Finlay, we're in the same camp on this. The Lebanese are glad reporters are here. It makes them feel people still care about them. It's as if they're not dead yet."

He shuddered. "What you're doing—putting them before Anouk—it's not right."

"It's exactly what I should be doing. Sunbeam is only one person. She's safe. My work matters to thousands."

How could she be so abstract about this? "Stop it. Please stop it. Anouk's worried stiff. She didn't used to be, but now she is."

"Tell her I'm safe with Zaki. Pretty safe, at any rate. Ha!"

"I saw your photo of that poor fellow being dragged along the street. Jesus, Mo! You didn't used to take shots like that."

"Now I know the score: If it bleeds, it leads."

"They could rape you."

"C'mon. You know Arabs aren't like that. Anyhow, it's not the end of the world if I get groped. Hey, your tic's acting up again; go take a Valium. There're lots where you left them." She drummed her fingers on the railing.

He reached for her hand; she drew it away.

Again she glanced at her wristwatch. "Look, I'm not enjoying this conversation. I'm going to bed."

He didn't follow. He pictured her brushing her hair while she listened to the radio with its reports of the latest checkpoints. He stared at the sea, which was nothing but darkness. The silence was profound. Above, a hundred thousand constellations gleamed and twinkled. A falling star streaked across the night sky. Mo was that star, pure and single-minded. What would become of her? Sadness overcame him, but then he noticed a larger star high in the firmament. Entranced, he gazed until he realized it was not one star but two: companion stars, like him and Colette. He yearned for her beside him.

When finally he went inside, Mo was already in bed. She had on pajamas—white with piping at the collar—and he noticed the pale strip on her wrist where she wore her watch. She was sleeping or pretending to be. He turned down the sheet on his side and crept into bed. He turned from her, his face to the wall. In the morning, he would tell her about Colette. He really would. He swore he would.

Chapter 19

Mo jiggled his elbow. "Wake up."

Groggy, he turned over. He propped himself on one elbow to check the time. Ten-thirty in the morning and already hot as Hades.

She got her photo bag from the closet. She didn't so much as glance at him, and he realized that she was now used to operating on her own.

"Where are you off to?"

"Zaki got a tipoff. Another sighting of Cinderella's Coach. We're off to check it out. It's probably a false alarm. Molly's in a bad way, so we don't want her along. Do me a favor? Stay with her till we get back." Mo grabbed her bandana, the one she wore in case of tear gas, and tossed it in the bag.

After she'd left, he made the bed. Rust-red smears stained the sheet where she must have scratched her mosquito bites. "Only hound dogs scratch their itches," Colette teased last week as she rubbed an ice cube on a mosquito bite above his left elbow. She told him to give Mo plenty of love so she'd have nothing to complain about, and straightaway Colette burst into tears. Wasn't it odd? He'd fallen in love with Mo in part because she was so decisive, and now he wanted someone with softer edges, more like him.

He left the apartment, went down the hall, and rang the Delacruzes' doorbell. Molly opened the door. Her face was pale, her red hair tangled, and her eyes red-rimmed with dark circles under them. She looked exhausted.

"Too hot for coffee," she said. "Want some lemonade?"

He nodded. In the kitchen, he smelled brownies—Danny's favorite—baking in the oven. Molly hitched up her sagging jeans. Juan used to call her his "sweet Irish potato," but she'd lost weight after his death and now after Danny's disappearance, she looked scrawny. Like Mo, she believed in women's lib. That was what they called it. Along with a dozen other faculty wives, they attended consciousness-raising meetings in which they would sit in a circle and—so he supposed—grouch about their husbands. All except poor Molly.

He followed her out to the balcony, where pink flowers blossomed on a trellis. She set the pitcher of lemonade on a small table made of turquoise and green tiles, which she and Juan had brought back from Spain on home leave a few years earlier.

"Here's what I wanted to show you." Molly touched the plant in the large terra cotta pot sitting on the tile floor. "It's a Star of Bethlehem. It flowers only one day a year. The rest of the time, it's drab leaves. Yesterday when I saw the bud, tight as a peony's, I dragged the pot out of its corner. And now look at it."

Finlay breathed in its pungent scent. The single bloom, the size of his hand, had broad white petals and a cluster of slender spears.

She touched his hand. "Do you believe in coincidences? First, the sighting of the VW bus. And then this rare bloom. Maybe the third thing is that Danny will smell it from wherever he is and come running. You don't think I'm crazy, do you?"

He wasn't going to discourage her. "My mother's people, they're Scots, believe in the fairies."

She smiled. "Sure you be Celtic kin."

They gazed at the seemingly miraculous white blossom. She poured him a glass of lemonade, the ice cubes clicking. It tasted sour, and he set down the glass.

"I kind of guess you've come back to persuade Mo to leave. The embassy is after me, too. They'd like all the expats out. Know why I can't go?"

"Danny."

"The second they release him, he'll come home," Molly said. "I better be here for him."

He kept his thoughts to himself. "It's sometimes hard to know what to do."

"Everything here is crazy. Boom. Boom. Boom. Everyone's cowering in the basement. And off goes Mo with all that gumption and zip and confidence. Nothing stops her. Know what I mean?" Molly ran a finger around the rim of her glass, and he noticed her ring, tear-shaped with glints of rose and green. "Mo's one in a million. When I couldn't recall Danny's smile, she searched her files and found me this." Molly opened the locket at her throat; inside was a photo of Danny carrying a peace sign. "It means the world to me," Molly said, snapping the gold case shut.

He made some banal optimistic comment.

"What's that?" She rushed to answer the door but came back a moment later. "Nobody there. I'm hearing things." She shot him a piercing glance as if imploring him to deny it.

"Are you able to sleep?" he said.

"With pills, but they give me nightmares. Last night I dreamt about warlords. They were in tuxedos and sat cross-legged on a Persian carpet. Mo was there too, wearing a pearl choker and little black dress."

He smiled. He couldn't imagine her wearing anything like that.

Molly continued describing her dream. "The warlords turned into penguins, and Mo begged them to agree to a ceasefire, a real one—not just time off for looting—but nobody said boo. It was turning into a nightmare when I woke up. You know how that goes."

The doorbell rang, this time for real. He put an arm around Molly and walked with her to the door.

Mo stepped in with Zaki, a black-and-white-checked keffiyeh around his neck. As they shook hands, Finlay touched the stump on the boy's finger and flinched.

"Anything about Danny?" Molly cried, clutching her hand to her throat. Her ring glinted. Where was it he'd read that opals brought bad luck?

"We better sit down." She walked Molly to the sofa and told how they'd located the VW bus in the alleyway opposite the Clemenceau Theater. They'd already waited an hour or so when a man carrying a briefcase got in and drove off. She and Zaki trailed him to the last gasoline station on their side of the Green Line and accosted him when he got out. "He claimed he'd bought the van last week for two thousand dollars cash. When I told him it was ours, he wanted to sell it it back to us for two thousand five hundred. The gall of the man."

"What about Danny?" Molly cried.

"I'm sorry, but he said he'd never heard of any Danny. He sounded like he was telling the truth. Five minutes later, he got back in the VW bus and drove off in it."

"It's diminishing returns." Molly rubbed her hand across her forehead.

"We'll keep looking. Keep hope alive," Mo said.

The platitudes, the keeping things going. Now that Finlay had been away, he saw how fragile it all was. People protecting each other in the midst of chaos.

When they got home, he turned on her. "Why can't you be honest with Molly? You know anyone not traded in the first few

days doesn't stand a chance," he said coldly. "Turns out poor
Danny wasn't much of a bargaining chip."

"So now you're talking about him in past tense? What kind of a
friend are you?"

"An honest one. Molly should cut her losses and get out. And
you, too."

"I know what I'm doing."

"You're enamored with this war."

"Look— for the last time. Beirutis are glad I'm here. It makes them
feel their lives count. The Napalm Girl in Vietnam. Remember
her? Stark naked, the clothes burned off her back, wailing as she
fled. Please, Finlay, be fair. Surely you haven't forgotten how we
were convinced deep inside how evil that war was? You felt it as
much as I did. Don't say you didn't. That picture helped stop it.
You ask why I keep on. That's why."

"And our own girl? What about her? It's tragic about Danny, but
he's a goner. Anouk's not. She needs you." He grabbed Mo by the
hand, half-dragging her into the hall.

"Stop it," she screamed. "Get your hands off."

He pulled her in front of her shot of the youths on Martyrs
Square hurling rocks and the tires sending plumes of smoke into
the sky. "So is this picture worth dying for?" He pulled her toward
the photo of a woman kneeling in the mud beside a child-sized
coffin. "Or this one? Is it worth making an orphan of Sunbeam?"
She wouldn't be pulled any longer, so he merely pointed at the
next photo down the hall. "How about this one? Nice caption,
isn't it? 'Son grieves father shot at roadblock.' An award winner,
I'm sure."

She wrested herself loose. "You didn't used to be a bully." Once
again she was cool as a cucumber, the woman in charge who would
let nothing stop her. "Look, I'm off. I've got a press conference at
noon."

"I get the feeling I'm not wanted."

"Could be," she said. "I wonder why."

The moment the door closed behind her, he felt ashamed of having lost control of himself. He remembered Freddy, her brother, killed in a rice field on the Mekong Delta in Vietnam. Once Finlay had come upon a box of loose pictures of Freddy —a gangly kid in a jungle jacket, his face still pimply, hair in a crew-cut. Mo never talked about him and never, to Finlay's knowledge, looked at the photos of him. Perhaps it was too painful. Perhaps her sense of pity and outrage over his death was the root of her crusading spirit and crazy belief that her photos would make a difference.

Discouraged, he left the flat and ran a mile along the Corniche before he showered and went to meet Zaki at Uncle Sam's Café. As he passed Nicely Hall, he thought of his students. He had loved them all— Yusuf and Nabeel, Emile, Jawad, Randa, Maria, and Reyhaneh the girl from Iran— with a particular fondness for the smokers in the back row. He'd not known who was Muslim and who Christian, who Palestinian and who Lebanese, who on the left and who on the right. Everything had unraveled so quickly. It seemed surreal that only a few semesters ago, he'd assigned the essay topic, "Marriage between Muslims and Christians should be encouraged/forbidden."

He passed through Main Gate onto Bliss Street. Nothing had changed. The Red Berets were still there. So was the graffiti, Free Palestine, scrawled in black paint on the wall of the Kodak store. A tattered poster of Danny hung half-on, half-off a telephone pole. A shoeshine boy waited for customers with an array of cans of shoe polish in front of him. The honking of cars set Finlay on edge, and he was glad to enter Uncle Sam's Café and get out of the noise.

Zaki was already there, waiting. Finlay took a deep breath. "I misjudged you. When Anouk went to you and stayed overnight, I assumed—"

"That I was a cad." Zaki set down his coffee.

Finlay winced at the old-fashioned word.

"I would never do anything to harm her," Zaki said.

"Of course you wouldn't. Please forgive me."

"It doesn't matter." Zaki seemed to harbor no resentment. He spoke about his prospects—a cousin he might marry, a chance of work in oil-rich Kuwait or Saudi Arabia. "And your life in France? Your wife says you've become a baker." Zaki said it in a manner that suggested Finlay had lost his mind. "Be glad you're not here. You'd get fed up with gunboys pushing their way in and making off with the bread without paying." He took a pack of Marlboros from his shirt pocket. "Cigarette?"

"No, thanks."

"Do you like it? Baking?" Zaki tapped the cigarette against his palm.

Finlay flexed his hands. "I do—the feel of the dough, the rhythm of the work, from feeding the fire to kneading the dough and forming the bread. And you'll appreciate this, there's time to read while the dough rises."

The waiter arrived, and Finlay ordered espressos. Zaki struck a match, and as it flared, he lit his cigarette. "It's too bad you left teaching. You were an excellent professor. My favorite."

"It wasn't for me," Finlay confessed. "I had to pump myself up at the beginning of each semester by giving myself pep talks."

"You sounded confident. You fit Chaucer's description of the scholar: 'gladly would he learn and gladly teach.' It's good to see you again, even if it's just a quick visit. Here we feel grateful when we see we are not alone."

Ashamed, Finlay said he'd come to persuade Mo to leave.

Zaki stubbed his cigarette in the ashtray. "Right to do so, of course. Take her away. There's nothing here. Poor Lebanon. It's become as sad as Palestine."

After leaving the café, Finlay arranged to ship their household goods to France once the port reopened. On his way home, he stopped in a bookshop and spent a long time looking through the postcards. He wanted to send one to Colette. Instead of a touristy one of the Cedars or the Roman ruins of Baalbek, he chose one with a picture of a red rose, and mailed it from the post office.

After he got home, he asked Mo to help him pack Anouk's things.

She looked up from the table where contact sheets were spread out in front of her. "You do it. I've got work to do." She circled an image with her grease pen.

"A woman would know better what she'd need."

"Please, Finlay. I'm sorry. I'd like to help, but I'm on deadline."

In Anouk's room, he looked through her closet. He chose a blue-flowered dress, a couple of board games, Monopoly and Risk. From her drawers he pulled out her school T-shirt, a pair of jeans and shorts. She wanted her books, so he found *Watership Down*, a story she adored about shipwrecked rabbits, *Little Women*, which she'd read three times, along with a novel set in a boarding school that Jilly had given her. He glanced at the lower shelf where Anouk kept the books she'd outgrown, and his eye fell on Dr. Seuss's *Horton the Elephant*. As a child, she'd loved the story of the Mayzie Bird flying off, entrusting Horton to sit on her egg until it hatched. It was the first book she'd read all by herself. With gusto, she'd sounded out the words, "An elephant is faithful one hundred percent."

At seven o'clock the cannon boomed from Bain Militaire. He sorted through his things and boxed up his suits, trousers, and dress shirts to give to the Red Crescent. Afterward, he poured himself a glass of Ksara wine and went to the balcony, where Mo was stitching her Shining Star quilt. As the sun gathered itself into an enormous orange ball and slipped over the horizon into the sea, she set down the patch she'd finished seaming.

"Finlay, we need to talk." He sat down beside her and took a sip of wine. "Here's the thing," she continued. "I'm worried about Anouk's education. You're nowhere near a lycée. I'm hoping she gets one of those scholarships Bill Newton's parents set up."

Finlay wasn't sure about that. "She's a B student. I don't want her applying if it's only to get turned down."

"Grade point isn't what they're looking at. It's school spirit. That was Bill's thing, and Anouk's got it in spades. And don't think I'm taking advantage of my connection with Bill. This isn't for me. It's for Anouk."

Already a few stars pricked the sky. When they'd moved to campus, Anouk was still young enough to trust that if she wished upon a star her wish would come true. "She misses you," he said.

"Well, I miss her too. But I need to stay."

"Even if you end up being in the wrong place, wrong time like Danny?"

"Look. Anouk understands what I'm doing. I wish you did." Mo selected a patch from the basket. The cotton was midnight blue with a print of tiny white stars. As she hemmed it in the dim light, Finlay closed his eyes and thought of Danny.

When he shall die,
Take him and cut him out in little stars,
And he will make the face of heaven so fine
That all the world will be in love with night
And pay no worship to the garish sun.

Mo put her hand on Finlay's knee. "A penny for your thoughts."

"About Danny? Doesn't look good."

"I'm not giving up. Not yet." She pressed his knee slightly. "How's the little break from me going?"

Finlay shifted uncomfortably. Did she suspect something? When he searched for the best way to begin, he drew a blank.

"Finlay?"

"At first it was hard," he said, deflecting the question. "She said I'd forced her to live with barbarians."

"Sounds like our Sunbeam."

"One night she woke up screaming. She'd heard gunfire. I told her that it was our neighbor shooting rats. That settled her."

"Uh-huh." Mo bent over the table where she was fitting eight diamond patches together to form a star.

"She has crying jags," Finlay continued. "You know how crazy adventurous she is, but that first month she wouldn't ride her bike on the highway. She'd only take the back roads, even though it took twice as long. She's better now but—"

"Remember how she left, screaming as if her life was over?"

"She still needs you."

"You just said she's better."

"It's a lot more than that. She misses you."

"So who's she staying with?"

"A neighbor. A widow named Colette." Finlay averted his eyes and looked out to sea.

"A merry widow?" Mo said, her voice mocking.

He picked at a stray thread on his sleeve. Now that he was on the brink, he was deathly afraid.

"Anouk's fifteen. Old enough to stay on her own for a few days," Mo said.

"That's what she said. But we still have rats. They run up and down the walls, and she's terrified they'll get into her sheets."

"That's disgusting."

"You know how kids are—they act as if they couldn't care less when we're around, but as soon as we're gone, it's a different story." Seizing upon Mo's concern, he tried again. "Come back with me.

Do it for Anouk."

"How many times do I have to tell you?" She pierced the needle into the cotton. "I've got work to do here."

"Our lease is up at the end of August. Our residency visas will have expired too. You'll have to leave then. Why not now?"

"Because it'll get worse. And you know how it goes—the greater the danger, the better the pictures." She cackled, her laugh eerily reminiscent of his mum's.

"Don't say that. Are you doing it to rile me?"

"No. But it's not that easy for me either. Sometimes I can't sleep for worrying about things. I feel guilty about how I'm making you miserable. But I can't stop now. You know how bored I used to get and how I hate the humdrum life with nothing ever changing, no novelty, no thrills. I'm making good pictures. And Zaki gets us out in time. We're doing the right thing."

"Aren't you ever scared?" He'd wanted to ask her that for the longest time.

"Sometimes. When a bullet whistles by, I get this little shiver, and then Bingo! It's over, and I feel, whew, I'm still here, and I zip in and get the shot." She was becoming animated. "I feel great! While I'm doing the work—composing the picture, setting the f-stops and stuff—I'm concentrating so hard that I don't sense any danger."

"What if they get you?"

"Well, tough Twinkies. Don't worry so much. Most of what I do is routine: checking in on the hospital, the morgue, and the cemetery. That's all safe."

"If you're close enough to get the picture," he said harshly, "you're close enough to get shot. Right?"

She pulled back her hand. "I'm doing what I have to do."

"Which is?"

"Haven't a clue. Come on, Finlay. You know what I'm after."

"You're so vain. What makes you think you can change the world? People here have been fighting forever."

"Eventually they'll stop, but I can help hurry up the process. Let's not argue." She fondled his knee. "Tell me about France."

He edged his knee away and her hand slipped off. Her ambition angered him, but he felt guilty because of his changed feelings about her. Restless, he went to the railing. "There's something I need to tell you."

"Oh?" She came and stood beside him

"I've met someone in France. Someone I like."

She didn't speak for a long time. "You can't ask someone for a divorce when a war is on," she tried to joke, but one glance at the misery on his face sobered her. "I knew you weren't happy. The thing is, well, I thought we weren't that much worse off than other couples." She put her head between her hands. "Don't do this to me, Finlay," she said, her voice low, insistent. "We never fight. We have money and sex and friends, and we don't complain about each other. And there's Sunbeam. She'll be the one who suffers."

"She doesn't know. I needed to talk it over with you first."

"This is crazy. What you want is for me to give you a pass, saying it's okay for you to have an affair."

"I didn't mean to fall in love," he said.

"Have you had sex?"

"No. But it's in the air. We flirt. The other day, well, she pushed me away."

"Fooling around, isn't that the Frenchy specialty? All right, I guess you can have yourself a little affair."

"Colette won't, not with a married man."

"Colette? That's her name? Isn't that the woman Anouk is staying with?"

"It's a small village. There aren't that many people." He dug his hands into his pockets. "Know what bothers me the most? How am I going to explain her to Anouk?"

Mo flushed. "That's your problem. Anyhow, it's not Anouk you're being unfaithful to. It's me." The gulf between them remained as wide as ever, and Mo suddenly realized it. "Look, it's late. I'm exhausted."

They lay side by side in bed. Now and then a car would pass, its headlights reflecting on the ceiling. After a while, she turned her back on him. He breathed a sigh of relief. The silence was total, so unlike the Espérac house with its creakings and odd noises. He found himself wondering how Anouk was faring. Once on seeing Colette with a red rose in her fair curls, Anouk darted to the rosebush, plucked a rose and pinned it in her own dark hair.

In the night he awakened, and Mo was gone.

He found her on the balcony looking out to sea, the full moon gleaming on her ivory pajamas. When she turned toward him, he saw she'd been crying, something he'd only witnessed once—when Anouk had convulsions as a toddler. He was about to comfort her, but she might misinterpret it. He stepped back.

"I feel so stupid," she said. "I thought it'd be easy to share you if this day ever came. But it's not. I'm jealous. I can't help it. I've been racking my brains, trying to figure out what to do."

He didn't know what to say. He wanted her safe, but out of his life. Safe, anywhere but Espérac.

"There's no way I can go now when I'm making it. It'd be professional suicide." She implored him, "Won't you wait for me to come when the lease is up? It's only a little over a month. That's not long."

"I don't know." He paced up and down the balcony.

"Finlay, you're like a caged animal. Come over here and tell me what you're thinking."

"Nothing much." In fact, he'd been thinking about her late grandfather, a gunner who survived World War I, blinded in one eye by shrapnel. "Crazy Ole One-Eye," the family called him.

On Finlay's wedding day, he had lectured him about loyalty and sticking to a deal even after it changed for the worse.

"Look, here's what we'll do. Have your little French fling." She looked away and when she turned to him, her eyes were wet. "I didn't mean that the way it sounds. I shouldn't have said it. You must love her. Of course you do. It's a wonderful thing for you. And I can deal with it. I know I have no right to ask, but promise not to let her get pregnant and to keep it a secret from Anouk. I'll save the plane ticket and come when the lease runs out in August. For now, let's take it as it comes. Both of us."

August was a long way away. As usual, Mo had the last word.

Chapter 20

Awakening at Colette's on Sunday morning, Anouk jumped out of bed. Mom was arriving today. After eating breakfast, some apricots and bread with fig jam, Anouk offered to help weed the herb garden. Behind the parsley, basil, cilantro, fennel, and sorrel lay a bed of nasturtiums, and she nibbled one of the peppery blossoms. She was about to take another when she noticed the statue of a winged angel at the back of the garden. Some kid must have shot at the angel with a BB gun because there was a hole like a bull's-eye right in the middle of the angel's chest. A small bird flew over, a green worm dangling from its beak, and darted into the hole where the angel's heart should be. A few moments later, out the birdie flew, a thread of black slime trailing from its beak.

"Look at that," she said to Colette.

Only when Colette said what a good maman the bird was to clean up after her chick did Anouk realize the slime was poop. Why would Colette want a baby? Why would anyone? No wonder her mom didn't.

"Would you like to come to church with me?" Colette asked. She was dressed up in a yellow blouse and a leopard skin skirt. Anouk begged off. She'd never been to mass, had no idea how to act, and didn't want to make any more faux pas.

After Colette left, Anouk tried out her new makeup, but she got mascara under her eyelids, which made her look like a raccoon. She cleaned it off. At least, her nails were trim and attractive. She searched for something to read. There were no magazines, and all the books were in French. She picked one, *Savoir Faire*, and settled herself in the hammock under the apple tree. She'd been reading a few minutes when the bird flew back with another worm for the hatchling in its hidey-hole. It made her think of Danny. She hoped his captors were taking good care of him. She touched the bracelet he'd given her. Some of its threads had unraveled, but she was determined to wear it until he was released. She shut her eyes tight and wished with all her heart that his captors didn't make him wait until the troubles were over before they released him.

She flipped through the pages of the etiquette book. There were tips on how to cut chicken and to bone fish, and on how to behave in a church, in a mosque, and in a synagogue. There were rules for everything—how to flirt, how to get along with older people, and even how to talk to the doctor. Danny would hate it. He'd scowl and shake his black curls and say that instead of copying other people, she should make up her own mind and do what she believed was right. That was Danny, freethinker. She didn't agree. Rules made life easier.

Her mom wasn't always polite. "I speak my mind," she liked to say. Mom thought that people should be able to take criticism. But what if she didn't fit in here? What if she hated Monsieur Noel and the Vamps and the whole setup? It could happen. She got on her bicycle and worried about it all the way to Issigeac. In the square, she leaned her bike against the back wall of the church and listened to the people inside singing "Alleluia." After a while, she left and meandered around the market stalls in the hope that she might bump into Pierre. She felt sure her mother would approve of him because he was earnest.

She decided to get her mom a present and went from stall to
stall to find the perfect gift. She inspected the painted wooden
fans, liking the way they clicked shut. She examined the boxes
of ribbons and barrettes, the silken scarves, the fancy soaps and
lotions, the sachets of lavender, and the flowers. She fancied the
potted gardenia with creamy blossoms and green leathery leaves,
but Mom might forget to water it, and it would die. She petted the
kittens up for sale, but Mom was allergic to cats. Would she never
find just the right thing?

She watched the girls strolling up the street arm in arm with
their mothers. She'd done that with Colette, but never with Mom.
Maybe people here might think that meant they didn't love each
other. But Mom said that just because you didn't show things on
your face didn't mean you didn't feel them. That was what made
photography so challenging—to catch the fleeting expression of
deep connection.

Right away Anouk knew what to buy. She hurried to the
stationer's and leafed through the photography magazines in the
display rack. She chose the most expensive one. Back home as
she wrapped it in turquoise tissue paper, she couldn't stop smiling.
She'd found the perfect gift. She didn't have a satin bow to tie the
package with, so she cut a strip of the pale green cotton she'd used
to make the curtains, and it looked beautiful.

When the bells rang at noon, she went straight to Monsieur Noel's.
Bottles of pills and foil-wrapped suppositories—whatever those
were—lay in a jumble on the kitchen table; sticky tape with dead
flies dangled from the ceiling. She took one look at the pots soaking
in the murky water in the sink and went out to the garden, where
a table was set up under the ash tree. When he saw her, Saucisse
stopped gnawing his bone and thumped his tail until she petted
him. Pierre was there, and she held out her hand to him—the

etiquette book said it was up to the woman to extend hers first—
but then she noticed his father was there and she should have
greeted him first. Luckily, no one seemed to object. When it was
time to eat, Pierre drew back a chair for her. During the meal, he
kept his hands on the table on either side of his plate exactly as the
book said. She liked it that he was polite, and she copied him so
as to be sure to follow the rules. She hoped he'd notice her shiny
red nail polish.

"A glass of wine?" Monsieur Noel held up a bottle of white.

She thought of her mom and refused as politely as she could.

"But it's a Monbazillac, 1958, to honor Pierre's success. It's not
every day a young man passes his Bac."

"Leave her be, Papa."

Pierre smelled nice, a woody scent. He was wearing his soccer
T-shirt with the whale insignia and rugged-looking sandals. He
was muscular, but his tortoise shell glasses made him look like an
intellectual. Colette passed around the plate of canapés, triangles
of toast with pâté, and pointed out the freckle of black truffle. The
pâté tasted velvety smooth, although her mom would say, "Poor
little goose never did anyone any harm."

"What did you think of the essay on the Bac exam?" Monsieur
Noel asked. "Should extremism in defense of liberty be tolerated?
I go along with Montaigne and the golden mean."

"Passion is more desirable," Pierre said. She didn't understand
all his points, but he knew how to argue. Monsieur Noel came
back at him, saying that Montaigne was no slacker and had ridden
all the way to Italy on horseback. That led Colette to talk about
her pilgrimage, crossing the Pyrenees and hiking through forests,
cornfields, and dusty plains, and the senior man who gave her a
caramel and asked her to pray for him at the cathedral in Santiago.
There, she had pressed her lips to the silver box holding the bones
of James, the brother of Jesus.

"Baf. Those bones were fake, just like the shroud in Cadouin, and the thousands of locks of Mary's hair and vials of her breast milk. And the same goes for the crumbs from the Last Supper."

Instead of being irritated, Colette smiled at him. "At Compostela, I breathed in clouds of incense in the perfect beauty of the church, and I got over Victor. Just like that." She snapped a finger. Anouk wanted to hear more about Victor, but she rambled on about pilgrimage. Sometimes a yappy dog would race after her, and she'd scare him off with her walking stick. She got blisters on her heels and lost two toenails. City people pointed at her and the other pilgrims as if they were freaks; at night they slept, sweaty and smelly, lined up in sleeping bags, so they looked like sausages. But those were nothing when set against the beauty and meaningfulness of the pilgrimage. In the Basque country, she'd seen storks perched on huge nests high up on the roofs of the houses with red shutters. And in a little church in a hamlet, she'd seen a carving of God with souls nestled in his lap. "Imagine that," Colette said. "Just like a mother."

Anouk tried to imagine God like that. Back in Beirut, she'd once seen a crowd of pilgrims all dressed in white as they set off, chanting, toward Mecca. Danny had once hiked the Santiago de Compostela Pilgrimage Trail to the town in Spain where his grandparents lived and where he and his mother had buried Mr. Delacruz. Danny wanted to go back there. Danny and all his big plans. She couldn't help but feel cross. He should have figured out a way to escape by now.

Just then Colette patted her hand. "Let me tell you the pilgrim's motto. 'The pilgrim does not ask. The pilgrim says 'thank you.'"

There it was again. Etiquette. It was unfair of Monsieur Noel to get so annoyed with Colette when all she cared about was being kind and pleasant. Just then Anouk felt something warm on her ankle. Could it be? Yes, Pierre's bare toes were touching her ankle.

He winked at her. Thrilled, she looked at him. He blinked his
jade eyes, and she slipped off her sandal, felt his foot, and quickly
pulled back.

"Enough nonsense about pilgrimage." Monsieur Noel fiddled
with the knob of his hearing aid. "Damn thing is no good. Can't
stop the ringing in my ear. Anouk, speak up and tell us about that
hellhole, Beirut."

"It's nice," she said. Flirting with Pierre was so exciting that she
couldn't think of what else to say. He rubbed the side of her ankle
and lightly ran his foot up to her calf. She felt herself blushing. She
forced herself to talk about Beirut so they wouldn't suspect, and
rattled away about the concerts and theater and movies.

"Tell us about Kansas and the Wild West, your maman's home,"
Colette said.

She knew she should talk about the grain elevators, tall as
skyscrapers, and the red-tailed hawks on the telephone poles, but
how could she when Pierre was making her tingly?

"Have you ever been to a rodeo?" Monsieur Lebon asked.

She slipped her foot back in her sandal. "Yes. And I wore a
cowboy hat, a red bandana and pointed boots with spurs."

"A cute little cowgirl," Pierre said, squeezing her hand.

Monsieur Noel shifted the talk to the Soviet landing on the
moon. "Humans don't belong there," he said. "They'll spoil it."

"I'd love to be an astronaut," Pierre said.

"Me too," Anouk said.

"Baf. The moon's no place for a girl."

"But if I had the chance to go and didn't take it, I'd be sorry
forever," she said.

"Do you have any regrets?" Pierre turned to Monsieur Noel.

He crossed his arms over his chest. "Ah, yes. At times I find
myself impotent."

"Papa, don't be gloomy."

"On the contrary. Did not Montaigne say we should admit this infirmity and speak openly about it, thus relieving tension? I follow his wise example."

Embarrassed, Anouk dipped her spoon in the soup and swallowed a mouthful. It tasted bland. Monsieur Noel listed the ingredients: goose fat, wine and vinegar, bouillon and four garlic cloves per person.

"That's a lot of garlic," she said.

"Best soup in the world. It cures hangovers, and garlic makes a man potent." He giggled. "I'll serve it on Colette's wedding night."

If Dad talked like that, she'd be mortified, but Colette just smiled. After everyone had finished, she cleared the table. While she was in the kitchen, Monsieur Noel poured himself another glass of wine and turned to Anouk. "Colette thinks your papa is chic," he said, a twinkle in his eye.

"My mom is pretty, too."

Colette brought out the main course. On the platter were four trout, caught at dawn by Pierre, their sides sprinkled with slivered almonds, their gray eyes open. Although she felt squeamish, Anouk copied the others, eating all the flesh on one side before flipping the fish and starting on its other side. "You must be an excellent fisherman," she said to Pierre.

"A lucky one." He rubbed his foot on hers. Again, it was thrilling. He was flirting with her; she was sure of it.

"In Pierre's honor, I will tell the legend of the whale of the Banege," Monsieur Noel said. Anouk glanced at Colette. She was too polite to roll her eyes, but Anouk figured she'd heard the story before.

"Once upon a time, an angler rose at dawn, tugged on his gaiters, waded in the muddy Banege and cast his rod. Not a bite. He cast again. Nothing. And so it went. He was about to leave when Boom! A whale breached, exploding water. 'Bozo! With your hook, you scratched my flipper.' The whale blew a foul, fishy breath on the poor fisherman, who cried, 'Spare me.' 'Ah, very well,' the whale said, clapping his flippers. The fisherman ran home, fast as his bandy legs could carry him.

'Cretin,' his wife yelled. 'That whale owes you a favor. You let him off the hook. Go tell him to lead our pigs to cepes, the most prized of mushrooms.'

So he did. 'O king of the Banege,' he called, 'my wife wishes a boon of thee.'

'And what does she want?' the whale roared.

The angler fell to his knees. 'Milord, she has a great desire for cepes.'

'Say no more.'

All week, his wife feasted on cepes, but she tired of them, and only truffles would do. Again, she ordered her husband to go down to the river.

The whale closed one blue eye when he heard the word truffles, and recalled their sexy, earthy scent. He told the angler to go home, for he would grant her wish."

Anouk glanced at her watch. It'd be seven o'clock in Beirut. Her parents would be at a buffet somewhere. In a couple of hours, they'd set out for the airport. She jiggled her foot and looked at Pierre, and he winked at her. Monsieur Noel droned on about the shrewish wife, who was now fussing about having to haul water from the spring.

"'Our water, not good enough for her?' The whale reared on his tail. 'She must be punished. Never again will a cepe or a truffle pass her lips, and all the days of her life she must fetch her water.' The end."

Monsieur Lebon and Colette both clapped, but Pierre said the story made it sound as if ambition was a fault. It made Anouk want to hug him.

"Baf. Young people seem incapable of understanding the need for moderation." He passed her the cheese plate. "Now, would you prefer the Brie or a wedge of creamy Camembert? Or may I tempt you with a bit of Roquefort or Gruyère? Or a sliver of this goat wrapped in grape leaves?"

"I don't care. Whatever."

Pierre looked sharply at her, and she bit her lower lip. He'd caught her being rude. Colette crooked her finger and beckoned her to come inside. "Papa went to the trouble of finding cheeses that might please you, Anouk chérie. He wanted everything to be perfect, so you'll be happy. Don't hurt his feelings by implying he's wasted his time on you. It's easy to make him happy. Smile at him. Say something like, 'Oh, a morsel of this Gruyère would give me such pleasure.' She put a finger under Anouk's chin. "Let him know you appreciate his efforts. It will make you happy, too. That is my lesson for today in charm and seduction."

When they went back outside, the cicadas were shrieking, and Monsieur Noel was rambling on about how Napoleon once begged his mistress not to bathe for three days because he reveled in her odor.

"Papa, please," Colette said.

"Only a bit of history," he said.

Anouk served the pastries, and exactly as Colette said, they cared passionately. Pierre's father had his heart set on the apple tart and said it was the best he'd tasted for years. Pierre selected a chocolate éclair, saying he infinitely preferred it to all the others. Monsieur Noel chose "The Nun," two pastry balls coated with chocolate to resemble a dark robe. "Here's what to do with the holy sister." He giggled and bit off the top ball. "Gobble her up."

At five o'clock, after four hours at the table, Colette served espressos followed by prunes in eau de vie, each in its tiny glass. Monsieur Noel and Monsieur Lebon leaned back in a fragrant haze of Gitane smoke, and Pierre invited Anouk to go for a walk. He had dark hair, like hers, and he looked as handsome as Tony in *West Side Story*. She felt shy and proud when he held her hand. When they passed the Vamps' house, she imagined them pulling back their lace curtains to peek at her and Pierre. She liked the idea.

"Did you have a good time?" he asked.

"Yes, except Monsieur Noel drinks too much."

"That's not such a bad thing when you're old. How many more times will he feast with us and savor that superior Carignan white?"

Old men shouldn't talk about sex, but she didn't say so. Still, it was easy to chat with Pierre. It seemed like minutes instead of hours before his father was calling him to leave.

After he kissed her on the cheeks, Pierre looked deep into her eyes. He smelled of the woods and she liked it. He said he looked forward to meeting her again at the July 14 celebration. Back home, she turned on her tape of *West Side Story*. She imagined it was Pierre singing, "Something's Coming, Something Good." She did a cartwheel. A cute guy and Mom too!

At eleven-fifteen that night, it was time to set out for the station. Monsieur Noel gathered the horse-racing magazines piled on the front seat of his Peugeot and tossed them in back, where Saucisse was curled up on the green blanket. Anouk got in front; Monsieur Noel revved the motor, and they were off.

At the station, they studied the timetable. The train from Bordeaux was on time, but she was so tense that she needed to pee. The toilet was still filthy, with fresh graffiti scrawled on the walls. "The male apparatus" was what her mom had called the penis the one time she explained about sex. The French name for it was zizi. Zeeezeee, they pronounced it. Jilly knew lots of names for it, but zizi was nicer than any of them. Before Anouk finished, the overhead light went off, and she yanked up her panties and, feeling her way along the clammy wall, made her way out in the dark.

"Platform Three," Monsieur Noel announced. They crossed the tracks. It was dark, and they were the only people on the platform.

"Attention. In two minutes, the Bordeaux train arrives." The clickety-clacking got louder, and a whistle shrieked as the train slowed to a stop. The doors opened, and a half-dozen passengers disembarked. She spotted her father on the platform, suitcases in hand, and she raced toward him and fell into his arms. Then she looked around. "Where's Mom?"

He bowed his head. "I'm sorry."

"What? Not here?" Anouk trembled, stunned by this betrayal. "It's not true. It can't be."

He squeezed her hand. "Steady now. She says she needs to stay in Beirut until Danny's found."

"So, it was all for nothing," Anouk howled and pulled away from him. "Did you say something wrong? You must have. Did you really try?" she accused him. "Maybe you don't want her around, but I do."

"Don't say that. If I had the magic words, your mother would be here now."

Dad gripped her arm as she slouched toward the parking lot. Monsieur Noel opened the back door, and she squeezed in beside Saucisse. She wanted to fling her arms around him and weep into his warm pelt, but he had fleas. Instead, she looked out the window. The streets were empty, the houses dark. They crossed the bridge over the black water of the Dordogne River. As they neared the bar with its sign, "Citizens, you who love good wine, go no farther," Monsieur Noel suggested they stop for a nightcap.

In the bar her father ordered a beer, Mort Subite. Monsieur Noel suggested she have a mint drink, a perroquet. "We call it that because it's green like a parrot. Colette liked them when she was your age."

Anouk imagined Colette nudging her, wanting her to be polite, and managed to smile. "I've never had a perroquet. Perhaps I should try it."

"Oh, yes," he said. "It's all the rage."

It tasted of mint and licorice, and the ice cubes crackled. "You're right. It's good."

"Is it not?" he said, smiling broadly.

That didn't change her attitude toward her father. He was such a dope. If she'd been the one to go to Beirut, she would have convinced her mom. She was positive of it.

"Any word of the lost boy?" Monsieur Noel asked.

"Nothing," Dad said.

Anouk sniffled. When they got home at two in the morning, she was too mad to sleep. Over the course of the long car ride, her thoughts about her two parents had balanced, and then tipped in the other direction. What was wrong with her mom? Maybe it wasn't her dad's fault, after all. She got the magazine, savagely tore off the pretty wrapping, and threw it into the compost heap. She ripped out the pages with all their prize-winning photos, tearing out a half-dozen sheets at a time and hurled them in. She grabbed the pitchfork and turned the weeds, vegetable peelings, and stinky melon skins over the beautiful pictures.

Once they were buried, though, she regretted what she'd done. She wrote a note to her mom. "What happened to Danny could happen to you. Can't you find work here? If you hate it, you can leave. Give it a try. That's what you always tell me."

She slipped out to the mailbox to post the letter. It might not ever reach Mom, but she had to try.

Chapter 21

On the morning of July 14, Finlay threw open the shutters. Colette
stood below, at the war memorial, a sheaf of blue delphinium,
white lilies, and red roses in her arms. As she stooped to lay them
at the feet of the bronze soldier, he wanted to call out to her, but
that seemed improper, like yelling at someone in church. If only
she would glance up and crook her finger, beckoning, as if to say,
"Come out and play." They would find some hidden place, twigs
prickling their bare arms, and she might run her hand over his
trousers and tease, asking why he had a zipper for a fly instead of
buttons. He quickly buried that notion, turning away from the
window.

Monsieur Noel had invited them both to watch the Bastille Day
parade on television, but when it was time to go, Anouk was still
in her pajamas, dawdling over a bowl of café au lait. She pouted,
saying the parade would be boring. So he left without her, telling
her to come as soon as she was ready.

Upon his arrival, Saucisse leaped up and slobbered on his thigh
until Monsieur Noel dragged her off and tied her to the kitchen
table. In the salon, it was dim and pleasantly cool, unlike at home
where Anouk insisted on keeping the shutters open in the heat of
the day. Finlay watched seven thousand soldiers march down the

Champs-Elysée. They looked about the same age as his students, whom he'd last seen hunched over their essays. It was impossible to imagine them as killers.

When Anouk arrived an hour later, she sat on the opposite end of the lumpy sofa, as far from him as she could while the French Foreign Legion in dress whites and black boots marched through the Place de la Concorde toward a towering obelisk. Monsieur Noel said Napoleon had brought it all the way from Egypt to please his Joséphine.

"He shouldn't have stolen it. The Egyptians would take as good— or better—care of it," Anouk said.

Monsieur Noel harrumphed, insulted. "It was their gift to us," he said and left the room.

Finlay tried to suppress his anger at Anouk's rudeness. Yet she was upset over her mother's not coming, and he would make allowances.

A squadron of armored vehicles clanked down the Champs-Èlysées, followed by sailors marching in blue-and-white vests and red pompom hats. When he said they were handsome, she rolled her eyes. Jets flew overhead, their contrails of red, white, and blue bright against the sky. He asked if she remembered the tracer bullets that lit up the night sky last New Year's Eve.

"Yeah. So what?"

"I'm worried about you."

"Don't bother. I'm okay. A-OK." A moment later, she turned to face him. "That's a big fat lie. Everything's crappy. I'm stuck here, bored out of my mind."

"It'll get better."

"Dream on," she said.

On the screen, the president of the republic and his entourage of generals and ambassadors stood on the platform decked out in red-white-and-blue bunting and watched the flyover. "Impressive, huh?" Finlay tried again.

"So the French know how to put on a parade. Duh."

He wasn't getting anywhere. It was like when they first moved here. "Did you have a good time with Colette while I was gone?"

"Why are you asking about her? You talk about her all the time."

"I do?"

"Yeah." Anouk straightened up on the sofa, her eyes intent. "Do you like her?"

"Colette?"

"Duh. Who else?" He paused, searching for an answer that wouldn't hurt her. "Forget it, just forget it," she cried.

"There's no need to be rude."

"Okay, sorry," she said grudgingly. "You haven't told me about Beirut."

He didn't dare mention Danny. "Everyone is trying to leave. There was such a traffic jam on the Airport Road that I almost missed the flight back. By the way, I ran into Pierre and his father on the train from Bordeaux."

"Really!" She sat up straight, her resentment about Colette forgotten.

"Yes. Pierre asked about you."

He could tell she was delighted. On the television, a dozen parachutists floated onto the Champs-Elysée, billowing clouds of red-white-and-blue nylon slowing their fall.

"Wow. Maybe they're the same parachutists we saw our first day here." She moved closer, her gaze never leaving the screen. "Know what? One of these days Danny is going to pop up. See, Daddy, sometimes things seem dangerous, but they turn out perfect."

It was the first time she'd called him "Daddy," or mentioned Danny in a very long while.

That evening a crowd assembled for the Bastille Day festivities: retirees, shopkeepers, and red-faced farmers from kilometers round about, their hair slicked back, ready for a bit of fun now that they'd finished the haying. Several of them came up to Finlay to congratulate him for reopening the bakery. Monsieur Noel basted a hog on a spit above burning coals, and one of the Vamps jabbed the tip of her cane into the meat to see whether it was cooked. On the far end of the square, below garlands of red-white-and-blue tissue paper flowers, the mayor served glasses of strong punch. People milled around, greeting those they hadn't seen since the Fête of St. John. When the bells rang at eight p.m., they all sat down at the trestle tables. Finlay unpacked the picnic basket and set the plates, glasses, and cutlery on the white paper covering the table. Not realizing that it wouldn't be needed, he'd brought along a tablecloth from home, and now he set it on the chair beside him to hold the place for Colette.

Pierre sat beside Anouk. "Did your mother come?"

Anouk flinched.

"You must miss her," Pierre said and at once changed the subject, remarking that the mayor was a charming man who greeted all and sundry, not only those who'd voted for him.

The lad had social graces, Finlay was glad to see. But what was keeping Colette? The hum of conversation—a constant murmur—continued until wrinkled Madame Licorne, who'd taught grades four, five, and six to everybody present under fifty, pressed her hands down on the table and pushed herself up. She rapped her knuckles on the table and raised a finger to her lips. "Shh. Silence for the mayor."

At once, everyone shushed as if afraid she would march over and pull their ears for chattering. The mayor marched up to the podium, adjusted the tricolor sash that stretched diagonally across the jacket of his navy suit, repositioned the gold-rimmed spectacles that had slipped down his nose, drew a folded sheet of paper from his breast pocket, and set it on the podium. He thanked them for attending this hundred and eighty-seventh anniversary of Bastille Day, celebrated each year, except during the shameful time of the German Occupation.

Monsieur Noel squeezed himself between Anouk and Pierre on the bench and settled Saucisse at his feet.

The mayor glorified the Revolution and the Declaration of the Rights of Man. Whatever the differences among the inhabitants of Espérac, they were all proud of their ancestors' courage in storming the Bastille and setting the prisoners free. "Long live the Republic. Long live France," he cried. He snatched off his glasses, waved them in the air, and they all cheered.

"Here you are, at last." Finlay stood up as Colette came and sat down next to him. Silver spangles sparkled on her dress of navy silk. She looked scintillating. He poured her a glass of Monbazillac.

"We thought you were never coming," Anouk chimed in. A girl her age placed a soup tureen on the table. It was Charlotte, Pierre's sister, who returned a few minutes later to ask Anouk to help serve.

As Colette stood to ladle the steaming soup, her dress rustled. Finlay felt her eyes lingering on his. He managed to avoid staring at her décolleté, but he could barely eat, and his soup bowl was still half-full when Anouk and Charlotte returned to take away the tureens. Then back they came with platters piled high with chicken legs. Children lit artificial snakes, making them arch, puff, and smoke. When it was finally dark, the fireworks began.

Colette exclaimed as Roman candles gave off sparks and colored balls. More fireworks flashed red, orange and yellow, making bangs and whistles and crackles. Saucisse ran off in fear. At the grand finale, a dozen bursts, Finlay flinched.

Colette touched his hand.

"I'm sorry. It's—it sounds like bombing."

"It's safe here." She smiled and patted his hand, and he recovered himself.

The accordionist slipped his arms into the straps of his instrument, and the older people cheered. First came oompah and polka music. Someone yelled for the Duck Dance, and within minutes the square was full of people of all ages. "Quin…quin…" they quacked, laughing as they flapped their arms to the music.

"Pierre must like Anouk to come back from Paris for this," Colette said. "Not many would give up the chance to see the fireworks at the Eiffel Tower. They're the best in the world."

After the accordionist left, a recorded waltz came over the loudspeaker. "Dance with me?" Finlay said to Colette. He drew her close, so they were cheek-to-cheek until Anouk and Pierre joined the dancers. Suddenly hyper-aware of the need for propriety, Finlay led Colette back to their table. At midnight, thunder rumbled, and lightning flickered. People packed up dishes, glasses, and silverware in their baskets and began to leave. Pierre and Anouk kept on dancing until the music stopped. Finlay and Colette watched as Pierre walked Anouk the few steps to her door.

"I think he likes her," Colette observed.

"Maybe." Was it his imagination, or did Anouk caress the boy's neck before she slipped inside? Should girls of fifteen do that sort of thing?

After he'd walked Anouk home, Pierre came back to help the men stack the trestle tables and benches against the wall that enclosed the square, and then he cycled home in the dark. There was another thunderclap, but not a drop of rain. Everyone had gone, leaving Colette and Finlay to gather the empty wine bottles, and carry them to the depository behind the church. When they got back to the square, Colette noticed the string of lights still lit. "We shouldn't let them burn all night. What a waste," she said. She helped him prop the aluminum ladder against the wall of the *Salle des Fêtes*. Lightheaded, he climbed, petrified.

"Be careful," she called.

On the top step, he stretched his hand toward the electric outlet. The ladder swayed, and he could feel himself leaning dangerously sideways. Heart pounding with fear, he reached farther and yanked out the plug. He began the climb down, the ladder wavering with each step. Near the ground, only two steps to go, he felt her hand between his thighs. He almost fainted with desire.

Back on terra firma, he placed his hands on her shoulders and drew her to him, feeling the silk of her dress smooth under his hands. Hand-in-hand they walked in the humid darkness. Halfway to her home, by the path that led toward the spring, he paused. "Shall we wait for the shower there?" he said lightly.

She lurched against him as they walked, a little tipsy, and he put his arm around her waist to steady her. At the spring, he took the tablecloth from the basket and spread it under the chestnut tree. She found a pebble and skipped it across the oval basin. "I'll not soon forget that day when I first saw you here," she said.

"Two months ago today." He tightened his arm around her.

"You were bashful at being discovered half-naked. I liked that."

He nuzzled her neck, breathing in her scent as the wind soughed in the trees. She kicked off her red heels and wriggled her toes in the dewy grass. She raised her hand to unfasten her tortoiseshell barrette. Her thick golden hair fell past her shoulders, and he breathed in its scent of almonds.

"Kiss me," she whispered.

They lay in each other's arms. In the tall grass, tiny green lights glimmered, glowworms blinking their presence to the universe. In the shrubs beyond, sparks flickered as fireflies sought each other. A thousand cicadas droned, their mating calls a pulsating plainchant. Finlay's eyes searched hers. His heart pounded as he undid the mother-of-pearl buttons of her dress and slipped his hand under the silky fabric. She wore no brassiere. That was new to him, a woman who anticipated what he wanted. He stroked her warm breasts, and she drew his face close, her fingertips grazing his throat. He pulled off his windbreaker and bunched it into a pillow for her. She slipped out of her dress and panties; he tore off his clothes and knelt on the ground to kiss her narrow ankles and up each leg—ankle, calf, and thigh—his desire ever more urgent as he touched her moist hair and heard her whimpers of pleasure.

"Allons-y," she breathed in his ear. "Off we'll fly to seventh heaven."

Chapter 22

A pebble pinged against her window. Anouk bounded out of bed, hoping that it was Pierre dying to see her, just as Romeo came to Juliet in the night. That would be so romantic. She peeked out the window and saw that it was only Monsieur Noel. The magic of the evening had utterly passed. She hurried down the stairs to open the door.

"I need to talk to your papa," he said.

She rubbed the sleep from her eyes.

"I'll wait. Go get him." Monsieur Noel sounded upset, and he hadn't even bothered to kiss her cheek.

Upstairs, she banged on his bedroom door. "Dad!" she yelled. When there was no answer, she opened the door. The room was empty, so she went back downstairs to find Monsieur Noel pacing in the narrow hall. "Dad's probably still at the party. So what's happened?"

"No, I'm not the one to tell. I need to explain it to your papa first."

She nagged him. Finally, he said that her mother had called, but they'd been cut off. Anouk pestered him, tugging on his arm, but the harder she tried to get him to tell her what had happened, the more upset he seemed.

"Maybe Dad's in the bakery," she said. "When Dad can't sleep, he sometimes goes there."

"Let's go." Monsieur Noel shone the flashlight at her bare feet. "Better put on your shoes. It looks like a storm is coming."

Puzzled and afraid, she obeyed. Outside, it was dark, and the lights in the houses were off as well as the single light high up on the wall of the *Salle des Fêtes*. She stubbed her toe against one of the benches stacked along the wall. Monsieur Noel plodded along, leaning on his umbrella as if it were a cane. "Please hurry," she said when he caught up.

"I'm coming as fast as I can. You run ahead," he said.

Her dad wasn't at the bakery.

When Monsieur Noel caught up with her, he remembered that Finlay had been with Colette and maybe they'd gone to her house.

"But what's it all about? Just tell me," Anouk said as they made their way in the pitch black. But he wouldn't.

When they arrived, he waved his flashlight over the house, from top to bottom. The kitchen and living room shutters were closed, but those upstairs were flung wide open. That was where Colette's bedroom was. As he shone his flashlight up toward it, a terrible thought seized Anouk: Daddy and Colette were up there. Doing it. She grabbed Monsieur Noel's hand and forced down the flashlight.

"Stop that," he said in a testy voice. "Be reasonable. We need to find your father. Your maman—"

"No," Anouk screamed. She turned on her heel to run off, but when she heard the crunching of footsteps on the gravel, she stopped short. "Look, someone's coming."

Monsieur Noel beamed his flashlight toward the path that led from the spring up to the square. There they were: her father and Colette walking side by side at arm's length from each other. Like neighbors. Like old friends. Platonic, like her and Danny. Colette was arranging a cloth over the picnic basket. Anouk sprinted toward them. "Daddy, Mom called. Something's happened, but Monsieur Noel won't tell me what."

They went inside Colette's house. She flicked on the kitchen light and sat Anouk in the Voltaire chair with the velvet leopard print. Monsieur Noel found a bottle of Armagnac in the cabinet where Colette kept her supply of spirits and dribbled two inches into a snifter. "Drink this, Finlay. Drink it all," he said. "There has been an incident."

"An incident?" Her dad's voice sounded gruff.

Monsieur Noel yanked his shirtsleeves down over his wrists. "Maybe I made some error, and I certainly hope I have. But if I understood correctly, she wishes to inform you that the young man is dead. 'Danny Delacruz, mort,' that's all she said."

Colette cried. "Anouk's about to faint."

She felt her dad's hands on either side of her face as he lowered her head to her knees. A moment later, Colette put a glass in her hand. "Here, drink it, all of it."

"It burns," she whimpered. She turned to Monsieur Noel. "What else did my mom say?"

"We were cut off."

"We need to call her," Anouk said.

It was still raining, fat drops hitting the pavement, as they hurried back to Monsieur Noel's house. When they entered, the half-dozen clocks struck two a.m. Anouk stared up at the boar's head, its yellow teeth pointed and menacing. She fiddled with her bracelet while Finlay dialed their number in Beirut, 961-1-340-482. His palms were sweaty.

There was no answer. "Try again," Anouk said.

"Go to the post office in the morning," Monsieur Noel said when they still couldn't get through. "The connection will be better."

At home, Finlay lay in bed and listened to the raindrops banging on the roof. Once Danny found a four-leaf clover, and Molly was thrilled, for she believed it would bring him good luck. But superstitions were nonsense. He recalled the lonely summer he'd spent as a boy in Scotland, where Mum had sent him to fish its cold waters with her father. Grandpa set Finlay to gut the day's catch. At first, he made a right mess of it. Later, more adept, feeling pleased with himself, he whistled a tune. "Hell and damnation!" Grandpa roared. "For the love of all that's holy, do you want to get us all drowned? Damn fool lad—didn't anyone ever tell you whistling into the wind invites a storm?" Grandpa grabbed a haddock lying on the deck and walloped him on the cheek.

Now, from Anouk's room, Finlay could make out the strains of "Danny Boy" playing on her tape recorder. The last time he'd heard it was during JFK's funeral on television.

Finlay turned to face the wall. He knew what was bothering him. You cheat. You pay. He had pledged himself to Mo for a lifetime, a promise fouled. Those first times he'd kissed Colette, he feared something bad might happen. Danny's father Juan, whose field was chaos theory, believed an odd bit of science: how the flap of a butterfly wing in Brazil could set off a tornado in Texas. It boggled the mind, but Juan, who had left Spain to train at MIT, was nobody's fool. They used to meet at Uncle Sam's Café and discuss the newspaper accounts of the previous day's battles over coffee. In those early days of the troubles, they were both convinced the papers exaggerated the atrocities. Neither believed the Lebanese were such savages. For if that were true, there seemed no hope for humankind.

Realizing he was thirsty, Finlay got up to get a drink of water. Back in bed, he mulled over John Donne's idea that no man was an island and everyone was connected. Could his dalliance with Colette have led to Danny's death? The idea seemed preposterous, and yet something about it rang true inside him. He'd crossed the line. His daughter had almost caught him in the act.

In the night, he heard the stairs creak and the front door click shut. He got up to look for Anouk, but she was nowhere in the house. He found her curled up in front of Monsieur Noel's house on the wet grass, Saucisse in her lap. He squatted beside her and put his arm around her. "You're sopping wet. Come home."

She was crying. "You know how deaf Monsieur Noel is. He might not hear the phone if Mom calls. And what he said about Danny. It's not true." She wiped her cheek on one of the beagle's soft ears.

"Your mother wouldn't lie."

"He must have got it wrong. It can't be true, because if Danny got killed, it could happen to Mom, too."

Suppressing the shudder that ran through him, Finlay helped Anouk to her feet. "I'm sure your mother's fine. We'll call her in the morning. Now let's go home."

He promised to stay with her. He lit a votive candle and sat by her bedside. Occasionally he'd nod off. When he awakened, he stared at the framed tapestry with its blue forget-me-nots and the words, SOUVENIR OF MY CAPTIVITY, embroidered in gold thread. Poor Danny. Could he really be dead? And where the hell was Mo?

In the morning, they went to the post office, and Finlay placed a call to their home number in Beirut. No answer. Becoming impatient, he asked the operator to put a call through to the Dean's Office. He closed the glass door of the cubicle, sat on the hard-backed chair and cupped the receiver to his ear. When Dean Sharif came on the line, Finlay turned so that Anouk was out of his line of vision and said their neighbor, who had received a call from Mo, had understood her to say Danny Delacruz was dead.

"I'm afraid so. I know you liked the boy," the dean said.

Finlay groaned. "Is Mo all right?"

"She's fine."

"And Molly?"

"She keeps talking about those days when Danny was still alive, when they could have done something. At least now that his body has been recovered, she'll feel she can leave. Better for her."

Finlay walked out of the cubicle. Anouk tugged on his elbow as she followed him out of the post office. He turned and, bending slightly, held her tight. "Sunbeam, I'm terribly sorry. Danny's gone."

"Dead?" She pulled herself away and rushed off into the rain. He ran after, throwing up huge splashes with his shoes until he caught up with her. When they got home, he turned on the BBC. First came the lead stories: the storm that followed the heat wave that made 1976 the hottest summer in decades; France's performance in the Olympics, where the Soviets and East Germans were scoring big; the Supreme Court's ruling that the death penalty was neither cruel nor unusual. At the end of all the stories came the war in Beirut. There were no details, merely the bare bones of the story: an American, Daniel Delacruz, had been found dead, and five U.S. aircraft carriers were sailing toward Beirut harbor to evacuate Americans and Europeans.

The news spread fast. An hour later the Vamps knocked at the door and tottered in out of the downpour. Dressed in identical print dresses, they furled their umbrellas and sat at the table in the kitchen. Finlay made dark coffee, and the aroma spread through the room. "Please accept our respectful sympathy," they murmured in unison.

Anouk gulped her mint drink and then ran her finger around the ring of water on the oilcloth left by the glass. "Your maman will be coming soon," both the Vamps repeated as they left.

"They're such phonies," Anouk said after they left. "They didn't even know Danny, yet they act so icky sympathetic."

"They mean well."

"So what? You think that makes it better? What if something else happens—" She looked on the verge of tears, and he was helpless to stop them. "Dad, take over, okay? I'm going to see Colette."

Colette was at home in the kitchen, scrubbing potatoes in the sink. She untied her apron and sat Anouk down. "You're drenched. Here, sit by the window. It's a sunny spot; the cat likes it." She fetched a towel, dried Anouk's hair and wrapped it in the towel. "Have you eaten?" she said. "No? I'll get you a little something—a slice of toast, a poached egg?"

Anouk spilled out what happened to Danny.

"Of course you can't eat. No one can, not after bad news. But a little cup of hot chocolate, wouldn't that hit the spot?" Anouk mutely agreed, glad for the sympathy.

As Colette warmed the milk and stirred in the cocoa powder, Minou jumped into Anouk's lap and lay there, purring.

"There now, try that." Colette handed her the cup.

The cocoa was so comforting that Anouk shared something she'd been holding in for a long time. "Know what I can't stand? The whole world feeling sorry for me because of my mom."

"Of course you feel like that. Anyone would."

"It's so fake." Anouk stroked Minou.

Colette gestured to the pile of knobby potatoes and the heap of nettles on the table. "It makes the most comforting of soups. You'll like it."

"Mom would hate how people here are worrying about her when they don't even know her. It's like they're saying she can't take care of herself."

"Pay no attention to them." Colette handed her a paring knife.

"Tell me honestly. What do you think?"

"About your maman? She's like Jeanne d'Arc. You've heard of her? Our patron saint."

"There's a street with that name in Beirut. Once a car bomb went off there, and my mom took a picture of the car, a Mercedes with smoke pouring out. She got it published."

Colette said nothing. She gouged a black spot in the potato in her hand and added it to the pile of peelings. She added the peeled potatoes to the skillet in which sliced onions and leeks were browning.

"It's sizzling. Smells good too," Anouk said.

Colette raised the flame over the pot on the stove.

"A watched kettle never boils. That what my mom says. She doesn't wait around. She's brave. She—"

"Know what Jeanne d'Arc said when the neighbors grumbled that she should be a normal girl, stay home, get married and have kids?"

"No, what?"

"'Enough women are doing that,' she said and sneaked off to become a soldier. She shed her blood for us—to rid us of the English. That's why there's a statue of her in every church."

"Even here?"

"Yes, I'll show you. We can go now if you like."

"How about the soup?"

"It needs to simmer." Colette lowered the flame until it was a thin ring of blue under the pot.

Anouk looked out the window. "It's still raining."

"Just a drizzle. It'll be dry in the church."

Anouk was reluctant to go. She wasn't used to visiting churches, and she worried she'd goof and do something inappropriate and Colette would frown.

"Come along, my flea," Colette said.

When they entered, Colette dipped her finger in the water in the marble basin at the entrance and touched her forehead, chest, and shoulders. A crucifix hung on the south wall near the door. Anouk averted her eyes from the dead, mostly naked man on the cross smack-dab in front of her. Why would anyone want to look at that? Especially Colette, who liked things to be cheerful?

"Come on." Colette took Anouk's arm, and they walked over to the statue of Joan of Arc, standing on a pedestal near the front of the church.

"She's pretty," Anouk said. Saint Joan looked about her age. She was slim with pink cheeks and straight brown hair, and she wore a sky blue tunic painted with silver fleurs-de-lys. Shiny plate armor protected her elbows and knees. She held a blue banner and wore a sword attached to the belt at her waist.

"Of course she's pretty," Colette said. "She knew it's important to look pleasant. That's easier when you're young. And she cared about fashion, too. They say she had a beautiful dress made for King Louis's coronation in Orléans. That was her moment of triumph."

"Why does the crucifix show Jesus dead, but the statues of the saints show them alive?"

Colette's mouth quirked. "Such questions you ask. They say her skin had the scent of iron. Blood smells of iron, so that may be why. She was always in the thick of battle."

Anouk touched the tip of the silver sword. "It's like she's got a gun."

"Sometimes you have to fight to be free. Our Joan was only a year older than you when she ran away from home."

"My mom was a runaway, too. But she'd never kill anyone. She's a pacifist."

"Not our Joan. Poor thing, well, you know what happened. To die like that. Now, if a man were so valiant, people would praise him and say he'd sacrificed himself for the greater good. That he died in glory, and that, at least, the children had their maman. While poor Joan, she was a virgin— no husband, no babies. Your maman is lucky to have you."

A surge of longing welled up inside Anouk. "I miss her."

"Of course you do." Colette patted her on the arm. "Here's what you should do when you feel sad. Come here, lay some flowers in front of Joan, and say a little prayer for your maman. Burn a candle for her, too. That's what I do when I miss my maman. Her name was Marie, so I pay a little visit to the Virgin in her honor. Come see."

The Virgin Mary, who stood on a pedestal a few feet from Joan of Arc, held an edge of blue mantle in her fingertips. Colette took one of the candles from the metal box fixed to a pillar, lit the wick, and knelt in front of the statue. Anouk stood, breathing in the scent of beeswax until Colette got up from her knees. "See, that's prayer," she smiled. "It's simple. I thank God that Maman loved me, and I feel better."

"My maman's not dead." Tears pricked Anouk's eyes.

"Well, the living need prayers too." Colette held her arm, and they strolled back toward the door. Light streamed through a roseate window and dappled the tile floor with patterns of blue, gold, and pink. It reminded her of Mom twisting her kaleidoscope. By the time they got back to Colette's, the nettle soup was a thick bright green. Plop plop plop, it bubbled. Colette stirred it smooth, poured it into a bowl, and added a dollop of crème fraiche. "Your father likes cream." She handed the tureen to Anouk to take home. "Tell him I miss him."

Anouk didn't.

The next morning, there was still no news from Mo. Finlay's fortnightly delivery of firewood arrived. He pulled on his red gloves with the leather palms and yanked the black tarpaulin off the stack of chestnut—bundles five feet wide bound with wire. He loaded them, armfuls at a time, and pushed the wheelbarrow to the woodshed, where spider webs over the window dimmed the light. As he rubbed his lower back, a trickle of sweat escaped his sweatband.

No one in Mo's family had worked at anything but farming. All her cousins married farmers, but she never wanted anything but photography. He imagined the editors stateside saying, "She's on the spot. She's one tough cookie. We've nothing to lose." So they published her pictures: pacifists on a hunger strike in front of a display of stiletto heels in Red Shoe's vitrine; a child squatting in the wreckage hugging a naked doll; a man in a red keffiyeh bent over a shrouded corpse; a kid in shorts tumbling head first from the Ferris wheel, blood on the nape of his neck.

Finlay wiped his eyes with the back of his hand and then continued stowing the fagots. Where the hell was Mo? Without him around, nagging her to be prudent, she'd say to Zaki, "Oh, let's go a little closer, and then we'll zip right out." If something were to happen, God forbid, Anouk would be damaged. Irreparably. He cursed himself once again for being so ineffectual during his visit to Beirut. But what could he have done differently?

After he stored the wood, he mixed the dough and set it to rise. He hiked to Issigeac, where he bought the *Herald Tribune* and read it over an espresso at the Café de la Paix. Two hundred Americans and Europeans were being evacuated from Lebanon. The paper ran one of Mo's photos on an inside page. Her ambition had been realized. Since the fighting had resumed last fall, every week she'd sent a choice half-dozen photo editors a few dozen prints on spec. At first they sent form rejections, later scrawled notes. Now she was a rising star. Like Byron, she'd wakened and found herself famous. The photograph showed a girl with a white ribbon in her dark hair touching a crucifix— Christ's iron torso blasted by shrapnel. Mo must have crossed the Green Line to get that shot. Why would she not listen? he cursed uselessly.

He left a few coins under the saucer and jogged back to Espérac. By the time he arrived at the bakery, the dough had risen. He cut and shaped the puffy mass into loaves. He checked the oven. The glowing embers were now ash.

"Like everything on earth, ash serves a purpose," his mother-in-law used to say. One weekend late in March years ago, he'd walked along the perimeter of Beulah's property and doused the edges with kerosene, setting alight her acres of tall-grass prairie. "Without fire, the prairie will die," so she said. He'd been skeptical, but three months later, in June, when he helped her harvest her crops of soybeans, wheat, and milo, he saw she'd been right. The fire had transformed the land into fertile, blackened earth.

He set the loaves on the linen cloths. Sitting in the bentwood chair by the window, he opened the newspaper and reread the reports on the combat in Beirut. His anxiety mounted, and he waited impatiently for the dough to rise. Once it was pliable, he shaped it, tucking it in and molding it, his fingers always moving. He sliced a wedge, plopped it on the scale, and cut or added bits until it was the correct weight. He shaped sixty-seven loaves.

Calmer now, he set the tungsten light in the oven and moved the loaves to a wooden peel, long as a vaulter's pole. The top of each loaf he sprinkled with flour and slashed with a razor. Balancing the peel on his shoulder, he maneuvered it into the oven and deposited each of the loaves. He clanked shut the oven door. For the tenth or twelfth time that morning, he swept the tile floor and tossed out the flour dust. Dust to dust. He worried for Anouk, grieving for Danny, terrified for her mother.

Yesterday, Colette told him these experiences would serve to make Anouk more nuanced, more aware of what Colette called the mysterious and difficult things of life. He really hoped she was right.

Chapter 23

After supper two days later, when he went to return the soup tureen, he found Colette in the garden pruning her roses. She set the secateurs on the ground as he handed her the soup tureen. She didn't thank him. Grim-faced, she took the dish to the kitchen. The curtain of bamboo beads rustled as she slid through it. Startled, a pair of turtledoves on the birdbath flew off in the direction of the statue of the angel. Colette returned to the garden with a bottle of white wine and poured him a glass. "Your wife will return. Oh yes. Madame Fortin will walk into your arms." Colette's voice was bitter, her face drawn.

He repeated his litany, how he wanted Mo safe with every fiber of his being, but as for his marriage, it was over. Whatever used to bind them had evaporated into thin air. He had loved her the first years of their marriage; then after he didn't, he pretended he did. But to imagine Mo dead? He touched his stomach; it felt as if someone was shoveling out his belly.

On the way home, he spied Anouk in a field. She stood atop a hay bale, cradling an imaginary machine gun in her arms, shooting up the fiery sky. He coaxed her down—her hands and knees red and scratched from having clawed and crawled up the hay bale. When he persuaded her to come down, he walked her home through a field of sunflowers. Their golden petals had fallen, and the flowers stood erect in rows on the parched earth. He thought of soldiers standing in formation on the killing fields.

"Face it, Mom's dead."

He pictured Mo's ginger hair matted, black flies feeding on her lips. It made him nauseous. But then, at the farther end of the field, he spied a couple of sunflowers, volunteers, their petals like golden rays. "Look at those over there," he shouted. "They're alive. And your mom is, too."

"You're wrong, Dad. She's dead."

"She's not. Trust me."

In the night, a knocking at the front door awakened Anouk. She went to her window, but it was too dark to see who was below. In her baby-dolls, she hurried downstairs.

"There's a telephone call for your papa. Hurry," Monsieur Noel said. "I'll wait for him here."

"It's gotta be my mom. I'm coming too."

She awakened her father and ran ahead, but Monsieur Noel's door was locked. When he and Dad finally got there, Monsieur fumbled with the key, and it seemed to take him forever to unlock the door. Why was he so clumsy? Why did he lock the door? At last, they went inside, and her dad picked up the phone.

"Mo, can you hear me?" he shouted. Anouk tugged his pajama sleeve and grabbed the receiver from him.

"Mom, it's me," she said. "What's happened?"

"Sunbeam, put your father back on."

"But I want to talk to you."

"Me too, but I don't know how long it'll be before the connection goes bad again."

She gave the phone back to her father and punched the button for the speakerphone. The static was so bad that Mom had to keep repeating herself.

"What's that?" Dad said. "Molly's coming?"

"Yes, for a short visit."

Anouk grabbed the receiver. "I wish it was just you."

"Sunbeam, Molly's coming especially to see you—"

The line went dead. Dad rubbed his forehead. He was probably worrying about what Mom would say to his two-timing her. But Anouk didn't feel the least bit sorry for him. She had to face Danny's mom. In Beirut, she'd done all she could to avoid her. Whenever Mrs. Delacruz dropped by to see her mom, Anouk would go off to her room, pretending she had homework. She always took the stairs instead of the elevator so as not to get stuck inside with her. Now that Danny was dead, it would be a thousand times worse. Mrs. Delacruz would be sure to scream, "Why did you tell him to take the van? Don't you have a brain in your head?"

The next morning over breakfast, Dad gave her the double whammy. The moment she saw the spasms in his left cheek, she knew it was bad news.

"I need to to tell you something," he said.

"Later, okay? I want to clean up the house for Mom." Anouk set down the slice of toast on which she'd slathered Colette's cherry jam. Her stomach churned.

"This is the thing—"

"Dad, I've really got lots to do."

"Hear me out. This is important. You know your mother and I haven't been seeing eye-to-eye. Not for a long time." He hesitated. "I won't go into the details, but the thing is, Colette and I like each other. A lot."

"Well, I like her too. Everybody does. Just what are you trying to say?"

"Only this. I can't be with two women at once. So when your mother comes, I want you to share your bedroom with her. Molly can stay in the guest room."

Anouk waited for him to ask, "Is this all right with you?" Apart from the move here, he'd always sought her opinion before coming to any decision that affected her. But now he didn't. She no longer counted. It was Colette's fault. Even the half-blind Vamps could see how he and Colette felt about each other. When people were in love, they didn't want anyone else around. That's the way it was. He would ditch her just as he was dumping Mom.

Anouk pushed her plate away, the toast uneaten. She ran out, slamming the door behind her. Upstairs, she flung herself on her bed and buried her head in her pillow. Life was fun with Colette around, but she better not butt in once Mom got here.

She wouldn't let Dad spoil her special day. She would still make the house sparkle. She wiped the doors and windowsills, cleaned the stove, and mopped the kitchen floor. Once it was dry, she polished the dining table until the kitchen smelled of beeswax. She swept the dust from the stairs and cleaned the flyspecks off the windows and gold-edged mirror in the salon. She removed the embroidery, SOUVENIR OF MY CAPTIVITY, from its place above the mantel in her room and hid it in the bottom drawer of her dresser. She felt blue. All the time Danny was gone, she kept telling herself that he was having an okay time, like her ancestor François in World War I. She had been sure he'd been able to persuade one of his captors to help him escape.

"Danny's dead. Dead. Dead," she repeated, hammering it into her head. She'd never see him again, his jade eyes, his tall, angular frame, skinny in his sailor jersey and Bermuda shorts. She'd never again smell his scent of ripe apples and or hear his breathy, crackly voice. On his last day, did he cry? Or sing? Or crack a joke, sure that Goldfingers and Fathead would never kill him? Even after his father died, Danny wasn't scared of death. Once he told her that cats purred when they were euthanized, and if cats didn't fear the hereafter, why should humans?

After lunch, she collected wildflowers—blue chicory and daisies— and arranged them in the green vase on the bedside table in her room, the one she would share with her mom. She cleared the dust bunnies from under the bed, emptied the top two drawers in her dresser, picked up her clothes from the floor and put them in the bottom drawer. She made her narrow bed, changing the sheets and covering them with a bedspread that smelled of lavender.

By late afternoon, the house looked spotless, and her mood improved. She bathed in Colette's big tub, using her bubble bath—she had permission. Afterward, she opened Colette's ivory-inlaid box in Colette's bedroom and checked out her cosmetics: half-dozen tubes of lipstick, small pots of cream, eye shadow, and eyelash curlers, and a powder puff, the shape of a pink pompom. Anouk looked at herself in the hand mirror, which was silver with a cherub decorating it. What should she wear?

Danny once said white was the color of mourning in India, so she put on her white skirt and blouse. She brushed her hair, put on the mascara and lipstick Colette had given her, and dabbed Jilly's perfume, Sweet Honesty, behind her earlobes. Her dad dressed up too. Instead of shorts and Birkenstocks, he had on a white shirt, black tie, black pants, and black socks in his black shoes. He looked so grim she worried even more.

In the station, the arrivals and departures timetable showed the 23:58 from Bordeaux was on time. To get away from her traitorous dad, she ran off to the toilet. More of the oxblood paint had peeled off the door. When she locked the door, the light came on, and she scrunched her toes and squatted on the footpads. Graffiti covered the rough walls where someone had scrawled in English: Big cock. Want to play? Call 05-59-99-26. She looked around for toilet paper. None. What did the French do? Just shake themselves? There wasn't even a sink. And why couldn't they keep their toilets clean the way the Beirutis did? She yanked the flush chain, and the water thundered down and splashed her toes. She managed to get out before the light turned off.

When the boxy yellow train pulled in, the half-dozen passengers disembarked, were met and whisked away. The stationmaster blew his shrill whistle, and the train chugged off into the dark.

Mom stood at the end of the platform beside her blue suitcases.

Arms open wide, Anouk raced along the platform. As they hugged, she caught her mom's scent of Ivory soap.

"You let your hair grow." Mom ran her fingers through it. "Makes you look grown-up."

"Exactly what I want," Anouk said, grinning.

"You're all grown up and beautiful, too."

It didn't sound like Mom at all, and tears welled up in Anouk's eyes. A moment later, everything was spoiled. Mrs. Delacruz waved. "Hi," she said, heading straight toward them.

Anouk shrank back. Danny's mother looked awful. Her freckled cheeks were gaunt, and her red hair had thinned, dulled and gone gray. Dad was kissing Mom—not a smooch, just a peck on each cheek.

"No hug for me?" Mom said.

Dad put his arms around her, but let go the instant he saw Mrs. Delacruz.

"Molly," he said.

She hovered a few steps away, her arms wrapped about a black backpack. Anouk gulped, and her throat hurt. Danny's ashes would be in there.

Dad drew Mrs. Delacruz to him for a hug. "You must be exhausted. I'll get the car." He rushed across the tracks into the station, leaving them on the platform.

"I'm going to catch up with your father. You keep Molly company." Mom gave Anouk a little push and hurried off.

Anouk kept her head down as she slouched toward Mrs. Delacruz. She didn't know what to say, and before she knew it, she was blubbering.

Mrs. Delacruz rummaged in her yellow handbag. "Here, take this." She handed a tissue to Anouk, who blew her nose. Then the words tumbled out of her in a great rush. "Danny wanted that foot, yeah, but he wouldn't have gone past the Green Line on his own. I bugged him to go," she whimpered.

"But Danny chose to go. It took me a long time to believe that. I still can't talk about it. It's no one's fault. Or everyone's." Mrs. Delacruz's voice faltered. "And maybe I'm to blame. I wanted to stay in Beirut. Even with Juan gone, it was home. Mostly, I didn't have the energy to leave. And now, oh dear. Did you know—when Danny was born, the cord was tight around his throat? He was deathly pale. He looked so withdrawn, so far away. And now he's far away again."

"You must want to kill me."

"Oh dearie, no. I never once felt that way." She stretched out her arms and hugged Anouk as if she would never let her go.

The comfort felt good. She and Mrs. Delacruz went out of the station to the parking lot. Dad was loading the suitcases in the trunk while Mom, hands on her hips, was supervising.

Dad asked Mrs. Delacruz to sit in front while Mom climbed in beside Anouk in back. He tore down the narrow highway. No one said a thing. Anouk looked out the window at the plantain trees. When she couldn't stand the silence another second, she told them how Monsieur Noel said Napoleon had planted the trees to shade his troops as they marched to war, but now the government was chopping them down because cars kept smashing into them.

And the awful silence continued.

"Turn on the radio, Dad, please."

It was one of Monsieur Noel's tapes of Edith Piaf singing how she had no regrets. The only one who didn't, Anouk thought as she looked out the window. They passed three of the iron skeletons the government put along the side of the road in spots where people had been killed to warn against speeding. She thought of Danny's jokes:

Who was the most famous skeleton? Bone-apart.

What do skeletons say before eating? "Bone appétit."

Why are skeletons so calm? Nothing gets under their skin.

She twisted her neck to see the speedometer. "Dad, slow down." That was a mistake because he took it so slowly after that, it seemed the drive to Espérac would never end.

When they got home, Dad carried her mother's suitcases up to Anouk's room. As she trailed behind them on the rickety stairs, he mumbled something about how rooming together would help the two of them get caught up.

"Oh." Mom turned pale. "So that's the way you want it."

Anouk was embarrassed for her. She would be extra thoughtful to Mom to make up for Dad. He shouldn't have sprung that on her. In the bedroom, Anouk showed her the drawer she'd cleared for her. "There's scented paper too. Smell it," she said.

"Not now, Sunbeam." Mom threw in her slacks and shirts and underwear any old way, which wasn't like her at all.

"I'm sorry the bed is small. It's a double, believe it or not."

Mom looked upset, her freckles standing out against her pale cheeks.

"Aren't you happy to see me?" Anouk asked.

Mom stopped unpacking. "Of course I am." She drew Anouk close, stroking her hair and snuggling her. When Anouk told her that there wasn't a proper toilet or even any hot water, Mom told her that it was a lot worse in refugee camps and asked her to check that Mrs. Delacruz was settling in.

Anouk found her in the spare room, unzipping her backpack.

"Can I get you anything? A glass of water? A blanket? It gets cold at night."

"No, I'll be fine." Mrs. Delacruz reached into the backpack, removed a white cotton bag and set it gently on the bed as if it held something fragile and precious.

Anouk stared at it. "Are they—? Could they be—? You know what I mean?" She couldn't bear to say it.

Mrs. Delacruz pressed the bag to her lips and then put it in Anouk's hands as if she were a brand-new mother passing around her baby. The bag of Danny weighed about the same as a sack of sugar. As fast as she decently could, Anouk gave it back, and Mrs. Delacruz set it on her pillow. Was she going to sleep cuddled up to Danny's ashes? Anouk shuddered, and her words tumbled out in a whiny voice. "Why did Danny have to die? Why?"

"I don't know." Mrs. Delacruz got up and closed the shutters. "Sometimes I think I'm losing my mind." She sat on the side of the bed, the bag of Danny in her hands. "I'll sing him a lullaby, the same one I used to sing when he was teething." She began, "'Hush, little baby, don't you cry.'"

It made Anouk want to bawl, so she ran off to her room, where Mom was sitting in the chair in her PJs. "I brought you something, Sunbeam. It'll bring you luck."

"Lucky?" She thought it must be the rabbit foot Jilly had once given her; instead, it was a letter addressed to her with an American stamp. She glanced at the return address: "The Bill Newton Memorial Foundation."

"Open it. Read it and tell me what it says," Mom said.

Anouk ripped open the envelope, unfolded the thick paper and read the typed paragraph. "We are delighted to inform you that you have been awarded one of the six scholarships for children of war journalists."

"You see," Mom said. "Aren't you glad you applied? I knew it. I knew you'd win."

Anouk was stunned. "But—"

"It's your lucky break. There's an international school in Paris. I could take you there on my way back to Beirut."

An image of Pierre flashed through her mind. "I don't know." She folded the letter, put it back in the envelope, and set it on the chest of drawers. Too much was happening all at once for her to take in.

"There's something else," Mom said.

"Oh?" She hated it when people began sentences that way. It was always bad luck. "Maybe some other time," she said. "I'm ever so tired."

"Well, let me spit it out. I've given it a lot of thought, and—"

"I'm really tired," Anouk said.

"All right, we'll leave it for tomorrow." Mom got into bed.

Anouk hid behind the armoire, changed into her baby dolls, and climbed into bed. The bed was far too narrow for both of them. Uncomfortable at crawling in beside her mom, she got a sheet from the armoire, and put it and her pillow on the floor.

"Don't be silly," Mom said. She pulled back the sheet and moved over in the bed. "Come on in. There's plenty of room. Pretend it's a slumber party."

Once in the narrow bed, Anouk clung to her side. Mom wiggled nearer, pressing her warm breasts against her. Then Mom turned on her side and fell asleep, making small snorts every once in a while. Once she even farted, and Anouk didn't mind. She was glad her mom was out of Beirut, safe at last, but she couldn't help but worry that Mom might blame her for Dad's falling for Colette. And it was silly to feel hurt that Mom hadn't noticed the green curtains that she'd made, but Anouk couldn't help it.

The next morning while Mom was still sleeping, her dad rushed off to the bakery even though it was his day off. His excuse was that he needed to catch up with his accounts, but Anouk knew the real reason: he wanted to stay clear of her mom.

After breakfast—coffee and toast with fig jam—Anouk showed Mrs. Delacruz around. Danny's mother didn't mind having to use an outhouse and wasn't scared of bats either. Anouk gave her a tour of the square—the tall, rusted cross in its center, the war memorial, the post office, the hall where the mayor kept office hours, and the bus shelter with its billboards of long-past concerts and dances. Monsieur Noel toot-tooted as he puttered by in his Deux-Chevaux. The Vamps strolled past, smiling. They lingered, looking expectant.

"I'm not up to talking to strangers," Mrs. Delacruz said.

"They're checking you out. You and Mom being here is the first exciting thing that's happened for ages." They left the square and Anouk led her down the hillside path toward the spring. Mrs. Delacruz dipped her fingers into the pool. At its edge, she removed her sandals and slipped in her feet. The frigid water made her gasp.

Sitting on one of the flat beveled stones by the pool, Anouk stuck in her feet and gazed at the image of the church tower wavering in the water.

"It's pretty," Danny's mother said.

"I call it the Church of the Crooked Cross." They rested there awhile, shoulders and backs warmed by the sunshine, feet numb with cold. She peppered Mrs. Delacruz with questions about Beirut: Who was still there? Who had gone up to the mountains? Were the gunboys still at the gate? Were the cinemas open?

After a while, it was time to go home. As usual, Anouk took the shortcut through the graveyard. As they strolled between the rows of graves, the headstones mottled with yellow lichen. Anouk read aloud the names she could decipher: Bois, Beaune, DeLorme, Bornat, Lescure, Mauriac, Delpech, Desmarties. Rain, the wind, and time had worn away many of them. On a vast vault of red-speckled marble, a lizard darted out from under a red-lettered sign: FOR SALE. ROOM FOR SIX. The idea of bodies stacked on top of each other made Anouk queasy, but she liked the inscriptions on the headstones: Eternal Regrets. Years pass, the memory of you remains. May your rest be as sweet as your heart was good. Little bird, if you fly near this tomb, sing your sweetest song for him.

"What's that stain?" Danny's mom asked when she noticed the yellow splotch on the Jabert family vault.

Anouk hesitated. Mrs. Delacruz would think Monsieur Noel was a creep to pee on someone's grave, and that would be unfair, so she explained how a friend's mother—she didn't dare say who it was—had fallen in love with a German soldier and how cruelly Monsieur Jabert treated her.

"Revenge by pee," Danny's mom joked. Something about her sardonic tone reminded Anouk of Danny, but it wasn't funny. "Still, don't settle for nastiness. Living well is the best revenge, Juan used to say."

"He was right," Anouk said.

As they passed Colette's mother's grave, Mrs. Delacruz sniffed the pink rose that ran along the iron fence enclosing the grave. She touched the glass-framed photograph of Marie Laforet. "What a pretty young woman," she said.

"That's the grave of the mother of a friend of mine," Anouk said.

"You mean Colette? Your mother told me about her. 'My rival,' that's what Mo calls her. With that cloud of dark hair, I'm not surprised the German fell for her. Poor Colette, it must have been hard for her, her mother sleeping with the enemy like that. People must have wanted revenge. Is she bitter?"

"I guess. She doesn't object when Monsieur Noel lets his dog pee on his tombstone."

It started to rain, great sheets of it, so they raced toward the lean-to at the far end of the graveyard and sat on the bench. The rain drummed on the tin roof, and the air smelled fresh and clean. Mr. Brown, who taught chemistry, would say it was because of all the ozone.

"I've got something I need to ask you," Mrs. Delacruz said. "You were the last person to see Danny alive. It sounds superstitious, but I feel he wants something from me—urgently. It's like when he was a baby, and I was slow getting him his mashed banana, and he'd scream. That's why I came here. Maybe he said something to you that might help me figure it out."

Anouk felt a prickling on the back of her neck. "I try to forget that day."

"The police found him shackled to a radiator," Mrs. Delacruz said, and her voice sounded haunted, faraway. "They found lists on foolscap paper on the floor: his friends—you were at the top; his teachers all the way back to kindergarten; the books he intended to read; his heroes. Your father was there along with the Buddha, Jesus, and Gandhi."

"My dad?"

"Yes. Those lists and the bag of his ashes, that's all I've got left of Danny." She lowered her voice to a whisper. "Please. Anything. Anything at all."

A silk poppy lay on the ground. It reminded Anouk of one of Danny's plans, to collect petals from the purple bougainvillea in front of College Hall and arrange them into a huge peace sign. He figured he'd need a few hundred, one for each dead person.

"That wouldn't be enough," his mother said.

"Danny thought so. Since most fighting occurred at night, the gunboys could go rat-a-tat-tat like crazy, and no one could tell they weren't shooting to kill. His theory was that nobody would want to kill someone he didn't even know."

Mrs. Delacruz smiled. "That sounds like Danny. Is there anything else? Try to remember."

"Yes." Anouk hesitated. "But it's gross."

"That doesn't matter."

"We got into an argument. I said we should dig up the graves, bring up the bodies, get my mother to take photos, and when people saw how the corpses all looked the same, the two sides would get the idea and stop shooting. Danny got mad. "The dead deserve to rest in peace. 'R.I.P., R.I.P.,' he kept repeating. I wouldn't let it go. I said that if we brought up the bodies, they'd stink up the place so that people couldn't stand it, and they'd give peace a chance." Anouk stopped short. "Oh, sorry. You don't want to hear it."

"Go on. Tell me everything."

"There's not much more. That day, before we went to the beach, he helped me with my homework. I had to do a study sheet on a Greek play about a girl who buries her brother even though the king said he would execute anyone who did so. Antigone, that was her name, buried him anyway because it was the right thing to do. Danny couldn't get over it."

"Did he talk about Juan? About his dad?"

"Yeah, about burying him in Spain and how you'd walked for miles. It was a big deal for him."

"Anything else?"

She thought of the other thing, but it wasn't something she could tell his mother. "We talked about the war. He said we had to stay out of them—even if it was to help the little guy—because so-called good wars always turned bad. When we bombed German cities, we killed good Germans, too. There must have been some. Instead of going to war, the States should have paid ransom for all the Jews and given them visas. He said it was the same with every war: people thought they had good reasons to fight, but they were all plain wrong."

Mrs. Delacruz sat there taking it all in. Anouk thought of the other thing. Long before Danny was kidnapped, the day when she'd come on to him, he'd told her how if he were to like any girl, she'd be the one, but he wasn't attracted to girls, not in the way he was to boys. His green eyes turned stormy, and his voice trembled when he said, "I'm sorry. I'm so sorry." She was positive he wouldn't want her to tell.

The rain let up. As she and Mrs. Delacruz left the cemetery, they passed a fresh grave. On the mound of dirt was a china plaque, shaped like an open book with the words: "To speak of you is to make you live; to say nothing would be to forget you."

Bicycle wheels squealed, and Anouk stood on tiptoe so she could see over the cemetery wall. Some teenagers came careening by, and as they rounded the curve into the village, Pierre and his sister Charlotte waved at her.

"You've got friends here," Mrs. Delacruz said.

"Yes, but no one who knew Danny. It feels good to talk about him. You sound like him too."

"I hear you got that scholarship. I'm glad for you."

"I'm not sure I'll take it. How about you? Are you going back?"

"To Beirut? Maybe."

"I loved it there," Anouk said tentatively, not sure how she felt about it now.

"Didn't we all!"

Anouk looked down at the worms creeping on the pavement. High above on the slate roof, a pigeon cooed. The sound reminded her of the last time she'd seen Danny. She turned to Mrs. Delacruz. "When we were hunting for that foot on the beach, Danny told me about an old lady whose name was Peace Pilgrim. He wrote her name in the sand, but a wave came up and washed it away. He said he had a funny feeling something might happen to him. I jumped on him and told him to stop taking himself so seriously. He made some wisecrack how he didn't want to be buried in Beirut. We argued. 'When I'm dead, that's it. You can dump me in any old garbage can,' I said. And he looked at me as if I were crazy. 'You dummy,' he said. 'Even Stone Age people knew everybody deserves a proper burial.'"

Chapter 24

Finlay sat at the blue table, topping and tailing green beans. Earlier this morning he'd seen a flash of Colette ahead of him in the Sunday market. He elbowed his way through the tourists in the narrow street to catch up, but a couple pushing a baby in a stroller ahead of him took up the entire width of the narrow street. Having to slow his pace, he lost sight of Colette. Now, the beans cool in his hands, he shut his eyes, abandoning himself to the memory of her warm breasts scented with musk, her full arms entwined around him.

"Finlay."

He blinked.

"Dozing off again?" Mo, lean and taut, reared before him. She tapped the bowl of beans. "Reduced to plastic, I see. A pity you gave up pottery." She sniffed the air. "What's that stink?"

He gestured toward the compost pit. "The melons."

"You should cut the rinds up before tossing them in."

She was picking on him the way his mum used to do. "We need to talk," he said, feeling a renewal of urgency. "There's a café in Issigeac. Let's go."

"Why not here?" Mo sat down facing him.

"It's private there. No chance of Anouk or Molly barging in."

"No, let's get it over with," Mo said.

He steeled himself. Do it now, give your little speech. He straightened his back. "For starters, I'm relieved you're safe, but you put us through a lot."

"We've been through this before." She snapped a bean in two and dropped the halves in the pot.

"Well, it's taken a toll on us."

"And how about me?" She ticked off her points on her fingers: the snipers on the roofs, the shelling, and mortar rounds, never knowing when the next shot would come. "Don't you think I'm affected?"

"You're addicted to danger," he said.

"So? It's part of the job." She grabbed a bean from the ones he'd topped and tailed. "Look. You forgot to remove the thread. Just get rid of it. Easy peasy." She pulled off the line of green fiber, no thicker than a hair. "See?"

"I want you to give me a divorce." The words slipped out, sounding so final.

"So!" She slapped both hands flat on the table. "I figured as much. With one sentence, there go fifteen years down the drain. Well, shall we discuss it? Don't I have any say? Or are you going to clam up as usual?" She drew her hand over her eyes. "Can this marriage be saved?" she said in a sepulchral voice.

Finlay knew what she meant, but she still seemed to be mocking him. "Don't be like that. Please."

She let out a sharp cry. "God, Finlay, I'm sorry. I don't want to be one of those bitter bitches."

"You're not. You've never been." He tried to recall the little speech he'd prepared, but it had flown out of his mind. "You can't duck forever. Someday some sniper will get you. Think about what that'll do to Anouk."

Mo put her face in her hands. When she raised her head, he

saw her eyes were red. "You think I haven't?" she said. "When I
saw Danny's body, his hair thick with blood, I told Zaki, 'It's over.
I can't bear it anymore. That's my last shot of a dead kid.' I was
on my way to the office to telephone in my resignation, when out
of the blue, one of those quotes of yours popped into my head.
'Attention must be paid.'"

"Arthur Miller. *Death of a Salesman.*"

"Can't help it, can you?" She sighed in a long-suffering way.
"That's what I do. Call attention to all those kiddos who get shot
up. It's a terrible thing. We can't pretend it's not happening. You
believe that, too. Don't think you don't."

"I do," he said.

"So why are you staring at me?"

"You used to hate it when I quoted stuff." He was astonished.
What was it that Willy's widow said? And it all came back: how
Willy never got rich, wasn't an especially fine fellow, but something
ghastly happened to him, and he shouldn't be allowed to die like
a dog.

At last Mo understood, and he told her that he was glad, but
this didn't seem to make her feel any better. They weren't talking
about what was at stake. Her hazel eyes darkened, and her hand
felt chilly on his. "I feel like such a hypocrite. I still believe in free
love. It's not wrong what you're doing. It's probably the best thing
that's ever happened to you—but can't you see, it's hard for me.
Have you forgotten that winter in Kansas? How you would come
in out of the cold, and I'd be leaning against the radiator. 'Cold
lips,' you'd say as I threw my arms around that bulky parka of
yours, and we'd give each other Eskimo kisses. Don't tell me you
don't remember."

He did, as a memory from another lifetime. He didn't pull back
his hand, even though he wanted to. "I didn't know this would
happen. This thing with Colette, I'm overwhelmed by it. You

know me; it's all or nothing. I want out."

"So it's come to that! Look. Here's the deal. You get your divorce, but I keep Anouk."

He did pull away this time. He rose to his feet, putting some distance between them. "What are you saying? Espérac is her home."

"A dump like this? After Beirut? Come on. She's a city girl. You can't expect her to stay in the boonies. With just a pit to pee in." Mo pointed toward the outhouse.

He glanced at the marigolds that scrambled up the side of it. The seeds Anouk had planted three months ago were now a wild outburst of orange and gold. He glared at Mo. "Anouk belongs here now."

"Sit down," she said, her prairie twang confident. "I've already arranged for her to attend a school in Paris, on a scholarship. You said the lycée is an hour away. Who knows if it's any good? This way she'll get a decent education. You can always catch the train and visit her. Looks like a good compromise to me."

He had to admit that he'd been worried about Anouk's schooling. Still, he didn't want Mo using that as a lever to pry Anouk away from him.

"Look, you had your turn with Anouk. Now it's mine. There's nothing for her here—no museums, no art galleries, no nothing."

"She doesn't care for art."

"How about concerts? No kids her age to speak of and nothing for her to do but ride around on her bike. And don't forget that blonde bombshell of yours. You'll want time alone with her. Plus, you've got Toujours Pain."

He flinched when she mispronounced it and corrected her.

She grinned. "You got the name right. That's for sure. Pain every which way. So. If you're the baker boy, guess it's up to me to bring home the bacon."

At that moment, he despised her although he couldn't tell her she was wrong about what was better for their child. Whatever he felt about it, Mo was still her mother.

"Anouk belongs with me," he said stubbornly. "I'm the one who's been here for her."

Mo turned to go. "All right, why don't we see what she has to say?"

When her mom came into the room, Anouk was in bed rereading *Little Women.* She'd come to the point where Jo sells her hair so Marmee can afford to travel to Washington to visit Father, Mr. March, who has been wounded in the Civil War.

"I've got something to tell you," Mom said.

"Can it wait?" She showed Mom the book. "I'm at a really exciting part."

"It can't."

Something about her mother's expression made Anouk give in. "Okay. Okay." She put the book on her lap.

Mom came and sat beside her. "I've thought about it for a long time and, well, I've decided to divorce your father."

Anouk jumped to attention. "You're kidding, right?"

"He gets in the way of what I need to be doing. Plus, there's that woman."

"But now that you're here," Anouk pleaded, "maybe Dad will get over her."

"You seem to get along with her all right."

"When they're together, it makes me uncomfortable," Anouk protested. "Even sore."

"There's a good reason for that," Mom snapped.

Anouk had never seen her so pale. Mom was furious at being dumped. She hated not being the one to call the shots, so she pretended she was still in control.

"It's a rotten thing," Anouk said. "I didn't suspect anything, Not for the longest time, honest."

"Ha, course not. Your father is sneaky." Mom grinned. "Don't worry about me, Sunbeam. I've always got my work."

Anouk got on her bike and pedaled fast—past the war memorial and the cross in the square, the kittens sunning themselves outside Colette's house, and the vineyard on the far side of Espérac. She took the back road into Issigeac. She spotted Pierre sitting cross-legged on the riverbank opposite the soccer clubhouse, the line of his fishing rod dangling in the muddy water. She got off her bike, and took off her sneakers, and walked over to him. After yesterday's rain, the ground had turned squishy. "Fish biting?" she asked, shoes dangling from her hand.

He stood up, smiled, and kissed her on both cheeks. "No. Not today," he whispered.

She put a finger to her lips. "Oh, yeah, we don't want to scare off the fish. Maybe there's a whale about to bite." She giggled.

"Some days they won't bite, and there's nothing you can do." He was sitting at the river's edge, and she sat beside him. "You're unhappy. Something's the matter." He ran his fingertips across her forehead.

She dug her hands into the pockets of her shorts. "It's my parents. They're getting a divorce." She gazed at the Banege, its water the color of lead.

Pierre made sympathetic noises. He looked into his creel, rustled around the fishing lines, bobbins, spools, and hooks, and pulled out a box of cherry chocolates. "Here, have one."

She sucked the chocolate off the stem and bit into the cherry. "It's liqueur."

"It helps with sorrow. Careful. Don't bite the cherry pit."

"Know what sucks? I've got to choose which one to live with, or some court will decide what to do with me."

"You're worried about which one to hurt," he said.

"How did you know?"

"I've been in the same boat."

She had forgotten. "You live with your father, don't you?"

"Yes. These days it's okay."

"Where's your maman?" Anouk asked.

"Off with her boyfriend." He made a sour face. "Still, I'm not a child any longer. I prefer to spend my time fishing. It's better for a guy to be with his father. And it gives maman some time alone with her little friend."

It sounded as if Pierre didn't like his mother dating another man. "According to my mom and dad, it's all going to be ultra-cool." She spat the cherry pit onto the grass. "Some crappy joke, huh? Well, I won't choose. They can't make me."

He extracted a wriggler from the can of earthworms, worked it onto the hook, and made a new cast into the river. "So when will you be eighteen?" he whispered.

She moved closer to him. It felt intimate to be talking so low to him. "Uh. I'll be sixteen next week."

"Oh." His face fell. "You look older. Well, you might not mind school in Paris. I boarded at the lyçée in Bergerac and came home on weekends."

"Did you like it?"

"Some parts."

"I've read tons of boarding school novels—pranks and uniforms and no parents to boss you around." That much was true. Boarding school was neutral ground, not with her father or mother.

"The City of Light. That's Paris. Lots going on."

"We stopped there on our way here, but I didn't see much. I thought I'd missed my chance forever." She was warming to the idea. Living in Paris could be fun. "I'd like to climb the Eiffel Tower, to check out the gargoyles on the top of Notre Dame

Cathedral and maybe see the catacombs. I'd rub Montaigne's toe
too. And there'd be concerts. I'd visit Jim Morrison's grave in Père
Lachaise cemetery. Would you come too?"

"I'm a country boy. I prefer to stay close to home." There was a
tug on the tip of the rod, and the water thrashed as Pierre reeled
in his catch and scooped it into the net. "That's it. I'm done for
the day."

A few bumblebees droned in the honeysuckle, and butterflies
floated about the purple spires of the buddleia. Pierre offered her
another chocolate-covered cherry. With his pinky finger, he wiped
a slight smear of chocolate from the edge of her top lip. He drew
her to him. "*Ma biche*," he whispered. "My doe with beautiful
brown eyes."

A doe. How grown-up that word made her feel. His touch felt
as weightless as a butterfly alighting. He pressed her gently to him
as if, skittish, she might startle and run off. As their lips touched,
she smelled the chocolate on his breath and slipped in her tongue.
They lay on the warm grass until the bells of Issigeac chimed, and
then he walked her to her bike, and together they cycled back to
Espérac.

Meanwhile, Molly and Finlay were drinking gin and tonics on
the terrace. He avoided talking about Danny because he worried
it would upset her. But there seemed nothing Molly wanted more
than to talk about Danny.

"When the word about his death got out, crowds of students
marched from campus toward the American Embassy. 'Danny,
Danny, beloved of God,' they chanted. Can you imagine what he
would have said?" she laughed. "'What a load of bullshit,' that's
what."

"He was brave," Finlay said, careful to keep his words measured.

"Well, it wasn't worth it!" She twisted the thin band of gold on her finger.

He pressed his lips tight. Molly was right, but it wouldn't comfort her to have him say so.

"First Juan and now Danny. The embassy shoved me out so fast I didn't even get to choose an urn for his ashes," she said bitterly.

She was spiraling back to a place he was sure she'd been many times before in recent days. "Would you like another drink?" he said.

She nodded, looking miserable.

"Same as before?"

When he brought it, she swirled the gin and tonic, the ice cubes clacking against the sides of the blue glass. "When they gave me his ashes, I intended to scatter them on the sea. I headed straight for the university beach, but the water was so cold and choppy that I couldn't bring myself to do it. Back when he was a toddler, he was fussy about the water in his bath. It had to be the exact right temperature. I used to stick my elbow in the water to test that it was warm enough. I know it's ridiculous."

"No. It's a nice memory."

She gave him a half-smile. "Coming through customs, the officer asked if I had anything to declare. I didn't know what to answer, so I showed him the bag of ashes. Anouk gave me the same look when she saw it on my pillow." She touched Finlay on the arm. "She thinks Danny wants a proper burial. She insists on it."

"I could make you a decent urn. I know a potter not far from here. I'll call tonight and see if I can use the kiln."

She was grateful for his offer. "There's this other thing. Anouk has this idea that Danny wants to be buried in Spain with his father's people." Molly gulped her whiskey. "Danny was born there in his father's village, a little place on the pilgrimage trail. His grandmother still hands out caramels to the pilgrims. I thought I might go. Walking, I mean, and alone, too, since I'm not fit company. It takes about twenty-two days, time enough to get myself together if you know what I mean."

He didn't reply.

"Finlay? Aren't you listening?"

"Sorry. I was thinking about a friend here. She said that pilgrimage helped her adjust to things at a difficult time in her life."

"You mean Colette? Mo told me about her. You know, Finlay, I don't want to meddle, but maybe you and Mo should consider something like that. Spending time with each other like that might help get you back together."

"Too late for that," he said.

"Mo will miss you."

He couldn't help the edge that crept into his voice. "She lives for her work."

"She does, I'll admit that." Molly's voice turned wary. "So tell me about this Colette."

How was he to explain his attraction? Was it because Colette cosseted him? Was it pure selfishness? He had searched his heart on this, and he thought it was far more than that. Colette respected him; it was a relief to be free of Mo's taunts. He should have never married her, but he'd felt comfortable with her bossiness. She was like his mother, which was perhaps why the two of them had got along so well. But was he hurting Anouk by leaving Mo? He did not see how it could be otherwise.

"This woman Colette, what's she like?" Molly said.

"Well, that's hard to define . . ." He wanted Molly on his side, so he took care not to glorify Colette. He did not dwell on her vitality, her freshness, and exuberance.

Chapter 25

The next morning, Finlay journeyed to Cadouin. The potter's kiln was in a cavernous garage with a dusty concrete floor. Apart from its walls of dressed stone, cold to the touch, there was nothing unusual about the studio: a stainless steel sink, a potter's wheel, an electric kiln tucked away in a corner, and a counter on which leather-hard pots rested, waiting to be fired.

Finlay leaned against the counter as he wedged the moist clay, pressed down on it with the heels of his hands, and lifted and twisted it. He rocked to and fro on his feet as he stretched and smoothed the clay, kneading it until the air bubbles were out. He breathed in the clean scent of the clay and wondered whether he should have talked to Mo here. Perhaps in the neutral territory of this garage, they might have discussed Anouk in a gentle, amicable manner.

He molded the clay into a ball. He wet his hands in the pail of water and went to the wheel, where he slammed the ball of clay onto the bat. Once the wheel got spinning, he braced his elbows against his inner thighs and squeezed the cone of wet clay, moving it up and in, down and out, concentrating on keeping it from wobbling as it took shape. Once it felt balanced, he centered it. He pressed his thumb and widened the opening, keeping the ever-thinning walls intact. In three pulls, the walls were up. He kept the wheel spinning until the pot was smooth. Then he removed it, trimmed the base with a wire, and placed the pot on the shelf to dry. The lid he fashioned from the same piece of clay. Later, the potter would set them both in the kiln along with the other vases, bowls, and cups now drying on the shelves. After sixteen hours of firing, Danny's urn would be dry.

Anouk sat with Mrs. Delacruz on the terrace, a map of the pilgrimage trail spread out on the blue table as Danny's mother traced her route. She planned to take the train from Bergerac to St. Jean Pied de Port in the Pyrenees, where she would cross into Spain and begin the arduous hike to Juan's family.

"Aren't you scared of wild dogs?" Anouk said.

Molly laughed. "I'll fend them off with a stick."

"When Colette went, she took one. 'Darlingstick,' she called it. Funny, huh?"

Just then Mom came outside, her camera around her neck, and Anouk felt guilty she'd been caught talking about Colette. Mom must be jealous. Anyone would. Anouk went over to her and asked if she'd like to look at the church, where she might find some photo ops.

Mom frowned. "Anything special about it?"

"You'll see."

The pavement in front of the church was thick with pink and white confetti left from Saturday's wedding, but the prettiness of it didn't impress Mom, who stared up at the steep slate roof. "Damn pigeons. Beware, or they'll drop on you—sticky white stuff."

"Actually, they're mourning doves."

"Whatever you call them, they're driving me berserk. All that crazy coo, coo, cooing."

Mom sounded harsh, but maybe it was she who'd grown soft.

"Come on. You'll see. It's a pretty church." Anouk pulled open the church door. Inside, she dipped her fingers in the basin. The holy water felt refreshing, but she worried that her mother might object and quickly wiped her hands on her Capri pants. Anouk gazed at the calla lilies and pink roses on the altar, and little bouquets of sweet peas, jasmine, and gardenia at the end of each row of chairs. "Smells nice, doesn't it?"

"The light's wonderful. No need for a flash." Mom adjusted her settings and strolled around taking pictures. She photographed the stained glass window and the flowers on the altar. When she stood in front of the statue of Joan of Arc, Mom said she needed silence to concentrate, so Anouk just watched. She wanted to tell her mom that she admired her for being brave and daring like Saint Joan. But she didn't dare. "What makes you think so?" Mom might say, a wry edge to her voice, and Anouk would have to admit it was Colette who had said that, which would spoil it all.

Mom put the camera back in her bag. "Maybe you'll be like Saint Joan when you grow up. Don't be a conventional girl." She ran her fingers along the edge of Joan's silvery sword.

"I'd like to be bold. Like you," Anouk said.

"Be yourself. That's all."

"Once I lit a candle in front of Saint Joan. It was for you."

"Thank you." Mom sounded odd—hesitant and quiet. She held out her hand, which was soft as corn silk. Anouk held onto it tightly as she showed off the bright brass chandelier and the paintings too dark to figure out.

"What's that?" Mom said.

The warbling was coming from the statue of the Virgin Mary, so Mom hurried over. In a nest wedged between Mary's bare feet was a brown bird so tiny it could have fit in Anouk's hand.

"It's a wren, just a fledgling. Don't touch it. You could hurt it. Its bone structure is still delicate," Mom said.

Colette would have said what a perfect spot the wren had chosen with Mother Mary's kindly eyes on her, holy water to drink and splash in, and hymns to soothe it to sleep. It reminded Anouk of Dad trying to calm her when she was little and couldn't get to sleep. "Twinkle, twinkle little star," he'd sing, or "Sleep, my child, and peace attend thee all through the night." She didn't want to lose either of them. Suddenly, she blurted, "Dad's nice. He's not hard to get along with."

"So you say. You and your dad, you were always the best of chums. And where was I?" she said sourly. "He made sure I was left out. Nowhere. In the dark."

"You yelled at him a lot."

"You were always on his side," Mom said.

"Someone had to be. You kept jumping on him for every little thing."

Mom looked sad, and Anouk wished she could take back what she'd said.

"Your father told me when he came to Beirut, but I didn't believe him. Then, at breakfast, I needed honey, and the cupboard was neat as a pin. That's when I knew for sure. It's not like you or your father to be so orderly."

Anouk felt guilty, like she shouldn't have let Colette tidy up in their kitchen. But Colette was always like that, doing things for people.

"Your father says it's too late for us, and you know him—once he makes up his mind, that's it." Mom sat in a rush-backed chair in the front row. "So tell me about that woman."

Anouk sat down beside her. "Colette's nice, but I wouldn't ever let her replace you."

"Of course not." Mo got up and wandered off toward the south wall while Anouk stayed put and looked at the altar with its lace cloth. When they got married, Dad and Colette would stand there,

and they'd expect her right beside them, which wouldn't be fair to
her mom. But her parents would be divorced, so Dad and Colette
would have to have the wedding at the *Salle des Fêtes* with the
mayor officiating in his fancy sash. It wasn't fair. She suspected
Dad lied when he said he'd tried his level best to persuade her
mother to return with him from Beirut.

Anouk went over to find her and found her looking up at the
stained glass window of the Judgment of Solomon. There was the
king with his crown and two women in front of him. A soldier
dangled a naked infant by the foot, ready to slice the poor baby in
two. Both women wanted that baby. But did her mother want her?

"You'll like Paris," Mom said. "It's a lot like Beirut, and you'll
enjoy being more independent."

"But I'll miss Dad."

"How about me?"

"You never wanted to do stuff with us, Mom. We'd ask you, but
you'd never come."

"I couldn't. I had my work."

Anouk must have looked askance because her mom frowned.
"Please, listen to me for once. I've been a crappy mother. I'm not
the maternal type, but when we found Danny dead, I can't tell you
how comforted I was that you were here safe." She reached out
both hands. "Please."

Anouk bit her lower lip to keep from crying and crept into her
mom's embrace.

The following afternoon, Mo accompanied Finlay to Cadouin
to retrieve Danny's urn from the potter. The man was out, his
door locked. While they waited for him to return, they visited
the cloister with its pretty knot garden—four squares of box
hedge enclosing roses and lilies. Priests in soutanes, breviaries
in hand, strolled along the pebbled path. Mo snapped pictures

of them. In the exhibit hall, they viewed the glass case with the holy shroud, brought back from Jerusalem after the First Crusade and for centuries believed to be Jesus's burial cloth. At nine by four feet and mended in spots, the linen was the color of wheat. Finlay studied the calligraphy. He could make out some of it. With humor lighting his eyes, he pointed to the words "Allah" and "Muhammad" embroidered in gold thread in Kufic, the ancient form of the Arabic alphabet.

"It's bizarre," Mo said, smiling as well.

They walked the few steps to the abbey. The word PAX was carved above the lintel. Across the threshold, they paused to let their eyes adjust to the dim interior. Except for an old lady mopping the floor, a priest in a cassock reading his breviary, and a man dozing in the back row, the sanctuary was empty. Mo photographed the statue of the Virgin smiling at the impish-looking baby in her arms. "First time I've seen him look like a real baby," she said. Then she walked to the statue of Joan of Arc, this one a dour-looking girl in a white tunic with a print of gold fleur-de-lys.

Afterward, she and Finlay seated themselves at the outdoor café on the square. The waiter, wearing a black bow tie and a white apron over his dark pants, brought the menus. "No vegetarian offerings, I see. Good thing I won't be stuck here," she said.

Finlay suggested they order a steak with French fries and salad. He'd take the meat; she the fries, and they'd split the salad.

She looked at him askance. He shouldn't have said the word "split." She got up from her chair as if she couldn't stand being around him one moment more and walked around the square. She looked the same as always, a slight, short woman in her late thirties with a rope of ginger hair. She was photographing a pair of the massive stone pillars supporting the roof of the open-air market building when their meal arrived. He called to her, and Mo came and sat down. She picked at the salad and fries. A look of disgust crossed her face when he cut into the steak and blood seeped out.

"You'll do fine on your own," he said in a quiet voice.

"I know. I won't have anything to hold me back. Still, it'll take some getting used to. Being single, I mean. It's like that song, 'You don't know what you've got until it's gone.'"

Surprised by the sentiment, he set down his fork. He wanted to comfort her and to thank her for what she'd given him, the ability to see things fresh, but the chasm between them wouldn't permit it. Maybe in the future, he could tell her. For now, he sat beside her in silence watching the tourists come and go on the square, where a fire was being set for the village barbecue that evening. As the men arranged the kindling and the logs, it reminded him of the prairie fire they'd seen in the Flint Hills when they first started dating. She didn't remember it, so he described it. "The flames shot up, the grasses crackled, and my eyes smarted from the smoke. I couldn't stand the heat and ripped off my windbreaker. But you were out in it, shifting your camera so as to get the angle of light right. You pleaded for a few minutes more, so I went to wait in the truck. I grieved for the voles and mice and chipmunks and all the wee creatures perishing in the blaze." He turned to her. "Remember what you said?"

"Course not, that was ages ago."

"You didn't say anything until you stowed your tripod in the back of the truck, and then you came and sat up front beside me. You said the fire purged the land of the dead grass to make way for the tender shoots. You said it mesalleant a person could try again. It might be painful for a season, but bright freshness would return as surely as the flowers in springtime."

She smiled as if pleased that he'd remember something like that. "Nice to think so."

He touched her forearm. "It'll be the same with you. You'll be fine, Mo."

She gazed at him with that intense, pure gaze she had when taking a portrait. A moment later, she smiled. "Of course. Nothing can stop me now."

It was already two o'clock, time to return to the potter's studio and retrieve Danny's burial urn. As Finlay cupped the tall rounded vase in his hands, a line from Schweitzer slipped into his mind.

"A penny for your thoughts," Mo said.

"It's nothing." He didn't want her to criticize him.

"Can I hold it?" she said, her voice subdued.

She touched it to her lips, and a wave of regret swept over him. Had he shown her greater tenderness, would she have been less brittle? He would never know. In the car, the burial urn between them, they drove in silence toward Espérac. At the edge of the hamlet, where the Vamps lived, a clutch of brown chickens was scratching the grass, clucking Buk Buk Bacagh.

"Look," Mo said.

A chick had sneaked through the gap at the bottom of the chainlink fence and was now on the verge of the road. The mother hen clucked frantically at seeing her chick in danger and tried to squeeze through the gap, but she was too large. After what seemed a very long time, the chick pressed itself close to the earth and made it back through the hole to find refuge under its mother's wings.

"Mo," he said, the words stumbling from him. "You wanted to know what I was thinking. It was about Schweitzer, the medical missionary in Africa. He was on a barge at sunset when he passed a herd of hippos in the river, and the phrase came to him: 'reverence for life.' That's what I feel in Espérac. And not only the lordly creatures like lions and elephants, here every little creature has its place. Maybe it's vanity—oh, it's impossible to put it into words, but I love baking bread for this village where my ancestors lived. I feel I've found my—" To say he'd found his "home," or "destiny" seemed grandiose, so he fell silent. He dreaded that Mo might say, "Ha, bully for you," but she didn't say a word.

The following morning, a cloudy day with on-and-off drizzle, they had a simple ceremony for Danny in the garden. Molly dipped a gold-rimmed teacup into the plastic sack and removed a cupful of ash. She closed her eyes, murmured that she would forever love her Danny boy, and slid the ash into the urn. Anouk, Finlay, and Mo did the same. Each said a few words: Mo—that Danny was the light in a darkened world; Anouk—that he was her best friend and she would never forget him; Finlay—the words his mum had murmured at his father's funeral: "You are not going somewhere strange. You are returning to the home that you never left."

Each touched their lips to the urn. They added their gifts: Anouk, Danny's red-and-blue bracelet, now faded and frayed; Molly, a curl of her red hair tied with a white ribbon; and Mo, a photo of Danny and his late father in a motorboat cruising the turquoise waters under Pigeon Rocks.

At noon, after the church bell rang twelve times, they set out on their separate ways: Molly, with Danny's ashes in her backpack, on the pilgrimage road to Compostella; Mo and Anouk on the fast train to Paris; and Finlay to the bakery, warm and fragrant, where his darling Colette was waiting.

About the Author

Jean Grant was born in
Montreal, Canada. She has
worked as a journalist and
teacher in Egypt, Lebanon,
and Saudi Arabia.
Jean Grant was living
with her husband and family
in Beirut at the outset of
its Civil War. After being
evacuated to France, she
returned to the Middle East to work as a journalist in Dhahran,
Saudi Arabia, the setting for her first novel, *The Burning Veil.*
She now divides her time between Lawrence, Kansas, and a small
village in the southwest of France, which is the setting for *Flight.*

Acknowledgments

The lines from "At Evening," by Mahmud Abu Al-Wafa are from *Modern Arabic Poetry: An Anthology with English Verse Translations* (copyright @1967 by A. J. Arberry) published by Cambridge University Press.

Special thanks to A. Manette Ansay of the Bordeaux Writers' Workshop, along with Mai Al-Nakib, Frances Lench, Martha Payne, Natalia Sarkissian, Laura Schalk, and Lisa von Trapp. For the past ten summers they have helped me along the writer's way. I am grateful to the Great Plains Writers' Workshop in Lawrence, Kansas, especially Phyllis Fast, Judy Graversen-Algaier, Margaret Kramar, Mary McCoy, Rebecca Powers, Lucy Price, Sue Suhler, and Sheryl Williams.

I wish to acknowledge my dear friends and first readers, Mary and Roger Allen, Darlynne Devenny, Anne Fuhrman, Priscilla McKinney, Gayle Sherman, and Deborah Singmaster. I am obliged to John Paine for his attentive and skillful editing. And finally, a *grand merçi* to the villagers of the Issigeac area, and to *Maître Boulanger* Laurent Poujet and Jim McGinness of Lo Pan del Pech in St. Quentin de Dropt.

Discussion Questions for Book Groups

1. The action of the novel happened long ago and far away. Did this make it hard to follow?

2. Finlay is downwardly mobile. He goes from professor to baker. Does this help or hinder his personal growth? To what extent does our work define us?

3. Does Colette successfully merge feminism and maternal sensitivity? If so, what helps her succeed?

4. The main characters are expatriates, each seeking the spot that feels like home. What does a place require before one can feel at ease in it?

5. Can one belong to two worlds? Is it better to be an expatriate or to stay in the country of one's birth?

6. Need 'the companion star' be a lover? Might it be a parent or child or friend?

7. What attracts Finlay and Colette to each other? Will they tire of each other?

8. Is Mo an admirable character? Are ambitious, idealistic women doomed to suffer? Can a woman waste her life on domesticity?

9. Who is the least sympathetic character in the novel? Why?

10. Do you like the alternation between Finlay's point of view and that of his daughter, or does it seem confusing?

11. What do we learn about the social and cultural differences between Lebanon, France, and the United States?

12. To what extent is the war the cause of the deterioration in Finlay and Mo's marriage? Should they have tried harder for reconciliation?

13. Does Finlay's use of great quotations help you to understand him?

As Saudia flight 113 accelerated down the runway at New York's JFK, a man's voice floated over the intercom. His cry—half-singing, half-chanting—sounded like that of someone yearning for a lost lover. Sarah listened mesmerized.

"Please, could you tell me, what is that?" she asked the girl in yellow silk shantung pants who was seated beside her. "It's hypnotic."

"That? It's the prayer for travelers." The girl rested her fingertips on Sarah's wrist. "I'm going home. And you?"

Surprised by this warm touch from a stranger, Sarah felt already in a foreign world. She glanced down at the teenager's fingers, hennaed orange up to the second knuckle. "I'm going to work in Khobar. Ever heard of it?"

"Oh yes, the beautiful city of Khobar," the girl said, giggling. Funny. Ibrahim had never once described it that way. She would have asked about it, but the girl had already put on her earphones and seemed engrossed in her music. It would be rude to buttonhole her. Even when the flight attendant passed out thimble-sized cups of cardamom coffee, the girl kept on the earphones. Sarah pulled out her Arabic phrase book from her backpack, studied irregular verbs for an hour and then stood up to stretch her legs. Most passengers were napping, their heads lolling to one side or the other. At the rear of the plane, she noticed a brown curtain with a sign saying Prayer Room. Curious, she sneaked a look inside and saw a man kneeling. It would be rude to intrude, so she went back to her seat. Halfway up the cabin, she saw a man with classic Arab features, handsome like Ibrahim. He was cuddling a toddler in pink pajamas and stroking her black ringlets. A gold bracelet glinted on the child's chubby arm. It seemed a good omen. She smiled at the child, then continued up the aisle, squeezed past the Saudi girl, and sank down in seat #12H by the window.

The girl took off her headphones. "I wish we'd hurry up and get there. These flights are too boring."

"Well, there's a lot of time to think," Sarah said.

"Think!" The girl giggled. "I don't like thinking."

Sarah was about to say the long journey felt like being in limbo, but the teenager would not know the meaning of the word. She was fiddling with the channel selector for the in-flight entertainment but stopped when she found a religious program; at least that is what Sarah assumed it was. Verses in exquisite calligraphy flickered across the screen, and the girl rocked back and forth, her lips moving as she read along. Would Ibrahim's family be religious like that? Sarah hoped not. She lifted the plastic shade, but outside the oval window, she saw no lights but only blackness, the dark Atlantic below. When she first met Ibrahim, he had commented on the courage of the Pilgrims crossing the Atlantic. It had been last fall when her brother Pete brought him home so he could experience an American Thanksgiving. Daddy stumbled over his name.

"It's Abraham in English, sir."

"I'll call you Abe then," Daddy said.

"As you like," Ibrahim said in a grave voice.

"No, Daddy, let's not," she said. "It's perfectly easy. Eee-bra-heem."

When she had studied Arabic for her foreign language at university, her classmates nicknamed their tutors—Yusuf and Mohammed—Joe and Mo. It riled them. Ibrahim did not look offended at the prospect of being called "Abe." She liked that about him, that he was not defensive.

"Pete says you speak Arabic," he said, turning to her.

"I used to be able to read a newspaper, very slowly."

He smiled, showing a tiny gap between his two front teeth. He had extraordinary eyelashes, the longest and thickest she had ever seen. She took his parka, the down lining still warm from his body heat, and hung it up on a hook in the hall closet. They talked about the weather. Snow was forecast, the first of the season, and he had never seen snow. What else? She could not remember. It was his voice that held her. She had never heard a voice quite like that, gentle, slow, and seductive. Pete, who was wearing his green-and-gold Packers sweatshirt, said Ibrahim was a Fulbright scholar doing graduate work. Perhaps embarrassed by the attention, he ran his fingers through his curly hair. Later, as Sarah lit the tapers at the dining table, she felt his eyes on her, but when she glanced his way, his eyes darted off. Hazel, they bulged slightly under those amazing lashes. She touched the collar of her lambswool sweater, wondering if it was too tight.

The Green Bay Packers were playing the Detroit Lions, and after supper they all went downstairs to the den to watch the game. Ibrahim was having a hard time understanding the rules. Apparently, in his country they played soccer, not football. Happily, the Packers won as usual, and when the game was over, he helped Pete bring in logs from the stack in the garage. Pete made a fire, and the three of them sat around awhile drinking hot chocolate, eating apple pie, and talking about the game. The telephone rang and Pete went off. The logs crackled as they burned, their edges brightly outlined. Sarah asked Ibrahim about his work, and he said he was a hydrologist.

"Not oil? I thought that's what the kingdom was all about."

"When I was in high school, I saw a crew drilling for water, but oil spurted up instead. In its crude state it is viscous ugly stuff, and I thought of how water was pure and clean. That is when I decide to study desalination. I feel I was put on earth for this," he said, touching his hand to his heart. "And you, Sarah? Did you always want to be a physician?"

"I was like any kid. I wanted to be a rock star. And if I couldn't be a rock star, then I wanted to be a waitress, bustling around, feeling in charge. Then my mother got breast cancer, and her doctor took an interest in me. Mom wanted me to be a nurse, but you need so much more compassion and patience for that. I insisted I was going to be very successful in medicine, and she couldn't argue with that. Medicine's been hard, but I love it. Still, I feel like I'm in a bit of a rut. I've been at the same hospital three years."

"My father's been at his forty years," Ibrahim said, smiling. "What's your field?"

"Emergency medicine."

He told her his father had trained as an orthopedist and that although he was too old to carry on an active practice, he still went into the hospital most days.

"That's nice." She toyed with an earring...

CPSIA information can be obtained
at www.ICGtesting.com
Printed in the USA
FSOW01n1902150517
34099FS